Before WE RISE

Before WE RISE

amy babiarz

ISBN 978-1-916529-14-4 (paperback)
ISBN 978-1-916529-15-1 (ebook)

The Unbound Press
www.theunboundpress.com

Hey unbound one!

Welcome to this magical book brought to you by The Unbound Press.

At The Unbound Press we believe that when women write freely from the fullest expression of who they are, it can't help but activate a feeling of deep connection and transformation in others. When we come together, we become more and we're changing the world, one book at a time!

This book has been carefully crafted by both the contributors and publisher with the intention of inspiring you to move ever more deeply into who you truly are.

We hope that this book helps you to connect with your Unbound Self and that you feel called to pass it on to others who want to live a more fully expressed life.

With much love,
Nicola Humber

Founder of The Unbound Press
www.theunboundpress.com

For Ashtin

Disclaimer:

Though the following information regarding withdrawal and recovery is well-researched, please be aware that I am, first and foremost, an author, not a professional addictions specialist. If you or someone you know is struggling with addiction, please seek professional medical care. While the holistic approaches mentioned in this novel are used around the world, they are not recommended to be used without first speaking with a medical provider. This novel is not meant to be a guide to holistic methods of recovery. Each person is different from the next, and there is no one-size-fits-all approach to recovery.

For help with addiction recovery in the United States, you can reach out to SAMHSA (Substance Abuse and Mental Health Services Administration at 1-800-622-HELP (4357).

For help with mental health, suicidality, and self-harm in the United States, you can reach out to 988 by phone or text, or online chat at 988lifeline.org

For help internationally, local helplines can be found by searching online.

You are not alone.

ONE

E104

Sepyphyr Raznik, third Commander of the Raznik
Dynasty, is dead. I know this because I am his killer. I am Commander now, and the transition has been just this side of disastrous. Which side of disastrous remains to be seen.

For all that my people did not trust Raznik in the end, they trust me even less. They watched me murder Commander Raznik in what appeared to be cold blood. They have no way of knowing what happened over the last four months that led up to that final, fatal meeting. They have no idea that while decrying magic and sentencing people to their deaths, he himself was practicing the most dangerous form of magic.

Unfortunately for me, this mistrust has ended in more than one attempt on my life.

Early into my second month as Commander, I am awoken by a pair of icy cold hands wrapping themselves around my neck like a vise. My eyes fly open, making sense of nothing in the darkness. Pressure against my windpipe makes me croak, desperate for air. I claw at the thick fingers on my skin, unable to pry them off.

A torch flares to light off to the side, and Ocin's face swims into view, feral and vicious. His teeth are bared in a terrible smile as he squeezes.

"Did you think you'd stay comfortable, Commander?" he asks, his voice dripping with derision. "You thought you'd get away with murdering our ruler and taking over?"

"N-no, I—" Ocin squeezes harder, cutting my words off entirely. Black spots are beginning to swim in my vision as I am pressed against my mattress. The softness of it provides me little aid in counteracting the force with which he holds me. Briefly, I worry that my trachea will turn to dust beneath his grip. At last, I manage to get a hold on the tender triangle of skin between his thumb and index finger and pinch it hard between my nails. I feel the skin break and he rips his hands away, cursing.

Like a flash, I roll to the left, away from him and off the bed. I land on my hands and knees and push myself up, letting my own curse out when I realize that I have significantly diminished the space between me and the wall. Ocin realizes this at the same time and his anger is replaced with that horrible, predatory grin. He rounds the bed and in a last-ditch effort, I throw myself back across it, scrambling to the other side.

Ocin reaches over the footboard and grabs hold of my ankle, trapping my movement. He keeps his grip on it as he clears the footboard, back to where he started. With a growl, he tugs hard on my leg, yanking me forward. Something pops in my ankle and a shout of pain tumbles out of me.

"I'm going to kill you the way I should have years ago," he sneers. With the way he stares down at me, I don't doubt him.

My doors crack open and Desnal sticks his head in. Of course they would be in on this together. I wonder if they drew straws of hay to determine who would get stuck on watch duty.

"Oi, hurry it up, will you?" he hisses.

"I'm working on it!" Ocin snaps back. The momentary distraction makes him loosen his grip on my foot and I rip it out of his hand, pulling back and kicking him in the stomach as hard as I can. The effect is somewhat weakened by the soft mattress absorbing my force, but it's enough to send him stumbling back.

From beneath my pillow, I'm able to retrieve my sword at last. The hilt is cool and reassuring in my grip. I jump to my feet, holding it out. Ocin eyes it warily, clutching his stomach.

"Get…out," I pant. My voice is weak and crackly from the pressure of his fingers on my throat. I try to say more, but the words come out a painful, garbled mess.

"You don't deserve to stand where he stood," he spits at me. "You're nothing but a murderous, treasonous—"

I cough a laugh of disbelief, tasting iron. My eyes flick to his side, where he is fingering the handle of his sepiwin. I step toward him, sword pointing at him. The blade glints in the firelight of the torch.

"I will always be loyal to the true commander," he says, unhitching his weapon. The curved blades turn into a blur as he spins it in his hand. We stare at one another, unmoving.

"I…am the true…commander," I say at last with great difficulty, narrowing my eyes and adjusting my hold on the sword. The words are barely more than a whisper, but he hears them all the same. Ocin leaps forward with a scream, raising his arm and bringing it down. My sword plunges into him, but not before the razor-sharp blade of his weapon catches the side of my neck. I yank my sword back out with a sickening squelch, stumbling backward away from his twitching body.

With a gasp, I fall to the ground, clutching the gash. Desnal rushes in at the cacophony, eyes widening at the scene. His eyes land on me and then on Ocin's unmoving body before flitting back to me.

"You bitch!" he shouts, charging me. It's not a fair fight, but I manage to raise my sword one more time, swinging blindly as I begin to sway. It catches something, but the scene begins to blur before me, and then it goes black.

My vision swims back into focus, and I realize that I am no longer on the floor of my quarters. The head healer, Healer Rex, is bent over me, adjusting some type of cloth against my neck. I try to clear my throat and wince. Noticing that I have woken, he turns his gaze to meet mine. He peers at me through thick-lensed glasses. His fluffy white hair sticks out in tufts from under his soft, velveteen cap.

"Try not to speak, Commander," he instructs me. I try to convey a question with my eyes. "You want to know where you are?"

I lift my hand, holding a thumb up to indicate that he has guessed correctly.

"The infirmary," he says. "I'm afraid you've suffered a nasty wound to the neck. You're lucky—if it had been even the tiniest bit back, it would have cut your carotid artery clear through. As it stands, you'll have a rather impressive scar."

My eyes dart about the room in thought as I digest his words and figure out how to convey my next question: how did I get here?

As if he can read my mind, Healer Rex speaks again.

"You crawled out into the hallway, and a warrior on duty happened upon you. Might I suggest regularly stationed guards until the novelty of your leadership has blown over?"

I make a face. He's entirely right, and I've been a fool not to have them already. I hold my hand up, making an O with my thumb and fingers.

"Ocin and Desnal?" Healer Rex inquires. I send him another thumbs up. He hesitates for a moment, fiddling with a square of gauze in his hands before he answers. "Ocin is dead. Desnal was not far behind him, but his injury was caught in time. Am I correct in assuming that upon his healing, he'll be imprisoned?"

My face turns dark and mulish as I thrust my thumb into the air. A stab of vindictive satisfaction shoots through me at the news of Ocin's passing. That man was nothing but a predator and a threat while alive. Healer Rex moves back to my side and delicately removes the dressing from my neck. The gauze catches on stitching and I wince. A cool alcoholic liquid burns against the wound and then a fresh piece of gauze is set atop it, affixed with a piece of tape.

"You're free to leave when you feel ready," Healer Rex says, "but I need you to take the next few days easy. You can speak in small measures, until the trauma to your throat heals. I'll send someone to redress your wound regularly."

"Thank you," I manage to whisper. Healer Rex places a gentle hand on my shoulder, smiles, and then whisks away. Slowly, I swing my legs over the side of the bed and rise. My ankle is tender, and I take a few test steps, a limp marring my gait. Grimly, I smile as I realize that I have survived my first assassination attempt. I pray there will not be a second.

......†......

The next day, I have barely sat myself before the fire when the door to my quarters slams open, so forcefully that it bangs against the wall and bounces off it. Aleca strides in, her face murderous. She softens when she sees me seated with my leg propped on the ottoman and drops into the space beside me, throwing her arms around me tightly.

"Who did this?" she demands. "I'm going to turn them into a frog and eat them for dinner."

"Disgusting," I say, wrinkling my nose. My throat burns with the effort. "You needn't worry. It was Ocin, and he's dead."

"Did you kill him?"

Willow's soft voice surprises me, and I look past Aleca's mop of colorful hair to find Willow hovering behind her. Her eyebrows are pinched together in anticipation of my answer.

"Yes," I say simply, and she frowns, disappointed. It would seem that her first kill was her last, that her willingness to harm was provisional. "I know it's not what you wanted to hear, Willow, but it was me or him."

"No, I—of course," she says, sliding into a chair beside the couch where I sit with my sister. She folds her hands in her lap, fiddling with her fingers as she looks at me. Her gaze does not linger long.

I do not have the energy to have the same argument we have had so many times, over Bhamet, over Raznik, and now, apparently, over Ocin. It's a fight we never stop having, and I itch for a drink of mead. Just a sip, enough to take the edge off.

"Can I choose your mark?" Aleca asks. I rip my gaze away from Willow to stare at her, shock arching one of my eyebrows. There is a vindictiveness in her face I've rarely seen; she's never had the stomach for violence. When she notices the way I stare at her, she sets her jaw. "You think I'd be okay with letting someone get away with trying to kill you? Get real, Jace, you're my sister!" She throws her arms around me again, and I wrap her tightly in a hug, resting my chin atop her head. I chance another glance at Willow, who stares resolutely at her hands. I sigh.

"You may choose it," I say.

Aleca pulls back, tugging my right arm toward her. There is some space on the outside of my forearm, between the belladonna and my newest mark from Raznik's death. She narrows her eyes, thinking, and then raises one finger, inspired.

"Where's your kit?" she asks me. I point at my desk, informing her which drawer holds my marking kit. She leaps up, rummaging noisily through the items. Willow watches, discomfited, and asks quietly,

"Is this truly something to celebrate?"

"I will not pretend I am not grateful for another day to live," I respond, just as quietly. "There was a time when I did not care whether I lived or died, Willow. I would not call this a celebration, but I also would not call this a moment of mourning. My desire to see another day is tenuous at best. There are plenty of reasons I could self-deprecate and prove why I do not deserve this life, and I won't allow myself to spiral in the name of false morality."

She does not respond and I inhale deeply, closing my eyes to prevent myself from further arguing with her. As time has passed in Battlewood, we've begun to argue more. She wants to change me, and the changes are too disparate from the changes I want for myself. Aleca returns, opening the wooden kit box and fitting a needle into a wooden handle. She sticks the tip of the needle into the fire to purify it. Once it begins to glow, she pulls it back to cool it some. I let her decide on the colors, and she twiddles her fingers above several small jars of ink before settling on the bright red carmine ink.

Very carefully, she begins the process of inking my arm; she has little practice, and her touch is not a tender one. The tip of her tongue pokes out of her mouth in concentration, and she is bent so far over my arm that I fear she may tattoo her face in the process. After many long, silent moments, she sits up and examines her work proudly. I twist my arm to see a crude depiction of an O with a sword stabbed sideways through it. The lines are squiggly, but it makes the mark all the more personal to me.

"I love it," I tell her, and she beams. "Perhaps you can offer your services as a tattooist when you return to Syiera."

"How can I leave you now?" she demands. "I can't go back knowing that you're not safe!"

"I am safe," I say. "I made a misjudgment, and it shan't happen again. You know your place is with her, in Apaiji. I made a promise to both of you that I would send you back after the first harvest, and I intend to follow through on that."

"But first harvest has already happened!" Aleca protests. "I can stay—"

"You will not," I cut her off. "Your place is not here, Al. It never has been. You cannot continue your studies here. I'll send for a guide to come for you, and you must go with him when he arrives. You are better than what Battlewood can offer you."

"What about you?" she asks me. I fiddle with the blanket that is loosely draped over my lap. The knit has begun to come apart from years of use, and I roll the fraying threads between my fingers.

"This is my payment for killing Raznik," I tell her. "I have a duty to this Court, and I intend to make good on it."

There is much I hope to do to bring some semblance of normal back to Battlewood, much I hope to teach the people of this Court. The difficult part is in how to teach them.

How do I tell them that they need to question whether the deaths of those closest to them were accidents? Raznik was incredibly clever in the timing of his murders. Spreading out the deaths of my parents over the span of a couple of years removed any consideration that their deaths were anything less than organic. He knew what was going on with me and Tally because he was used to dealing with us in the dungeons. Raznik was many things, but unintelligent was not one of them. He knew to manipulate and isolate the most vulnerable citizens, turning them into faithful followers.

"Killing Commander Raznik was an accident," I continue, and I hope that Willow is listening. Sometimes, when she thinks I am not looking, I see her eyeing my marks, see the way doubt flickers on her face. I didn't enter that room with the express intention of slaying our leader, but I fear there will always be a part of her that feels she cannot fully trust me. "I won't pretend it wasn't a particularly motivating thought at times, but never in my wildest and angriest dreams did I plan for this. Now, all I can do is focus on breaking this cycle of lies and hate. Battlewood will rise again, as one. Healing will not happen overnight, and I must be okay with that."

......†......

The comfort I've begun to find in my new life does not last long. When Aleca and Willow are apart from me, either in the village or on the castle grounds, I realize how isolated I am here without them.

It brings with it a realization that I am truly alone in solving the mysteries left by Raznik, alone in pulling my Court back up out of the pits of corrupt despair. Knowing that my time with Aleca draws to a close, I begin to turn in on myself. The feeling is overwhelming, and for the first time in the several months since his death, I turn to the only thing I know numbs me.

There has been an aged bottle of juniper mead sitting on the drink cart in my office for months. I've left it there as a test of wills, but as I reach for the slim neck of the bottle, I know it's a test I've failed. Before I can talk myself out of it, I am lifting the bottle to my lips, drinking directly from it.

My eyelids flutter, the burning liquor a balm for my disconsolate anxiety. The sips become easier after that. Soon, my body feels loose and detached from itself, as if I am floating on a honey-colored sea.

I stand at the massive window in my office, staring down over the snow-covered grounds. In the distance, I spot patchy smoke rising from chimneys in the village. It would be a picturesque scene if it was anywhere but here. It's difficult to find beauty in a place that has caused so much pain. With a sigh, I bring the bottle to my mouth again, hissing against the sweet bite of the mead.

"Are you drinking again?"

Willow's voice sounds from behind me, cutting through the silence. I startle, making liquid dribble from my mouth. Wiping quickly at it, I turn, carefully hiding my right hand behind me.

"No, I'm not drinking," I say, the words tumbling too fast from me to be true. She raises her eyebrows, accusation painted across her face. "Don't."

"Don't what?"

"Don't look at me like that."

"How am I looking at you?" Willow asks. There is a patronizing sort of lilt to her voice, and it makes me set my jaw. It doesn't happen often, but every once in a while, glimmers of sanctimoniousness shine through. Now is one of those times.

"You know what I'm talking about," I say, my grip on the neck of the hidden bottle tightening. "Like you're this perfect, moral human and I'm some pitiable failure. You have no idea what I'm going through right now."

The temporary relief the mead had brought me is sour in my stomach now, and I feel everything more acutely than before. Fighting with Willow always twists something in my chest, and we've been arguing more and more lately. I feel sweat prickling at my hairline and down my spine.

"Jace, I understand—"

"No, you don't!" I cry, sweeping my arms wide. The nearly empty bottle appears from behind me. Willow's gaze narrows on it, a flicker of grim triumph on her face. It only further angers me. "You can't understand, Willow. I'm not—I know you've killed someone, too, and I'm not saying that it didn't matter, or, or that I—that you—" I flounder as I try to find my words, but the alcohol has made them difficult to grasp. My tongue feels swollen in my mouth, and the beginning thrum of a headache has taken up behind my eyes. I exhale shakily. "I didn't want this. I didn't want any of this. If I—the only reason I'm not dead right now is because I murdered the person who could have executed me, and, if I'm being perfectly honest, I wish he had."

"Don't say that," Willow says, stepping further into the room. She shakes her head, curls falling from their bun. "Don't say you wish you had died."

"It's the truth!" I cry, a humorless laugh falling from me. I am on the brink of hysteria; I can feel it rising in my throat. "I'm alive, and Raznik is dead, and even though I wanted him dead, I hate that I killed him. I hate that he's gone, and I'm here, and I'm drowning."

The last words tear from me with a sob. The bottle slips from my slackening hold, shattering on the hard floor. I fall to my knees, covering my face with my hands. The thin fabric of my pants soaks up the spilled mead, and glass crunches beneath me as I sink back onto my heels. I double over, my face so close to the floor that my nose nearly touches it.

There is a rustling of cloth and then Willow is kneeling beside me, a soft hand on my back. The weight of it is unsure against me, as if Willow can no longer figure out how to comfort me.

"All life is worth something, Jace," Willow tells me softly. I can read between the lines and I shake her hand off me, shifting away and rising. Even at my lowest, she can't help wielding the moral code she ascribes to, and it twists like a knife. Inhaling sharply, I do what I do best and shove my emotions down until they are little more than a dull pulse in my chest.

"Sure," I say. I wipe my eyes, turning away from her. "I should clean this up."

"Okay," she says. "I'll see you at dinner?"

"Sure," I say again, toneless. There is a long pause, a sigh, and then she is gone and I am left standing in the middle of a mess I fear I'll never be able to clean.

13

Near the end of the week, a guide bearing the Apaiji emblem on his left arm stands in the entrance of the castle, awaiting my sister. He is handsome in a youthful sort of way, his bronze hair in messy waves that do not seem to lay flat. He has his hands clasped behind his back, staring around the gilded entrance hall with great interest.

I make my way down the staircase, painfully slow in comparison to my usual gait. I am slowest to move in the early mornings when my body is still stiff. My ankle is terribly tender, and I have to rely on the assistance of a walking stick as I move so that I do not go sliding down the marble steps. A guard walks with me, my newest shadow. I hope that it will only be temporary.

"Good morning, Commander," the young man says. "I am Keiran. I serve the empire as one of the guide masters."

"Good morning," I greet the guide, extending my hand for a shake. "You may call me Jace, there is no need for titles. I thank you for getting my sister home safely."

"Think nothing of it," he says. "Will she be joining us soon?"

"I'm here," she calls from the balcony. She looks as if she has just woken, sleep lines still pressed into her cheeks. She has tied her hair back in a high tail, ready for her long trip. As she trots down the steps, her eyes brighten. "Keiran! I didn't know you were my guide. He knows everything about the Nautilus, he's like a walking encyclopedia. You'd never know he was my age."

Keiran flushes under the compliment, and I pray silently

that this means she has gotten over her crush on the older and off-limits Obsidian.

"You're too kind, Apprentice Grimme," he says.

"It's Aleca, we've been through this," she reminds him. She turns to face me, and her face crumples as she meets my gaze. "You're sure you're going to be okay?"

"I promise," I tell her. I take hold of her hands in mine, squeezing tightly. "These are much better terms under which you're leaving Battlewood this time. Enjoy this."

"Miss you already," she whispers tearily. I pull her into a tight embrace, and she squeezes me so tightly that it forces the air out of my lungs in a wheeze. I grab hold of her head, dousing her face in so many kisses that she finally pulls away, scrunching her nose and laughing. "Okay, okay! Mercy!" she cries.

"There she is," I say, smiling softly. "I love you, Al. Be safe, and send me a letter when you arrive back."

I face my guard and hold out a hand; he places a large cloth bag in it. I turn back to Aleca and hand it to her.

"What's this?" she asks, testing the heft of it.

"Some provisions for your journey. Soup balls, powdered drink, extra socks, cloaks. It's getting colder out there, and I won't have either of you falling ill on my watch."

We part with a final embrace, and I stand at the top of the steps to the castle, watching my sister and Keiran go until they are little more than specks on the horizon, marveling at the differences in the circumstances this time around.

Had things gone as Raznik intended only a few months ago,

Aleca would have been taken out next in the name of punishment. Aleca was a great threat to his hold over the Court. She stood to upend everything he'd built by working to uncover the corruption he wove into our Court. Though neither of us had known about the secret alliances my parents had formed with Apaiji, it seems Raznik must have known. Killing them had not been the end to the threat issued by my family, and he turned to his next target—my sister.

He could blame it on her learning magic right under his nose and then running off at a critical moment for his reign, which threw the entire Court into a spiral, but now I know the truth. Now, I understand that he never intended to let my family survive. Raznik never expected that I would turn against Battlewood, and that was where he began to misstep.

The moment he underestimated my sister, it began a downward spiral. He knew me as the warrior, as the delinquent-changed-loyal guard of our Court. I have never been known for being amenable to new mindsets, the least of which being an acceptance of magic and the unknown. He did not expect me to grow and change in the ways that I did in my time away from Court, and that was a critical mistake.

It is revitalizing to watch Aleca now leave for Apaiji as a free woman, a freedom I fought tooth and nail for. Filled with a renewed commitment to my Court, I turn and enter the castle, smiling when the heavy doors snap shut behind me.

......†......

Later, I find Willow in the greenhouses of the castle. She has been taking the opportunity to study under our master gardeners while here, learning about the flora of our Court which differs from Garyn's. She is alone in the greenhouse today, standing before a worktable with a mortar and pestle and several open jars. She has twisted her curls up and out of her face with a thin stick. I clear my throat and she jumps before turning around.

"Oh, Jace," she says, laughing a little. "You frightened me."

"Sorry," I say. I lean against the wall, hands behind me. She wipes her hands on the front of her skirts, leaving behind powdery gold and brown streaks. "What are you working on?"

"A tincture of marigold and cinnamon," she says. "I think it could be useful for inflammation."

I nod, chewing on my bottom lip. The air between us is tense. Unsure what to do, she slowly measures out the ingredients into separate vials before pulling out a bottle of carrier oil from a hidden pocket in her skirt. I clear my throat again before speaking.

"You need to leave, Willow."

She whirls to face me, hurt scrawled across her face. I realize instantly the way my words sound, and I yank my hands out from behind me, waving them as I shake my head.

"That's not what I meant," I say quickly. "Not like that. What I meant to say was that your village needs you. You can't stay here just because I've bitten off more than I can chew. My messes are not yours to clean up. You've been here for months now, and I can't keep being selfish."

Willow does not respond. She stares intently at a large, leafy plant, tracing the shape from top to bottom.

"I'm afraid that there's been much change between us," she finally says, dragging her gaze away from the plant to look at me. "I thought…maybe our differences didn't have to be so terribly different, but…"

"They are," I finish. "They're too great to ignore. I see the way you still look at me when you don't think I'm looking."

She flushes, looking down at her feet. Shame creeps across her face, guilt tugging the corners of her mouth down.

"I don't mean to," she says in a small voice.

"I know," I tell her earnestly, "but you want changes from me which I cannot give you. I'll never be able to live up to the idea of me in your mind."

This core difference has always been between us. We have argued over it many times, never finding resolution. The truth of the matter is that there will always be a threat of death by my hand, and despite the justifiability of it, she will never—can never—be okay with it. She's all but admitted that while she does not regret saving my life, she regrets taking the life of another to do so.

"Where do we go from here?" she asks, though we both know the answer.

"You go back to your village, and you serve your people. You find love with someone else, someone who will call you on instead of holding you back. You'll create transformative healing magic that will become the stuff of legends, and I will get to brag that I once shared the journey of my life with you."

My words are choked at the end, and I swipe at the moisture gathering in my eyes. Willow does the same. We both know that to remain together would be to hold the other back. We will never fully be able to bridge the gap between our lives. I cannot heal the chasms between my Court and the Courts around us if I am too focused on cobbling a patch over the chasm between myself and Willow.

"And you will do the same," she says, reaching forward for my hands. Hers are far warmer than my own, and she squeezes firmly. "You will find love in the arms of someone who can be a fighter and a defender, someone who can challenge you better than I ever could. You will transform the relationship Battlewood has with the Nautilus, and I will get to brag about the fact that I was there when it all began." She lifts my hands, pressing a kiss to the back of each one. A single, salty tear slips down her cheek and glances off my skin. Silence stretches between us, a string of unspoken emotion in it.

"I don't know how to say goodbye," she says. "It feels like a more permanent farewell, not just an, 'until we meet again.' I've never felt this before. The only other person I ever loved was Adler. He had been a friend since childhood, someone I never thought I'd lose, and we broke up because he didn't want me to become a healer."

"The only other person I loved was killed," I say, "so I don't have the best experience to draw from." I inch my pinkie over until it links with hers, and she curls hers around mine. "I cannot ask you to stay, though. It isn't fair for me to ask you to give up what you've spent years working toward."

"And I cannot ask you to abandon your Court at its most

vulnerable," Willow agrees. "It doesn't make this any easier, though."

"I know," I say quietly.

We look over at one another at the same time, and I know that our remorse is reflected in each other's faces. There had been a time when I would have thrown every responsibility away to pursue the thing I wanted, but that is something I can no longer do. Sometimes, the best thing that can be done for the person you love is to let them go, and it's a bitter pill to swallow. A farewell does not need to be permanent for it to still hurt, and I tell Willow as much. She nods, squeezing my pinkie with hers, and then lets go. I watch our pinkies fall away, knowing that our hands will not join as lovers again.

TWO

By the end of the day, two guards become my constant shadows. I do not intend to keep them forever, but the healer was right: until the novelty wears off, I am an open target. Many people are still furious about the shift in power, and I cannot allow my own hubris to be my downfall. I become grateful for them when, within a fortnight, another attempt is made on me. It is foiled in time by Llewyn, my newest and most dedicated appointee.

I enter my office to find him restrained in a sitting position on the floor by ropes, Llewyn standing at attention beside him. His blue eyes are wide, as if he cannot quite believe his success in capturing this man. I take in the scene before me, looking between the man and Llewyn. Unlike Ocin and Desnal, who had their own vendetta against me from long before I killed Raznik, I have no idea who Llewyn's captive is.

"What's this?" I ask.

"I caught him in your quarters, ma'am," Llewyn says. He brushes at an unruly lock of his fawn-colored hair which has sprung loose to droop between his eyebrows. The curl falls right back down and he jerks his head, shaking it out of his face. I'll have to remember to send him hair oil.

"What is your name?" I ask the man. He spits at me, and I raise an eyebrow. "Charming."

He scoffs, turning his head away from me. He's dressed in the same clothing as the kitchen staff, but I've never seen him before. His dark hair, thin and chin-length, sticks up at odd angles as if it has never seen a brush. His facial hair is no more kept than his hair, the wiry hairs overtaking his thin lips. Beneath woolly eyebrows, his eyes are bright and crazed.

Llewyn motions to a cup of tea on my desk that was not there when I had left that afternoon. I make my way over, examining the liquid from a careful distance. It looks like any cup of tea may look.

"Poison?" I ask. The man does not respond, nor did I expect he would. I send Llewyn to find our apothecarist, drawing my sword and keeping it trained on the man while we wait for their return. He sends me a glare that could melt steel, and I make a show of yawning widely. He mutters a very creative name for me.

It takes some time before Llewyn arrives with Nils in tow. Nils greets me with a nod, sparing a glance at the captive man before pulling out his travel kit and assessing the tea. I sheath my sword again, flexing my fingers; the joints have gone stiff from my grip on the hilt. With a grim look, he reads out his findings.

"Aconite, ma'am," he says. "A single sip of this would have

killed you. He went above and beyond with his dosage. He works for you?"

"Unlikely," I say, shaking my head. "I've never seen him before. If I had to wager a guess, I'd say that he stole a kitchen uniform and impersonated staff to gain access to my quarters. Would that be a correct assumption?" I turn my attention back on the man, who has remained silent and fuming in his ropes. He turns his nose up at me, and I take it as confirmation.

"I'm going to leave this with you," Nils says, placing the travel kit on my desk. "I'd consider familiarizing yourself with poisons and their antidotes." He eyes my neck, still healing from the attempt two weeks prior. "A salve of lavender and lemon juice will assist in fading that, if you wish it to go away."

"I'll see to it," I say. I reach into my pocket, withdrawing a small pouch of coins. I hand it to Nils, shaking my head when he tries to refuse. With a grateful sort of look, he pockets it, and then he leaves.

"What do you want to do about him?" Llewyn asks, nudging the man with his toe. I sigh, running a tired hand through my short, silver locks.

"To the dungeons with you," I say. "I'm awfully sick of putting my own people behind bars."

······†······

Though the threat of danger lingers, I do my best to settle into my role as leader of the Court. I fear there will always be a level of discomfort there, but there is no growth in comfort, and I must learn to be okay with being uncomfortable, if only temporarily. I return to what I've been trying to do since I took over: figure out what Raznik was hiding.

With winter settled over Battlewood, now is the time to refocus energies. My Court is weak and does not know where to turn for guidance. The disappearance of Elouned, Raznik's bloodthirsty Valkyrie, weighs on me. The mystery behind the deaths of my parents and Tally still lingers and in my spare time—which is admittedly scarce—I do all I can to untangle the knotted web of lies woven by generations of Razniks.

Evening finds me staring down at the floor, hands on my hips. The circle of runes and symbols are still etched into the warped wood, as deep and as bright as the day they were laid. I can make no sense of them. I narrow my eyes and walk around the circle, same as I have done every evening before. It has not helped yet, but it makes me feel better to know that I'm not actively ignoring the problem, which is historically a particular strength of mine. The bottle of juniper mead lingers ever-near to my person. Since the departures of my sister and Willow, it has been my only true companion.

There is a dull throb behind my eyes that has been threatening to overtake me all day. Even in his death, Raznik is nothing but a headache to me. I give up and unroll the carpet to cover the images back up. I have not shared this discovery with anyone yet—I cannot be sure who is my ally and who is still an enemy in my home. I climb the single step up to the corner platform where my desk sits. Behind it, a massive window stretches from floor to ceiling.

The sun has already made its descent behind the mountains

and stars twinkle in the dark, cloudless sky. I stare with my hands clasped behind my back to relax my mind and hold off the headache. I can hear muted pounding and for a moment, I cannot tell whether it is my head or someone outside of my door. I rub my temples and the pounding continues.

"Commander Grimme?" a voice calls.

"Enter," I call. I suppress a sigh. I haven't had a moment alone all day, and now it seems I will not. I turn away from the window as the door creaks open. Parin, the second guard I've appointed to be my shadow, enters with a rolled piece of parchment and a wrapped package in his hand. He stands at attention before me, and I wave my hand. "Parin, we've been through this," I tell him. "Unless we are at some formal event, you are free to be at ease around me."

"Yes, Commander," he responds with a sharp nod. He does not change his position and I stare for a moment before cracking a smile. He is one of the fresher warriors that have turned out for Battlewood, and he is afraid to misstep. I remember those days clearly. There was a mass exodus when I took over, and it left a wide gap in service. Truthfully, I'm glad for it; there was mean blood in our military under Raznik, and that is not the mark I want to carve for Battlewood under my rule.

"What can I do for you?" I ask.

"These just came for you," he tells me, handing me the items. "There is also someone here to see you. He says he knows you. He is with the guards outside."

"Who is it?" I ask, breaking the wax seal and unrolling the parchment. I scan it quickly and roll it back up. It is nothing of pressing importance. The package is left unopened; it is a tome on battle magic, and it will have to wait until later. If I try to read now, my migraine will become incapacitating.

"Aureus, Lady Commander," a voice lofts from behind Parin. I look over his shoulder and see Aureus walking through the double doors of my quarters like he owns it, hands outstretched and a grin on his face. My heart leaps at the sight of him, excited.

"How did you gain entry? My guards will hear about this," I say sternly. Parin blanches for a moment, convinced he's misstepped, before I break into a grin and meet Aureus' open arms. He wraps me in a hug tightly before letting me go. I have not seen him since my time at the temple, but it feels as if we have been friends forever. I am surprised at how pleased I am to see him. I had enjoyed my time with him, but never expected we'd meet again. We found kinship in each other during my brief stay in that tiny village, a bond over our own carefully suppressed emotional demons. It's nice to know that our time together was not for nothing.

"Ah, don't go too hard on the guards," Aureus says. "I am devilishly charming." Aureus winks at Parin, who stands gaping like a fish out of water.

"You've done well, warrior," I tell him. "You may be dismissed." Parin hesitates and then gives me a mixture of a bow and a salute before turning and leaving. I press two fingers to my lips to stifle a laugh. "What brings you to the wintry mountains of Battlewood?" Aureus drops into a chair by the fire and holds his hands outstretched, warming his fingers. "Shouldn't you be annoying villagers somewhere?"

"The joy of being alive, Commander," Aureus says, "is that you call the shots on what life looks like. You don't have to just do one thing or another. I submit my humble services to you. I had heard that you were the newest commander of Battlewood, wanted to see if it was true—which it looks like it is. Congratulations?" His statement ends in a question, unsure. I shrug at him with a half-smile.

"Thank you, I think," I respond. "It was not planned."

"What happened?" he asks. He leans back in his chair, his thumb and index finger propping his face up on one arm of the chair; his other hand drapes lazily over the other arm of the chair, and the firelight glints off the many gems on his ringed fingers. He stretches his legs out on the ottoman, more comfortable in ten minutes than I've yet to be in this office. A current of jealousy shoots through me—why can I not find comfort and peace in my new role? The jealousy is quickly overtaken by guilt. It is not Aureus' fault that I am so uncomfortable and anxious. I doubt if I'll ever truly be comfortable here.

I motion to the decanter filled with a tart juice and he nods. I've tried to move away from alcohol, but the urge to drink is ever-present. A small bottle of mead rests hidden inside an opaque carrier bottle. As surreptitiously as I can, I tip it over my glass; the juice swallows the color of the liquor. I do not pour much, only enough to quell the worst of my anxiety and keep the shaking of my hands at bay. It's disordered, but I am only one incredibly flawed human.

"Do you want the long version or the short version?" I ask. He makes a go-ahead motion for me, inviting the long version, and I fill him in as quickly as possible, handing him his glass as I speak. "I had no intention of remaining in Battlewood," I finish, "and now, in the most twisted series of events, I am the leader of the entire Court. My village, and all the smaller villages spread throughout our Court, are looking to me for guidance, and I have no idea where to turn."

"Gods damn it all, Grimme, you don't do anything halfway, do you?" Aureus asks me. His voice, teasing as it is, cannot fully keep out his edge of concern. His eyes trace the jagged and still-healing scar along my carotid. There is only so much that a honey and lavender salve can do to fade it from an angry red to a puckered pink line. I have been pacing throughout the duration of my story, and now I drop into the chair opposite his with a groan. I throw an arm over my face, out of words. "Well, as next-in-line for the throne at home, I can tell you—,"

"I'm sorry, as what?" I ask, shooting upright in my seat. Some of the drink in my glass sloshes over the rim and I lift my hand to suck the liquid away. "Is there anything else you'd like me to know, Your Royal Highness?"

"Oh, did I not mention that when we met outside the temple?" he asks me innocently. I level him with a gaze.

"I think you are well aware that you did not tell me that, Aureus," I deadpan.

"My apologies, Your Commandership. Would you still like my advice?" I mimic his earlier go-ahead motion, rolling my eyes. "You have to give them a reason to love you. No Court does well when they are frightened."

"How do I do that?" I ask. "It seems that no one can get past who I used to be, and on top of that, now they think I'm a murderer—which I suppose technically, I am."

"Who did you used to be?" Aureus asks me.

"A drunk who made bad decisions," I say flatly.

"Well, there's your first course of action, then, isn't it? Prove that you aren't that girl anymore. You can't be going around telling people you've changed and that you're looking out for their best interest if they can't see your change. Get out there. Meet your people. Host a banquet, if you must, but do something. And, in the meantime, you will hire me on as your right-hand man to assist and guide you however I may."

I know that he is right, but it does nothing to quell the anxiety that rises in my throat. I am not a people-facing type of person. Many of my people still hold Raznik's death against me. I have allies in pockets of Battlewood, but they are scattered and quiet. The last time I faced everyone at a gathering, I wound up in a ball on the floor, overtaken by a panic attack. He must read it on my face because he says,

"Let me help you, Jace." It is the most serious I've ever heard his voice.

"Okay," I say in a small voice. It is humbling, verging on embarrassing, to need help, but I know that I am in over my head. "Okay."

Gently, he leans over and pulls the glass from my hand. His eyes glint with understanding, a sad smile tugging at his mouth.

I swallow hard, nodding. Aureus moves toward the fire, pouring my glass out over the flames. They flare with a sizzling hiss before receding again.

"We'll get through this, Jace," Aureus says, pulling me up into a bone-crunching hug. I sink into his hold, and we stay like that until the fire begins to wane.

......†......

My hands begin shaking within hours. My roiling stomach is the next thing to betray me, and I make it to a bin just in time to purge the contents of my stomach. This continues through the night, and my eyes are dry with exhaustion as the sun begins to rise. Aureus keeps vigil in a soft chair beside my bed, holding my hair back and alternating out cool compresses to wick away my sweat. With a gentle brush of his hand on the top of my head, he tells me he will be back shortly and then leaves.

I make the decision to stay in my bed, wishing for some form of mercy. Instead, I have to lean over the edge of my bed just as another wave of sickness sweeps through me, though it is little more than bile and acid at this point. I wipe my mouth with a quivering hand, cursing Aureus for this. I know that he is not to blame—he did not force me to drink—but he is the one who convinced me to stop, and it feels better to blame someone else.

As if on cue, Aureus enters my quarters. I manage a look halfway between a glare and a grimace. He places a mug of something on my bedside table. Steam rises from it and reflects off what tiny bit of light has broken through my drawn curtains.

"Passionflower tea," he tells me. "It will help you sleep and will also help you with the shaking."

"Thanks," I say. The tremor in my hands has found its way to my voice. Still twisted and draped over the side of my bed, I sit up with a struggle and sip quietly while Aureus watches me. Satisfied that I've finished the tea, he sits on the edge of my bed. "How do you know these tricks?"

"We are none of us without our demons, Jace, and I pray that when the day comes and mine finally catch up with me, you'll be there to catch me. We must take care of each other. It's a cold world, otherwise," Aureus says.

My eyes begin to flutter, heavy with sleep. Aureus pats my leg and rises.

"Try to sleep. I'll be back in a few hours to check on you. Your head guards have been told you're under the weather for a couple of days. Take this time to try to find yourself again. I know you're going to feel like trash for a while, but you have people in your corner. Use them."

I mumble incoherently as sleep overtakes me. When I wake again, I am soaked with sweat. My shakes have returned and every part of my body aches. My joints feel frozen, and it takes great effort to unfurl my clenched fingers from the fists they've formed in my sleep. I have been grinding my teeth uncon-sciously; a sharp ache in the hinges of my jaw radiates up into my ears.

I do not remember feeling like this the last time I stopped drinking. Have I truly gotten so much worse, or did I lose those days to sickness? It frightens me to think that parts of my past are gone from me without my knowing.

Another mug sits on my table, but it is not passionflower tea this time. A scrap of parchments reads, "St. John's Wort. – A." I sniff before tasting it. It is not as bitter as it smells. I finish off the drink in two large gulps and toss the heavy blankets off me. I am shaky and unsteady as I rise; I assume the tea is to help minimize this. Stripping from my sweaty clothes, I kick them aside. The cool castle air is refreshing and I do not redress myself immediately. I can feel a sticky sheen of sweat on my body, despite the lack of fire in my hearth. I separate the curtains a hairsbreadth and notice that a fresh dusting of snow coats the ground and village below the castle. Snow continues to fall lazily from a grey sky.

From where I stand, I see directly into the village where I grew up. It looks like ants from here, but I can clearly make out the training grounds, the forest where Tally and I used to hide out, and my charred home. I have had barely a second to spare in my investigation into their murders. There is a lack of justice in doing so—their murderer is already dead. I will never get my answers. Guilt rises in me as I realize how much I've allowed my vices to supersede the things that matter most; not for the first time, I've chosen myself over my family.

I allow the curtains to come back together and turn my back on the window. As goosebumps begin to erupt over my body, I reach for a fresh tunic and sleep pants. Without a fire in the hearth, the room has grown icy cold. Barefoot on the slate, a chill begins to rise through me.

The fever seems to be breaking, even if my shaking is still there. I fuss with some tinder in the hearth and sigh with contentment as heat begins to climb up my numb fingers. I stretch out on the carpet that lays in front of the fireplace before curling onto my side and staring into the flames, sending a prayer to Karishua that I break the hold I'm in soon.

For three more days, I cycle between sleep, sickness, and, at my lowest point, begging Aureus for something to take the worst of the edge away. I can do little more than protest weakly as he goes through my room, leaving no crevice uninvestigated. When at last he's finished, he sets the collection of bottles out for me to see. Shame turns my stomach at the number of them, all with varying amounts of liquor.

Taking a drink here and there had made it seem I was functioning without issue, but confronted with the reality, the severity of my drinking leaves me squirming. In a fit of embarrassed anger, I fling them into the hearth. They shatter against the back of it and the fire swallows the glimmering shards of glass.

My office is the same. He carefully places each bottle on the small table before the hearth and looks at me.

"I want you to tell me who you're doing this for," he says, handing me a bottle as he jerks his head toward the fire. I take it unsurely before turning to face the flames.

"For my parents," I say, throwing it. Aureus hands me another. "For my sister!"

Over and over, we do this, our voices rising as we go until we are shouting.

"Who are you really doing this for, Jace?" Aureus demands, handing one of the last bottles to me.

"Myself!" I cry, flinging the bottle into the flames as hard as I can. My chest is heaving with exertion, still weak from withdrawal, but I feel on fire for the first time in weeks. Aureus throws his arms around me, squeezing tightly and pressing a kiss to the top of my head. I hold him close, and though I am crying now, the tears are not accompanied by the despair I've been feeling for so long.

"It's okay to be selfish sometimes," Aureus says, his words muffled by my hair. "It's not a dirty word. You have to look out for yourself as much as you do anyone else."

"I don't feel like I have the right to be," I say, turning my head and pressing my cheek against the soft velvet of his shirt. The rising and falling of his chest is soothing. I try to match my breathing to his.

"There's an age-old adage, 'You must love yourself before you love anything else,' and while I hate how trite it is, there is truth there. Recognizing that you're worthy of goodness doesn't mean no one else is. If you spread yourself too thin, you'll have nothing to give to yourself, and a Court is only as strong as its leader."

I am quiet as I absorb his words. Aureus pulls away, scrutinizing me with those sharp sapphire eyes. I know I must look like I am on the brink of a breakdown. It's been days since I brought a brush to my hair.

"Choose yourself sometimes, Jace," he tells me. "If your cup is always full, you'll never find peace."

He kisses my cheek, his bristly beard scratching my face. I nod and step away, reaching for the final bottle of amber liquor.

"I choose myself," I whisper, softly dropping the bottle onto the flames. They accept the offering greedily while I close my eyes, letting the heat of it wash me clean.

······†······

A quarter of the next day passes before Aureus comes barging back into my office the way he did upon his arrival. Warrior Parin—the poor kid—follows hot on his heels, flushed and irritated.

"Commander, ma'am, I'm sorry," Parin says. He sounds breathless, as if he has just been chasing Aureus. Aureus, on the other hand, stands calmly with his hands behind his back. This man is a trickster, through and through. "He did it again. I swear, I was watching—"

"I have full faith in your ability as a warrior, Parin," I tell him, cutting him off. He ducks his blonde head, shooting a glare at Aureus. "Aureus can—and does—fool even the wisest of people. He can't help himself. It's like a child who has been given a penny in a sweets shop." Parin presses his lips together, unsure whether he is allowed to laugh. I turn an eye on Aureus. "If you don't stop terrorizing my staff, it's to the dungeons with you, young man, and I'll have Parin himself accompany you."

"I'm innocent, your Commandership," Aureus insists. He holds his hands in front of him as if to prove it.

"You are anything but," I correct him. "Stop terrorizing Parin," I add. "I need all the warriors I can get, and you're making the job harder than they need it to be!"

"I make no promises," Aureus tells me. "Though for what it's worth, Parin, you've had my number from the start. You're a good one. Now out with you!" Parin hesitates, looking between the two of us.

"Aureus!" I cry. "I'm the one who gives orders here!" I pause for a moment, and then add begrudgingly, "You may leave, Parin." Parin snaps his feet together, saluting at me. I fight a smile as I raise my hand to my forehead in a salute, releasing him from his stance. He nods curtly, turns on his heel, and exits.

"I should be Commander," Aureus tells me, entering further into my chambers and settling himself at my desk. He plays with my quill, soft and grey, and then tucks it back into its holder. "What cute guards you have."

"Don't you have an entire kingdom to take over some-where?" I ask him. Aureus has moved on to rifling through the drawers of the desk. He pulls out a rolled leatherbound map and a stack of letters.

"Your belongings are awfully boring. I would expect much less…mundane from you," he complains, fanning himself with the letters.

"Catch me four years ago," I tell him. "Are you going to tell me why I have the misfortune of your company today, or am I just stuck with you?" There is no bite to my words; I enjoy every moment with him, and he knows it.

"You wound me, Commander," Aureus says, clapping a hand to his heart. "Here I am, offering my most humble ser-vices to help you lead your people, and you accuse me of nothing but mischief and mayhem." I level him with a look and he smiles waggishly at me.

"You are as humble as a preening peacock. Why don't we take a walk?" I suggest. "I could do with a change of scenery."

I bring Aureus through the cavernous halls of Battlewood Castle. Living here is ostentatious, but with my childhood home burned to dust and an expectation to lead, I have no choice. Raznik's old quarters, situated in a tower two floors up, are left untouched. I want to sort through his belongings before I cast them, and all memory of him, from this place. I suspect that he's hiding more in his quarters, where there was little chance of anyone entering unless he chose to allow them. I have only held office for a couple of months, and the last two weeks have entirely been a wash; withdrawal is a nasty battle to fight. There is one room I've wanted to investigate and have not yet, and this is where I bring Aureus. On the first floor, straight across from the entrance to the castle, is the grand hall. It is where galas, feasts, and events are held—though there have been few of those in recent times.

We enter the room. The doors open with a massive groan, the hinges long since used. It's dim, lit only by the light that manages to come in through the windows. Five chandeliers hang from 15-foot ceilings, the brass oxidized after years of neglect. Cobwebs drape between them; it is difficult to tell where the stands of crystals end, and the strands of webs begin. The stained-glass cathedral windows have been here since before the Raznik Dynasty took over. The trading between lands used to be bountiful and amicable until Raznik's grandfather, Eambroch Raznik, murdered the leader of Battlewood, as well as his only heir, to usurp the throne. Eambroch was a young, proud man. He took reign of the Court at only 22 years old, headstrong and power-hungry. Had the windows been installed after, I'm sure they would depict stories of destruction, power, and might. Instead, they are beautiful images of flora and fauna, a rainbow of bright reds, cobalt blues, golds, emerald greens, and silvers.

Several windows depict the images of people. The one nearest me is a depiction of four leaders, a representation of each Court, kneeling before a woman with the image of Apaiji pressed into her forehead. I stare at it with a furrowed brow, drawing nearer to it. At the center of the bottom of the window frame, a plaque reads, "The Courts before their Empress." My eyes widen as I realize what it means: the entire Nautilus answers—or should answer—to Empress Syiera. The woman who hosted us at her palace, who is training my sister, is the one who oversees us all. Why did she not say something before? And why did I never think about the fact that there must have been a higher command over the lands? I know that I should not be surprised by the lengths the Raznik family went to in order to isolate and manipulate our people, but each time I learn something new, I am surprised once more.

Beside this window, another depiction shows 10 people in hooded cloaks seated at a large table, a massive crystal floating above the center of it. A chain of what I assume is meant to be silver-and-golden light stretches between each person, linking them all together. "The Council of Elders," reads the plaque attached. When Eambroch created the Pact of Silence, he left no stone unturned, disrupting the progress of the Council in a large way.

Almost overnight, Battlewood became an isolated Court, one forced into self-reliance before it was ready. In a bid for power, Eambroch cut off all contact with the Nautilus, decreeing that outside influence would destroy our culture. We went from being unified to becoming a sovereign Court, one which created a name of austerity and fear. The sudden breakaway led to nearly five years of famine before our farmers could rework the land and livestock to meet the needs of the Court. The loss of life was a justifiable means to an end for the new dynasty.

The full history has been lost to time, and there are questions which will never be answered. I do not understand why Apaiji allowed such a high form of treason against its empire. I trace the dark and dusty engraved letters of the plaque with a whisper-soft finger. The metal is cool against my skin. Shaking my head, I turn away from the windows to observe the rest of the room.

Like the amphitheater, the floor boasts a mosaic inlay of the Battlewood crest—the old one. As the Raznik Dynasty took over, everything was changed. Prior to Eambroch, and the shifting of titles, Grand Chancellor Lysaar Tumis commissioned the crest in the image of an elk head with sprigs of juniper berries and lily of the valley, our Court's flower, draped off of his antlers. Grand Chancellor Lysaar, who ruled for nearly 50 years before his murder, valued the fruits of our land and forests.

This is the image pressed into the floor of the grand hall. The tiles are cracked in several places, but the image is still beautiful. It is much more welcoming than the crest Eambroch created, which features a sepiwin crossed with a sword hovering above an open book. It drives the point home—know your Court and die by your Court. It is this crest that is inlaid into the amphitheater floor.

The sharp clack of Aureus' hard-heeled shoes echoes off the high, empty walls as he walks through the Hall. Along the left wall, tables have all been pushed together. The tablecloths atop them are moth-eaten beyond repair. Chairs are stacked haphazardly, looking more like a barricade than anything else. Across the hall in the right corner, a small, raised step still holds instruments from the musicians of past parties. It looks as if a party was abandoned halfway through. To the left of the instruments, on a platform raised even higher than the instruments, is a throne. Like the brassy chandeliers, it has oxidized into a blue-green color. The seat cushion is a faded red, threadbare. Tips of the feather filling stick out of the worn cloth. This room speaks to the glory that Battlewood used to have before being turned into a cold, emotionless place. I turn to Aureus.

"I know what I want to do," I tell him. I point out the crest on the ground. "Do you see this? This is who we used to be. We used to be leaders, hunters, foragers, traders. We used to be a people united not out of fear, but out of comfort and loyalty. I want to get back to that. I want to bring back our roots."

Aureus nods thoughtfully, stooping to examine the crest closely. He brushes his hand over it, wiping away the decades of dust and grime that have settled. I grimace—who knows what is in that dirt?—but he continues until the entire image is unearthed. He rises and steps back, staring down at it. Against the dust on the rest of the floor, the mosaic circle shines brightly. A sudden beam of sunshine radiates through the stained glass, illuminating the crest in sparkling, multi-color lights.

"Well, if that's not a sign from your goddess herself, I don't know what is," Aureus remarks.

THREE

As it turns out, Aureus is a wealth of knowledge. His royal upbringing and years of training have put him in a unique position as my unofficial advisor. If he weren't expected to be in his own kingdom, I'd hire him permanently.

I make the official decision to host a celebration. It is there that I will announce the plans for the future of Battlewood. I anticipate quite a bit of unhappiness from Raznik's most ardent supporters, but there is no movement forward without action. I pretend that the threat of dissension does not fill me with apprehension.

I create invitations to the banquet for each Court. Aureus suggests that I bring in the leaders of the Crescent Isles, which he offers his assistance with. The Isles are a great distance from our own Nautilus, further south and led by a monarchy. It means he will return to Alymere to speak with his family and use his influence on them to make the journey to Battlewood. Should he succeed, they will become new allies to our Court. It will take some time, and we settle on a festival at the Spring Equinox. It gives us several months to make changes, overhaul the castle, and prepare Battlewood for its first guests in over a century.

Before he leaves, Aureus and I take supper in my private dining area, away from where the warriors and castle staff eat. He is pensive as he plays with the spoon in the bowl of thick soup.

"Where does Battlewood get its name?" he asks me, finally lifting the wooden spoon to his lips. "If there was a time before the iron hand of the Raznik Dynasty, why name your Court as it is now known?"

"It is a part of the changes made by Eambroch," I say. "Prior to his theft of the Grand Chancellor's rule, Battlewood went by a different name for centuries. Islilja. It did not carry the weight of might and power like Eambroch wanted, and so we became Battlewood. Our entire history was erased nearly overnight. Anyone who fought against the changes did not live to see the next sunrise."

"Another change you plan to undo?" he asks, curious. I nod. "How do you expect your people to react?"

"Poorly," I say without hesitation. "Though the tides were beginning to change here even before his death, Raznik still has a devout following of people. He, and his father and grandfather before him, weaponized charisma."

"Might I make an observation?" Aureus asks. His tone is gentle, and I have the feeling I will not enjoy this particular observation. I make a sound of affirmation. "There might…you've been through a lot in your life," he changes course. "Your parents' deaths, Tally's death, this," he says, motioning his arms all around him. "That's a lot for someone to have to deal with. It may not seem like it, but I'm willing to bet that all that trauma rears its head at unexpected times?"

I listen intently, thinking as he speaks. I remember the feelings of hopelessness on the ship, the fight I got into with my sister, the way I was overtaken by a panic attack at Raznik's death. I think about the constant urge to drink, the way that I wish I could go back to those destructive, self-soothing behaviors. It sneaks up on me when I do not expect it to and is triggered by things that are seemingly senseless. It never used to happen. Not until death started following me. Now, the slightest change in someone's tone sends me into a panic that I've done something wrong and will have to pay for it.

"I'll take your silence as confirmation," he says. "I want you to be prepared for the fallout. Some of your people will take well to the changes, but many will not. How will you handle that? Trauma makes us behave in ways we cannot explain. You've done a fine job at using harmful coping mechanisms, but you cannot be that person anymore. How will you protect yourself, and your mental wellbeing?"

"I don't…I dunno," I say, uncomfortable with his pointed and accurate assessment of me.

"You must figure it out," he says, reaching over to place a hand over mine. His hands are rough and warm, so different from my icy-cold hands. I never seem to be warm in this castle. "Consider seeing a mind healer. Do you have those here?" I snort derisively.

"Mind healers, in Battlewood?" I ask. "Please, admitting

you need a mind healer here is worse than death. It means you're weak, that you cannot control yourself. I know that's not what it actually means," I add as his face screws up in distaste, ready to reprimand me, "but that is how it has been seen here for decades. Mind healers have been reserved for those who are nearly incapacitated mentally. It would not do for the Court to learn that their leader is seeing one."

"Consider a private healer," Aureus presses. "No change without action, right? How can you remove the negative ideas unless you do the work to lead your people to change?"

He begins to eat his soup in earnest, disregarding that it's gone cold during our conversation. I watch as he eats, leaning back in the armed dining chair. I settle my arms on the armrests and slouch down.

"Something to think about," he says, finishing his bowl of soup and pulling my untouched bowl toward him.

······†······

Instead of making a decision, I delve back into the mystery of understanding what transpired in Raznik's last few months. The book which I had delivered proved to be useful as nothing other than kindling when all was said and done. I had hoped it would be a comprehensive look at battle magic and its applications, having come from the epicenter of our Courts. Rather than a history of battle magic, it turned into more of a fiction-alized history, and nothing I could pull any information from. I was back at square one. Annoyed, I threw the book into the fire and turned my attention to my plans of overhauling Battle-wood to its former glory.

We get to work on refurbishing the grand hall. It is a massive undertaking, and I have enlisted the help of warriors and skilled laborers alike. It takes the better part of a week before the grand hall returns to its original beauty. Watching it unfold before me inspires me to try to do the same for the rest of Battlewood. I have tossed the idea of a mind healer around since Aureus' departure, though I am no closer to a decision one way or another. In my heart of hearts, I know that a mind healer is a healthy answer, not a shameful one. My irrational side continues to drive home that mind healers are for weak-willed and unhinged people, which I am not. The battle never quiets between the two sides.

One evening, I find myself walking the familiar path past the funerial Pyre, into the trees behind it. The sun hangs low and heavy in the sky, piercing through clouds that promise snow. I pause at the Pyre, last aflame with the body of Commander Raznik. The memory of his burning body, the stars on fire in the sky, the shouts and jeers and sobs from our people, it all comes racing back to me. I walk toward it as if I am in a trance. The carefully carved stone stage is as clean as ever. There is not so much as a streak of soot to be found. A soft dusting of snow gathers on the stage, gathering and then blowing away, glitter in the wind. I circle the perimeter, running a finger along it. This is where so many have been honored. I walk around it twice, slowly, taking note of eroded stone to be repaired come spring. I pray we do not need to use the Pyre, even then. I pray that no one else may die.

As if led by a force other than my own, I move toward that

shrub where I found Tally, cold and unseeing in death. I drop to my knees, squeezing my eyes shut. The ghost of her body, curled into a small, fragile ball, rises like smoke behind my eyes. A rush of cold air and her giggle fill the air. My eyes snap open and I gasp. I am alone. I know I am alone. That laugh, though…it sounded so close. So close. So real. Why am I here? Why am I kneeling in the ice and snow at dusk? What could I possibly have expected out of this? I don't even remember making the conscious decision to come here.

"Tally," I whisper. My throat tightens. "Tally, I'm so…I'm so lonely." I begin to cry, too overcome to care about the overt emotional expression. "I miss you, Gods, I miss you."

"You don't have to, you know."

A scream catches in my throat. I scramble away from the shrubs, landing on my backside. My palms catch rocks and ice, burning.

"C'mon, Jay, am I really so frightening?" I can hear the pout in her voice, and I know she is twirling one of her rich black curls around her finger.

"This isn't real," I whisper. I don't sound convincing, even to myself. I press my palms into my eyes so hard that starbursts dance in them. I'm going insane. That's the only explanation. If I'm not going insane, then how is she talking to me right now?

A giggle starts back up. I pull my hands away from my face with dread. Before me, dancing on the tips of her bare toes in the snow, is Tally. She is as beautiful as the last time I saw her. If I look too closely, though, I see that she is nearly translucent, glowing around the edges. She wears nothing more than the sundress I found her in, strappy and far too light for the winter cold. A fine golden bracelet that I cannot recall her ever wearing before is clasped around her thin wrist. A strangled sob wrenches out of me as I stare. She spins around, lifting her delicate fingers to the sky, a spectral ballerina.

"I'm real," she tells me. She drops to her hands and knees in front of me, her bright blue eyes sparkling. She leans in, that wolfish grin of hers spreading. My heart is racing. My hands tremble as I reach out to touch her, but before I can make contact, she darts away again, picking up her dance.

"Tally, come back," I say, struggling to my feet. I follow after her, deeper into the thicket of trees. The last feeble rays of light disappear entirely after only a few steps in. Tally's skin still emanates a soft, champagne-gold glow. She flits between the trees; in contrast, I stomp and stumble to keep up with her. Branches snap and echo in the tall trees. "Tally, wait! Where are you taking me?"

"Follow me, Jace," she whisper-sings. "I have so much to show you!"

We break through the trees into a small clearing, where a small stone cottage sits. I've never been to this part of the woods, never even knew that this was here. The windows are lit, warm and inviting. Smoke rises out of the chimney. Who lives here? Through a frosty window, I can see flames dancing in a hearth. Beside the cottage is a water pump and a bucket. Remnants of water drip into the bucket slowly, as if someone was just retrieving water. A small pile of wood sits under the overhang of the cottage. The smell of food cooking from inside makes my stomach rumble.

"Tally, where are we?" I ask. We stand side-by-side, staring at the cottage. Instead of replying, she walks up to the door and knocks. I stare again at her bare feet and bare shoulders. She should be freezing cold by now. I should have given her my cloak. I unclasp it and bring it over to her. Tally shakes her head.

"I don't need that, Jay," she tells me. "Temperature can't hurt me." I falter and then resituate the cloak around my neck.

"Please, talk to me," I say. I reach for her hand, grab hold of it without a moment's hesitation. In an instant, everything changes. Her hand, soft and supple, turns to ice and bone. The lights in the windows go out, and they are black and opaque. The cottage, so cozy and welcoming, becomes stony ruins. Tally turns to face me, and I let out a proper scream. Her right cheek is exposed bone, as well as the hand I hold and the wrist attached to it. Her eyes turn fearful, her curls lose their luster, and her dress becomes tatters. Only the golden bracelet remains as bright as if it were brand new.

"Please help us," she cries. "Jace, please help us!"

A terrible, heart-rending screech fills the air, metallic and awful. The noise comes closer, and I turn to run.

"Jace!" Tally cries again.

I sob as I run. I move as fast as my feet can carry me, ignoring the stitch in my chest and the tears that have frozen on my cheeks. Howls tear through the night. Branches rip at me, catching my hair and cloak. At the edge of the thicket, a branch snaps back into my eye and cheek. Blood blinds me and

I trip over a stone. I land flat on my stomach, my arms and legs sprawled. Whatever made that sound has not given chase. I lift my head, vision blurred red by my blood, and realize that I'm back by the shrubs where this started. I am shaking, frightened and exhausted. I lay my head back down, giving in and letting out a scream. It rips at my throat, every ounce of emotion in my body pouring into it. I scream again and let it turn into sobs that wrack my entire body. If I freeze to the ground tonight, I will not care.

······†······

"I found her!" a voice shouts. It is distant and sounds like it is underwater. "Grimme, can you hear me?"

I try to move, but every single joint is immovable. It is as if I am paralyzed. I try to lift my head and cannot. I try again and finally manage some movement. I am stiff and, I realize as I come to, sore and freezing cold. My left eye is crusted shut. Bits of memory come back to me. A shot of adrenaline sends me scrambling to a standing position; my body screams in absolute resistance at the movement. A dusting of snow falls from my body as I rise. My breath comes in desperate gasps. I look around wildly. It is pitch black out, nowhere near morning.

"Jace?" another voice asks. A hand rests on my shoulder and I shout out, jumping away from the contact. Linota's concerned caramel eyes stare at me. "It's just me and Galter, Jace," she says. She holds her hands up as she walks toward me, as if she is approaching a skittish creature. In a way, I suppose she is. One hand extends out toward me; the other holds a lantern burning bright.

"Lin—" My voice cracks as I try to use it. My throat is tender and burns. "Linota," I manage to croak out. I rub at my eye, breaking apart the blood and dirt and ice that has cemented it shut in a gruesome glue. It stings as the tight skin around the wound is pulled and twisted. For the first time, I realize that I'm shivering. Linota shoves a metal stein into my hands.

"Drink," she commands me. I do so immediately, like I'm back in her command and at her service. Like I'm a young and fresh warrior, not an exhausted and broken commander. I expect it to be filled with hot coffee, and I grimace when I taste lukewarm coffee instead. It pools in my stomach, warming my core, regardless. My fingers begin to thaw as they wrap around the stein. "What the hell were you thinking, spending the night out here?"

"D-didn't…mean to," I say through chattering teeth. I feel like a wounded child, surrounded by adults who are far more stable and wiser than I am. I clutch the mug of coffee tightly. My teeth begin to chatter in earnest from poorly repressed emotion and the freezing cold. I cannot fall apart in front of them. "I n-need to get b-back to my qu-quarters," I say. I try to imbue as much strength and command into my voice as possible, but I hear the quiver that lingers around it. "I th-thank you for your h-help."

"Grimme," Galter starts.

"That's enough, Galter," I say. I begin to hobble back toward the foot of the mountain. Climbing it to return to the castle is a daunting task. I wish my real home was not a pile of moldering wood. It would be so nice to sit at the rough wooden table, warm and dry and surrounded by my and my family's belongings. Instead, I live in a stranger's home. Before I can make it more than a few steps, my legs give way beneath me. Galter scoops me into his arms gingerly. "Pumedown," I slur. The adrenaline has worn away and I feel weaker than before.

"You know how we got to be where we are?" Linota asks, joining in step with Galter. "We knew when to accept help."

……†……

I am ordered to bed rest with a diagnosis of hypothermia. It doesn't matter. I find no rest or peace of mind. At night, my dreams are filled with Tally's terrified screams. I cannot shake the sight of her cheekbone peeking out of her skin, nor her bony fingers wrapped around me. She begged for me to help her. Help them, whoever the rest of them were. I worry that it was a hallucination—perhaps I had been outside for longer than I thought. The longer I spend time thinking about it, the stupider I feel. I should have known that there was something suspicious about it. Even if it were normal to see and speak with ghosts, I should have seen that it was a pale imitation of who Tally was. If I had been in my right mind, I would have seen it.

The Tally I knew never stopped talking. She was bright and outgoing. She was the type of person who thrived with physical contact: a hug, holding hands, anything that could connect her to another person. The skeletal Tally I walked through the woods with was aloof and shied away from touch. I know why, now. The moment I touched her, the illusion shattered. Was that really Tally? Did her body somehow survive the Pyre?

There is no way. I watched her burn. I sat at the Pyre for hours after her burning, refusing to allow anyone near it.

I feel like I'm going insane. I cannot trust my own memories anymore. Faced with endless time to think, I make up my mind. I have to talk to someone.

Finally, after nearly a week, I am given the all-clear by Healer Rex. As he prepares to leave, I hesitate and then speak.

"Excuse me, Healer, but I have a question," I say. My heart skips anxiously. I could change my mind. Take it back. He doesn't need to know what I am about to ask.

"Yes, Commander?" he asks. Gnarled hands hold tightly to his medicine bag. I pause a moment too long. "Commander?" he prompts.

"What do you know about mind healers?" I ask. The words taste like tar in my mouth. I know my face burns with shame. He eyes me for a moment, cocking his head to the side as he processes what I've said. I contemplate telling him that it is not for me, but Aureus' words come swimming back into my mind and I stay quiet.

"Quite a bit," he finally says. He adjusts his glasses on his face and sets his medical bag down. "What would you like to know?"

I gnaw on my lip, and then capture it between my index finger and thumb. I tug on it thoughtfully while I work out my next statement.

"Just how it works, I suppose," I say. "Where one may access them, the confidentiality of it, basic information."

"Pardon my candor, Commander, but if you're seeking a

mind healer, you may say so," he responds. Blast, he has seen right through me. I used to be so much better at throwing people off my trail. "Shall I send my wife to see you this evening? She is quite a talented healer—though I will confess, this old man is biased."

"Please," I say. "Though do impress upon her the need for privacy." He nods and sweeps out of the room in a rush of velveteen.

Anxiety gnaws at my stomach all day. Every knock at the door makes me jump. What if someone sees her come to my office? The healer said that she is one of the best—does the best also mean renowned? The day stretches into dusk, and then into twilight before there is a soft knock on my door. I hurry over and yank the doors open. A tiny woman cloaked in a hooded swath of burgundy velvet stands patiently with a serene smile on her face. I hurry her in and slam the doors shut behind me. The loud sound rings in my ears but the mind healer does not so much as flinch. She is as calm as I am anxious.

"Commander," she greets. Her voice has an interesting timbre—the first thing that comes to mind is a soft flute. If it is meant to set me at ease, it has its intended effect. She lifts the hood from her head; soft droplets of melted snow drip onto the carpet where they disappear into the design. Short, spiky hair the color of a fawn appears. "My husband said you were interested in meeting with a mind healer."

"Uh, yes," I say. "Well, no. Well, maybe. I—"

"I know that mind healers have a bad name for themselves,

Commander Grimme, but you would be surprised at the people I have seen in my time. May I sit?"

"Oh, yes, of course!" I start. "Please, let me take your cloak. I can dry it by the fire while we talk." She undoes the clasp at her throat and delicately hands the cloak to me. Every single move this woman makes is calculated and decisive. I rush to hang it across the mantle, far enough that no embers can catch on it. "I'm sorry, I don't even know your name," I say as I perch on the chair across from hers. I cannot quite find it in me to settle.

"Lilith, Commander. Or Healer Lilith, should you so choose," she says. She crosses her ankles and stares closely at me. Her eyes, the color of cognac, narrow as she takes me in. I shift uncomfortably, unsure what she's looking for—or finding. At last, she breaks her gaze and I exhale slowly. "What can I do for you, Commander?"

"To be honest, Healer Lilith, I didn't even want to talk with you," I say. Healer Lilith quirks a thin eyebrow, a small, wry smile on her lips. Realization dawns on me and my mouth drops open with mortification. "Oh, no, that came out wrong. What I meant to say was that I've been…struggling, lately, and I've been trying to deal with it on my own. However, I don't think I'm succeeding." I slide down the arm of the chair I've perched on into a scrunched-up ball. I tug a leg up underneath me and fiddle with a stray thread poking out of the braided embroidery of my tunic. "I'm not saying that I want to see a mind healer, but I wouldn't mind knowing more about it."

"I see," Healer Lilith replies. Her voice maintains that calm neutrality. She is the epitome of put-together. Is that a result of years of mind healing, or does she come by that naturally?

"What I can tell you is that it comes with hard work and a willingness to be honest and vulnerable. You'll forgive my saying so, Commander, but those are not two traits I equate with you."

"Forgiven," I say. "You are entirely correct."

From a fold in her shirt, Healer Lilith pulls out a journal. She holds it out for me, and I eye it. The cover is embossed in charcoal markings. Situated in the center of the journal is a large blue stone with flecks of white and gold. A simple metal latch keeps the book shut. She wiggles the journal at me impatiently and I take it from her hands. The leather is much softer than I anticipated. The deckled parchment papers inside smell fresh and new.

"I'm not much of a diarist," I confess.

"It is a first step in mind healing," Healer Rex tells me. "I find it helps to get all of my thoughts out onto a page in one place than to spiral and intermingle until I cannot tell one thought from another."

"I'll try," I say, though it is a feeble promise.

"Your success will only be as good as your effort," Healer Lilith tells me. "Mind healing is a serious undertaking. You must be ready to do the work."

She has settled back into her seat, and she watches as I analyze the journal. It's quiet in the room, too quiet for my comfort, and I speak to fill the silence.

"How do I know this will work?"

"You don't," Healer Lilith says. "No one does. Mind healing is not a precise thing. It can be messy, emotional, and bring up things you may rather keep hidden. I would encourage you to keep yourself surrounded by those closest to you, Commander. You've been through a great deal in a relatively short life. I hate to see you become more isolated."

Healer Lilith seems to have a better understanding of me already than I had expected; I feel I may need to reapproach my thoughts on the validity of mind healing.

She rises and removes the still-drying cloak from its place in front of the fire.

"Until you are fully ready to engage, I shall wait. I can see myself out, Commander. No need to accompany me."

I watch her go, trying to make sense of her. She may have felt our session was informational and successful, but I'm left with more questions than before. I add her to the list of people who prefer to speak to me in riddles rather than clear, concise language.

I place the journal in the center of my desk and douse the fire. The hallway is quiet as I leave my office. Only two guards are present; I send them off for the evening. The hall is dimly lit by sconces along the walls. They flicker but cast a strong light along the walkway. Portraits line the walls. I have never given much attention to them. A cool current of air wafts down the corridor. I suppress a shiver from the sudden shift in temperature. I am still fighting off the effects of my run-in with hypothermia.

A sudden soft and feminine humming gives me pause. It is haunting, ethereal. An echo hovers at the end of each note as it rises and fades away. I turn around to find the source and see no one. I shake my head. Perhaps my ears are ringing. I continue my journey to my quarters. The moment I have refocused myself, the humming begins again. The voice is so familiar to me, though I cannot place where I have heard it before. I try to figure out the song before reminding myself that it is just ringing in my ears, and not someone singing. There is no one in this part of the castle at this time of night except for myself and my guards, and there were no female guards on duty tonight.

I have nearly convinced myself that it is in my head when the humming grows louder. I turn around again, and the sound stops once more. My pace quickens as I walk. The slap of my leather shoes against the stone reverberates off the high ceilings. The humming is directly behind me now. There is no denying it. I do not bother to look behind me. I break into a run. The candles in the sconces go out one after another, as if something—or someone—is blowing them out. I half-expect to be overtaken by some spirit.

I have never been so grateful to see the door to my quarters. I rip the door open and slam it shut. The humming ceases entirely and the only sound I can hear now is my labored breathing. I lean against the door, panting.

Something dark has taken hold of this land.

FOUR

I am out the door the next morning with no real plan, but a need to get out of the castle. It is early, but not so early that the Court still sleeps.

Wind whips and howls around me as I make my way down the cliff and into town. The snow whirls in all directions, impacting my visibility and making it difficult to walk. My feet crunch against the snow and rocks. I tug my cloak more tightly around me and duck my head, continuing my trek. Sun tries to peek through the heavy grey clouds, though I do not think there is a likelihood that it will break through.

There are few people outside in the village. A couple of children run, throwing snowballs. A farmer leads his livestock through the streets. A wheeled stall has been set up by a child and her father selling hot drinks. I stop at their stall. The child's eyes light up, excited at the prospect of business. The father stiffens and bows to me.

"Commander," the father says. His voice is low, and I can hear the nervousness in his voice. Aureus' words come back to me once more: I must get to know my people and show them that things are changing.

"Good morning," I greet.

"We're sellin' hot cider! You want some?" the child asks. Her father nudges her. "I mean, you want some, Commander?"

"Ellisana, do not bother the commander," her father chides. She bows her head, tugging at one of her brown braided pigtails.

"This is just what I need on such a cold day," I say. "Please, you don't need to be so formal with me. You may call me Jace." I hold my hand out, which the father shakes.

"I'm Ellisana, and this is my papa, Merrid," Ellisana says. "I'm tryin' to raise money for my mama. She's sick, and we need help." There is a small lisp to her voice from a missing front tooth.

I stoop to Ellisana's level. She is young, maybe seven. She takes after her father's dark hair and eyes. There is an earnestness in her little face. She opens a small locket that is on a long chain around her neck, showing me a small painting of who I assume is her mother before clipping it shut again.

"I'm sorry to hear that your mama is sick, Ellisana," I say. I put a hand on her shoulder. "One of my dearest friends is a healer in Garyn. Do you think it would be okay if she stopped by your home sometime to see your mama?"

"Really?" Ellisana asks. She turns to look up at her father. "Can she, Papa?" I look up at Merrid, waiting for an answer. He regards the both of us closely. I know that he is concerned—we have been taught for so long that Garyn is not to be trusted. He tugs at his salt-and-pepper beard. I rise again, not breaking eye contact with Merrid. I nod almost imperceptibly at him, an offer of trust. He relents with a sigh.

"I suppose," he says. "Understand that we can make no promises for you or your mama, Ellisana."

"I understand, Papa," Ellisana says.

"Here," I say, tipping a handful of gold and silver coins into the money tin. I've found that I have access to more money now than I could ever need. The Raznik Dynasty sat on money like a dragon atop its hoard. I do not plan to do the same. There are plenty of families and villages who could use the assistance. "Please take this. Give a free drink to everyone in the village—if it turns out that I have not paid enough, come to me and I'll get you the rest. We will get help for your mama, Ellisana."

I am sent stumbling backwards as Ellisana launches herself at me. She wraps her arms tightly around my middle and squeezes.

"Thank you, Miss Commander!" she cries. My hand hovers for a moment before patting Ellisana on the head. I have never spent much time around children, and this one is as exuberant as they come. I lock eyes again with Merrid. He bows his head to me with a smile. It does not completely reach his eyes, still unsure how far to trust me, but it is a start. Ellisana lets go of me and fills a small paper cup with steaming cider. She shoves it into my hands with her own mittened ones. I can see flecks of cinnamon and nutmeg floating in it. Merrid unlocks the stand and readies the stall to be wheeled about.

"We live near the pub," Merrid tells me. "Two homes up on the left. If your friend chooses to help us." He cannot keep the doubt out of his voice.

"We will be by within the week," I promise. Ellisana waves brightly at me before setting down the street. I watch them pause at a home and hear her knock on a door.

"Here you go ma'am, free cider! It's on Commander Jace!" she exclaims, pointing a wooly hand at me. A curious head pokes itself outside of the door and looks toward me. I raise a hand in silent greeting. I leave Ellisana and Merrid to their work and continue through the town towards the outskirts. I had not planned on going into Garyn, but suddenly, the prospect of seeing a friendly face is too tantalizing to ignore, even if we ended on painful terms. I stop a guard on patrol and quickly write a note to Linota, giving her instructions in case I am not back quickly. He promises to deliver it straight away and heads toward the training field. I return to the castle, throwing together a bag of food, clothing, and supplies to make the trek to Garyn. It won't be a long trip, but it won't do to go unprepared.

I can just make out the outline of Devent Forest. It is my hope that I can cover enough ground that I do not have to camp out in this weather. The trek is made more dangerous than I would prefer by the wind, snow, and ice. Despite the cold, it is nice to be away from the castle and feel the fresh air on my face. I am away from ghosts and fear, away from the mysteries and lies. Perhaps I can finally get a decent night's sleep.

As the sun continues climbing behind the clouds, I stop to build a fire and make lunch. The coffee I brought in my travel stein is still hot. I drink deeply from it, feeling it warm my core. I do not let myself settle for too long. If I do, I will not want to start again. I can already feel the cold stiffening my joints and muscles. I force myself to rise again, dousing the fire with snow. It goes out with a hiss, and with it, the warmth. I sigh and start back down the sloped land toward the gorge and forest.

I hit a patch of ice and go sliding down the hillside, coming to a stop just past the first line of trees in the forest. I've never been so grateful to be traveling alone; having a witness to that would have been mortifying. I could swear I hear a giggle behind me, but I chalk it up to winter wildlife in the forest. I know for certain that there is no one here—who else would be foolish enough to tramp through the forest in this weather? I stand up and brush myself off. I let out a forlorn sigh as I real-ize that my pants are damp from my impromptu sledding. I consider lighting another fire, but the trees are so dry that I worry rogue embers will catch and spread.

A crack sounds from my right and I snap my head toward it, listening closely. There is nothing for a moment, and then another crack. I move toward it, damp pants forgotten. Another crack sounds, and there is no mistaking that it is the result of being stepped on. Is there another person here? Perhaps it is wildlife? It couldn't be a bear, certainly. This is not their season. The next crack comes from directly next to me and then again behind me. I turn around and find nothing. I hear a giggle again and know now that it was not a chittering animal at the mouth of the forest. I press my hands to my face and drag them slowly down my cheeks with an uneasy sigh. I bring my hands together directly under my chin as if in prayer and look up at the sky. I don't want to look back down. I don't want to know what is in this forest with me.

"Won't you at least say hi to me, Jace?"

I slowly lower my face from the sky, dread filling my veins. Adrenaline turns my mouth metallic. Tally stands in front of me, blue eyes bright and a smile on her face. She is still in her sundress, still barefoot. In the daylight, it is impossible to make out the soft glow from the other night, but I know that it is still there. I know that I am looking at a ghost. I know that this is not really Tally.

Even knowing that, it does not stop my stomach from flipping or my heart from stuttering. It is jarring to see her standing here, looking so alive. I stare closely at her cheek, trying to find any indication of a gaping wound or a show of bone. I find none. If I ignore her weather-inappropriate dress, I can almost believe that she is here with me, that she never left me. That she was never taken from me. The belladonna tattoo burns beneath my cloak, a hidden reminder of her death.

"Tally," I say. "What is happening?"

"What do you mean?" she asks me. She scoops up snow and holds it over my head, letting it fall onto me in a gentle drift. I shake my head, wiping the errant flakes from my numbed face. She giggles and repeats the action.

"Stop," I say, grabbing her wrist. It turns to bone in my hand. I suppress a gag. There now is the split in her cheek, larger than before. Her lips turn blue, her eyes milky and afraid once more. Her dress is more tattered than the last time, and I see a new wound exposing part of her clavicle. Still glinting in the sun is that golden bracelet, and I'm confident now that it was not hers in life. "Why are you here?"

"I'm not supposed to be here," she whispers. I have never heard her so frightened. The trees bend and sway in a sudden gust of wind. "I'm not meant to leave the woods. That's where she lives. That's where they keep us." Her voice quavers, and tears streak down her gaunt cheeks.

"Why?" I press. "Who is doing this to you? What is happening?" I press a hand to her left cheek, tenderly brushing her mousy hair out of her face. The wind continues blowing, sending glittering swirls of snow up around us.

"Please help us," she begs. The tears turn to crystals on her frozen face. The wind picks up in earnest now, howling through the empty branches of trees. She tries to pull out of my grip on her wrist. I tighten my fingers like a manacle on her, afraid to hold too much tighter. Her bones are so delicate in my hand. "Jace, please," she says. "I have to go." I release her and she darts away, disappearing into shimmering nothingness as she goes. The wind stills again, and I am left standing in the middle of the forest entirely alone.

I make it through the woods and to Devent Gorge in record time. I never move so fast as when I am chased by ghosts, it turns out. I stop at the gorge, panting and clutching at a sharp stitch in my ribs. As I catch my breath, I scope out the surroundings. Devent Falls has frozen over, the movement of water arrested in ice. Icicles drape off the cliffs where moss usually grows. It promises a difficult border crossing. I am more dexterous this time than the last, having full sobriety and thus full command of my body movements. There isn't a chance of my scaling the cliff wall down to the bridge safely, and I choose the overturned log instead.

I test the wood, which holds fast and firm. I must talk with Garyn about agreeing to build a true bridge in place of this dead tree. Abandoning all humility, I sit on the tree and scoot myself across the way. Small pieces of ice and wood break off and drop onto the frozen river below with a tinkling echo. The first time, I watch them go. The height is dizzying, though, and I cling tightly to the tree to avoid falling. I keep my gaze resolutely ahead, watching the cliff of Garyn creep closer and closer. This is certainly not a swift or precise means of travel, but I do not trust myself any other way. Had I tried to walk, I would have lost my footing in an instant.

My thighs burn by the time I find land again. They quiver when I stand. I feel like a colt taking its first steps. The snow is untouched here, a pillowy blanket. It comes up mid-shin, and I am grateful for the thick, fleece-lined leather boots on my feet. I march my way through the forest and realize only a few steps in that I do not actually know the way to Willow's village. I suppose it must be near here, since she had been harvesting ingredients when she found me last summer. I start walking again, hoping that I'll find some indication along the way.

It does not take long for that to happen. As I walk, I begin to see trees marked with runes. In the barren winter, the color-ful flags and strings of glass and stones are bright. The chimes that hang from the branches come together and fill the air with a ringing knell. This must be her village outskirts. Bolstered by the promise of seeing a friendly face, I find a spring in my step that was not there before.

Soon enough, I find the circle of huts where she and her townspeople live. With a curse, I realize I have forgotten what her hut looks like. I suppose I was not in my best mind the last time I was here. I enter the circle, looking for any sign of which may be hers. A villager standing near the firepit eyes me suspi-ciously. She leans over to the person standing next to her and whispers something in his ear, never looking away from me. He follows her gaze as well. I make my way over to them. They both take a step back.

"Hello," I say. "I'm looking for Healer Finch. Would you be able to point me toward the direction of her home?"

"What do you want with her?" the woman asks. It seems the time I spent here last year did little to change the minds of the villagers. I wonder if they feel I had a bad influence on their Head Healer.

"I'm sorry to have frightened you," I say. "My name is Jace—Commander Jace Grimme, of Battlewood. I'm not here to cause issues or harm. Willow—Healer Finch is a close friend of mine, and I've only come to pay her a visit."

"Why should we believe you?" the man asks me. I fight a scowl, trying to remind myself that they have no reason to trust me.

"I know that Battlewood has caused great harm in the past. I cannot change that, but I can apologize for it. Words do not carry near the weight as actions, but I can only offer my sincerity," I say, trying to sound every bit the magnanimous leader I'd like to be some day. I stand, waiting as patiently as I can while they make their decision to trust me or not. Finally, the man points at a hut behind me. A small placard reading, "Head Healer," swings back and forth in the calm breeze. "Thank you," I say. My tone is more brittle than I intend, but I'm cold and annoyed.

I make my way over to the hut and knock on the door. A fractured reflection of myself stares back at me from the large garnet crystal inlaid on the door. The door opens and a young man answers. He looks around our age, perhaps 18 or 19.

"Yes?" he asks. He is dressed in a tan tunic and breeches, an olive-green apron wrapped around his midsection. His caramel hair has been fastened up in short tail, a small cloth cap atop his head. His sleeves are pushed up to his elbows. I get the distinct impression I've interrupted him mid-task.

"I'm looking for Healer Finch," I say.

"Are you ill?" he asks.

"No," I say, "this is a social visit, not a medical one."

"Who is it, Briar?" Willow asks, coming to the door. Her eyes widen when she sees me. "Jace!"

"Hi, Willow," I say. Briar moves out of the way for Willow, who greets me with a tight hug. I breathe in her scent, spicy and earthy. Her curls tickle my cheeks and ears. I let out a sigh, happy to see her. I wrap my arms around her as tightly as I can, as if I can pour out all of my anxiety and fear in one hug. Many unspoken things are shared in the embrace, and we hold on for a moment longer before releasing one another and taking a step back.

"What are you doing here?" she asks me. She grabs my hand and tugs me into the hut. Warmth washes over me so suddenly that my entire body is wracked with a shiver. Briar hands me a cup of something steaming. I sniff it; it smells floral. Willow takes my cloak and small bag and hangs them both by her fireplace. I look around the hut. Her table is covered with open jars, some filled and some empty. Briar picks a pot and ladle up and works on filling them.

"I have a family who needs your help," I tell her. "Do you think you could come to Battlewood for a few days?"

"Briar, when you've finished with that, would you please prepare my traveling bag?" Willow asks, answering my question with one of her own. I clutch one of her hands in thanks.

"Of course, Willow," he replies.

"My thanks," Willow says. She leads me to a cushioned bench beneath a window and we sit. We both tuck our legs beneath us. I stare down into the mug of tea in my hands. Now that I am here, I feel even more like I am losing my mind. Will Willow feel the same way? I sip from the mug for something to do. The tea blooms floral and sweet on my tongue. Briar flits around, pulling jars, tinctures, and poultices from their spaces. Carefully, he fills the bag and then clasps it shut. He unties his apron and folds it carefully over his arm.

"I'll see you tomorrow morning?" he asks, hesitating unsurely before Willow and twisting his apron in his hands.

"Not tomorrow," she says. "I will be heading to Battlewood for a short sabbatical. I'll call upon you the moment I return."

Briar nods. Willow rises with a soft smile to press a single kiss to his lips before she turns her attention back to me. I swallow hard, surprised by the surge of unwarranted jealousy; we made it clear upon our goodbyes that we were freed to meet another, and I've no right to begrudge Willow a single thing. I swirl the tea around in the mug until she stills it with a soft hand.

"You seem troubled, Jace," she says. I sigh, considering whether to tell her about Tally.

"I'm just tired," I lie instead.

She says nothing, instead busying herself at the table. After a moment, Willow sits across from me again, wrapping her hands around her own mug.

"You know," she says, "I've found that I tend to turn within myself whenever I most need to talk. Would you say that's something you do, as well?"

The question would be an innocent one, if she didn't know me. She knows me well, though, and I narrow my eyes as she sips her tea. I press my lips together peevishly, but she waits for a response anyway.

"Yes, you might say that," I mutter. I can already feel my resolve weakening, and I hate that she can still work her way into my head.

"Perhaps it might help to share what's weighing on you," Willow suggests.

I stare down into my mug as if I can drown my thoughts away. Tired silver eyes stare back at me.

"I'm not drinking anymore," I say. Her face brightens, a warm, proud smile curving her pink lips upward. "I want you to remember that while I tell you what's been happening." Willow nods encouragingly, and I relent at last. Downing the rest of my tea, I begin to speak. I do not stop until I have gone hoarse. Willow rises as I speak, hands clasped behind her back as she paces back and forth. She's a captive audience, speaking only when I have finished.

"This is…" Willow trails off, pausing at last in her pacing. The candles have burned into near nothingness in their holders. The wax pools around the metal bases, threatening to spill over onto the rough-hewn wooden table. Outside, the sun has set and darkness presses against the windows. Despite my concerns that I will sound as if I've lost my mind, Willow accepts my story without question. Not for the first time since my arrival, I feel a wave of gratitude for her steadfast loyalty.

"I know, it sounds like too much work," I say. I am face down on the window bench, one arm draping toward the ground. My knuckles scrape against the wooden flooring. I trace the grain of the planks with my fingernail. A sliver of wood embeds itself beneath the nail. "Ow!" I say, yanking my hand up. Willow comes over and sits on the floor. She removes the splinter from my finger and then wraps her fingers between mine. Her hand is soft, but I feel the callouses of hard work there.

"I don't think it sounds like too much work," Willow says. "I think it sounds like there is much good that could come from change."

"I think so too, but I don't think that people will be too pleased with me," I say. "People are used to the Battlewood of present. Better the evil you know, and all." I roll off the bench and join her on the floor. A candle burns out near us, and then another. Long shadows fall across the single-room hut. I cling to Willow's hand like a lifeline, watching the snow fall through the window. She sighs but remains silent. Though I do not say it, I'm not sure how I am supposed to be able to figure out my ghost problem and figure out how to get my Court to trust me at the same time.

"I think it is up to you to show that there is no evil to know," Willow finally suggests softly. I don't have a response.

The final candle goes out in Willow's hut and darkness swallows the room. My eyes grow heavy as we sit silently; the scent of sandalwood and cinnamon hangs heavy in the air, the smell I've come to associate with Willow. Before long, I drift off to sleep.

When I wake, it is still dark in the hut, but a small fire burns in the hearth to keep the room warm. Willow is curled up beside me in her bed—she must have moved me at some point. She makes small snuffling sounds as she sleeps. She shifts, pressing into me. I do not think she realizes she has done it. I stare up at the ceiling, trying not to let my mind wander too far. It would be so easy to steal moments of comfort here in this dark room, but I know that when the sun rises, we would be back to where we were before: two life paths that cannot converge. I will not bring ghosts, fear, and trauma into her life. I will not come between her and Briar.

Instead, I turn on my side, careful not to touch Willow. She is much freer with her shows of care and affection, blurring the line between friendly and romantic, but I've never given it freely. Here, in this hut with her, I realize how alone I am in Battlewood. It does nothing to help my thoughts.

Morning arrives more quickly than I would like. I awaken to an empty bed, though the spot where Willow slept is still warm. Through bleary eyes, I watch as she fills two cups with coffee and sets small pastries on a plate. She tiptoes them over and places them beside me before realizing I'm awake.

"Oh, you're up!" she exclaims. "Did I wake you?" She sits next to me on the bed. Her hair has been tied up out of her face with a colorful band of cloth. She has pushed the sleeves of her shirt up to her elbows, and I notice that she has transformed her mark from the death of my would-be killer into a bouquet of herbs and flowers. I press my lips together, trying not to feel guilty for her own contrition. She has learned how to transform the emotion, and I must too.

"No," I say. "Thank you for moving me last night. I don't think I'd have fared well on a wooden floor." I push a lock of silver hair out of my face and tuck it behind my ear.

"It's been so long since I've seen you," she tells me. She moves her hand to trace beneath my eyes, where I know there are shadows from poor sleep and anxiety. Her fingers move to trace the scar on my neck, a frown pulling at her mouth.

"These last few weeks have not been easy," I admit. I sit up, letting the blankets pool around my waist. Willow hands me a mug of coffee. I take a deep sip. It is warm and nutty, with a sweetness that I did not expect. The surface reflects a warped and rippling likeness of my face, and the blackness of the drink is not enough to cover the lines that gather at the corners of my eyes, nor the dark circles beneath them. I stare at myself, the picture blurring and disappearing as my mind begins to wander. A soft hand on my shoulder brings me back to present. I smile weakly at her when she frowns, but the moment she turns away, my smile fades.

The home is silent as she packs for her trip to Battlewood, and it confirms what I already knew—our journeys were destined to remain separate. She was never meant to help carry my burdens.

My ghosts will always be my own.

FIVE

I have one additional task in mind before we head back to Battlewood. We set off for the center of Garyn where the head of their Court lives. Garyn is not necessarily a large Court, but there is quite a bit of land to cover. The homes of citizens are scattered throughout the land, unlike Battlewood where all the homes gather together in clusters. Willow's village, Bharasus, is one of the few who have chosen to live in close quarters together. They've adopted a mindset in which they all work together to raise one another. It's quite refreshing to see—Battlewood is a firm believer in every person for themselves.

The land is beautiful, which is no surprise to me. Small waterfalls and creeks pepper our trail, though much smaller than the one in the gorge. Some are frozen and some still trickle stubbornly. The firs and maples here are shorter but are also lusher than the ones in Battlewood. Runes and other shapes are carved into every trunk we pass. Small buckets rest beneath some, catching the syrup that drips from the taps in the thick trunks of the maple trees. Willow balls some snow and dips it into syrup.

"A Garyn specialty," she tells me. "Fresh fruit is hard to come by in the cold months, so we make sweeties another way." She hands it to me. I take it, careful not to get the sticky syrup on my gloves.

"It certainly is sweet," I say through a mouthful of sweet and melted snow. The maple is fresh and has an undercurrent of spice to it that I cannot identify. It is different from the syrup we have in Battlewood. It takes me a moment before I identify the warming spice in the flavor. "Clove?" I ask.

"From this tree," she says, pointing to one marked with a straight line. "The ones with this line all taste that way. Over here, with the circle, is cinnamon. The ones with an X are all-spice."

"How do you flavor the tree?" I ask. She stoops to make two more balls of snow, each dipped with a different flavor. I eat it all greedily. They taste exquisite.

"Our arborists work closely with our green witches," Willow says. "They work together to imbue nature with magic. It started as something of an experiment, and then the land took to the magic. Almost overnight, the forests of my village were filled with it. It's interesting to see how nature and magic balance and grow together."

"What about those times where there isn't balance?" I ask, thinking back to Tally and the cottage-turned-ruins. Inevitably, it brings me to thoughts of Raznik and his hidden battle magic, how it consumed him until his final breath. How was he able to keep such a secret hidden from our Court? The image of the rune circle masked by the ornate rug in my office swims to the forefront of my mind. Did anyone else know about it? "Does the land then become poisoned?"

Willow draws her hooded cloak around her more tightly as a surge of wind blows through the trees. Her copper curls spring out around the material, never able to be fully tamed. The tip of her nose and her cheeks are stained rose from the cold, swallowing her freckles. The wind makes her eyes bright and alert. Not paying attention to my feet, I stumble over a rock hidden by the snow. I right myself quickly, feeling my face warm. She laughs in that soft, feathery way of hers.

"I suppose it would," she answers. "I should think it would depend on many things, though. For instance, how long has it been imbalanced? What kind of magic is causing the imbalance? In this case, I assume you're talking about Battlewood."

"Yes," I confirm. "Though I'm no closer to answers now than I was months ago. Bless," I add with an awed sort of whistle, stopping in my tracks.

Before us, an elaborate home built into a massive oak tree rises into the sky. The home is three stories, joined together by a spiral staircase. A second staircase has been built into the hollowed trunk of the tree, protected from the elements. The windows are aglow with lit lanterns. A creek flows between us and the home, and a curved wooden bridge has been built to ford it. Strings of softly glowing orbs are draped between bare boughs of the tree. I dreamed of a hideaway like this my entire childhood. Is it too late to give up the castle and live here instead? Vapor leaves my agape mouth in puffs against the cold air.

A dog comes running from around the back of the tree and

barks when it sees us. Its muzzle and cheeks are white, and it reminds me of a small wolf, especially with the grey and cream fur. The dog stands at attention, its ears and curled tail alert and upright. A man follows, calling for the dog to relax. He's young, maybe early thirties, but not much else is discernible between the full beard and bulky winter clothing he wears. The dog trots back over to his side, and he pets it.

"Hullo there," he calls. He beckons us forward and we cross the bridge to the yard that has been landscaped in the area surrounding the base of the tree. He carries a sack of firewood over his shoulder, watching us as we amble over.

"Grand Chancellor Felix," Willow greets, bowing her head. "I apologize for dropping in on you so unexpectedly."

"Not at all, Healer Finch," Felix responds. "Why don't you both come inside? Lupa, come!" He whistles one sharp note and the dog races inside ahead of us. Both he and Willow have to duck as they enter the hollowed trunk, but I enter easily. We reach the top of the stairs and I let out a strangled sound.

"This is…incredible," I say. I spin around slowly, taking in every last inch. Along the perimeter, rising in a spiral, is the continuation of the staircase we are on. The landing where we stand expands into a full floor, anchored by supporting beams that run the height of the home. Along an entire wall, rows of books are tucked into shelving. A table sits nearby, covered in jars and herbs. In the hearth near it, a pot of water hangs above the flames. I assume the stairs lead into their sleeping quarters.

"Thank you," Felix says. "We're quite fond of it, ourselves."

He pulls his hands out of their thick leather gloves and reaches a hand out to me. "Grand Chancellor Felix Eltzer."

"Jace—I mean, Commander Jace Grimme, Battlewood," I respond, shaking his hand. His eyebrows disappear beneath his hat.

"Ah," he responds. I make a confused face, unsure how to read his response. He enters the home and hangs his gloves in front of the fire. He swipes his hat off his head and hangs it as well. Melted snow drips off it onto the ground.

"Um," I say in return. Felix reaches around and pulls loose the tie around his hair. Shoulder-length dirty-blonde hair hangs in a curtain, blending in with his blonde beard. He tugs his wet boots off with effort and they land on the ground with a dull thud.

"Forgive me for saying so," Felix says, stepping into a pair of slippers that have been warming on the stone in front of the fire, "but we were all pleased to hear of the shift in power. The loss of a life is never something to celebrate; however, given the history between our lands, we look forward to what may come."

"I only hope I can do well by the other Courts," I say.

"Then you are already miles ahead of where we were," he responds. He leads us to a round table that has had intricate designs carved around a floral filigree in the center. The legs have also been carved into an intricate pattern. "Please, take a seat. Tea?"

"Please," Willow says. I nod. Felix busies himself with pulling down ceramic mugs and a bag of herbs. "Where is your wife?"

"Otherwise occupied, I'm afraid," Felix says, setting three

cups on the table. He brings over the teapot and pours steaming water into them and then drops a small cloth ball into each. I watch as the water bubbles around the sachet. "Wren is on a retreat with the newest group of healers hoping to attain head status in their villages."

"Oh, I loved that retreat," Willow says wistfully. I poke at the bag as it floats on the surface, watching as the herbs release a swirl of olive-green water. The smell of peppermint rises; I inhale deeply, and the cool mint fills my sinuses. "Wren is the healer who oversees all of Garyn's healers," Willow explains to me. "She taught me everything I know."

Felix sets a plate of crackers and fruit in the center of the table and then takes a seat across from me. If I didn't know better, I would not think that I was sitting in the home of the Chief of Garyn. I would have expected more grandeur or more stringent protection, not a mountain man and his dog living in a treehouse—though that feels like a gross understatement for what his home truly is. He settles comfortably in his chair and breaks the ice by popping a piece of fruit in his mouth.

"What can I do for the new Commander?" Felix asks me. His voice is kind, open. He does not regard me with the suspicion I'm used to receiving.

"That's a great question," I say. "If I'm being honest, I came here to ask you about creating a bridge between our Courts, near Devent Gorge. I suppose a letter would have sufficed."

"There hasn't been a bridge between our Courts for—"

"One hundred years, since the first Raznik set fire to it. That's a long time to let enmity fester, and personally, I feel that it's time to bring that to an end," I say.

"What would Battlewood stand to gain from access to our land? Or, for that matter, what could Garyn stand to gain?" Felix asks. The accusation is softened by the earnest curiosity of his voice and the crinkles at the corner of his eyes, the lines of a good-humored man.

"I'll admit that I would prefer easier passage between the Courts for my own selfish pursuits, but your land inspired the change that has led to those selfish pursuits. My friendship with Willow aside, Garyn forced me to see the lies we were fed for so long. It is my hope that in building this bridge, it may serve as a metaphor for greater things to come." The words are stiff and sound foreign in my voice, as if I'm borrowing them from someone else. It still feels as if I am only play-acting the role of a commander.

Felix's deep brown eyes regard me carefully. I do not look away from him, from the sudden challenge I find there. Change and trust are a long game, and I am in it whether I want to be or not. He's not wrong to be hesitant—easy access means easy onslaught and coups. However, under my watch, I intend to shift the culture of Battlewood from one of bloody victory to one of peaceable trade.

Unsure what to do with herself, I catch Willow slide from her seat onto the ground to pet the dog, which has curled up at Felix's feet. Anxiously, I begin to pick at my cuticles, dry from the bitter winter air. If this is a power move on Felix's part, I will not be the first to give in. Finally, Felix leans forward and rests his arms on the table.

"I'm sure we could break ground in the spring," he says. My heart stutters in relief and excitement. This is the first real task I have broached as Commander outside of Battlewood, and the success leaves me feeling better about my position than I have in some time. "At a cost, of course."

"I would be happy to pay for the cost of construction," I say with breathless excitement. "The first of many reparations. I fear there are many people owed for the sins of my land." Felix nods, stroking his beard. The room is silent except for Lupa's panting and the crackling wood in the hearth. I take a long sip of the peppermint tea, grimacing at the bitter and oversteeped taste.

"We will look forward to continuing to build bridges," Felix tells me, "Both on land and in life."

······†······

Conversation is stilted as we enter back into Battlewood. I wonder what Willow is thinking as we approach the gorge, but I do not ask her. With her unwillingness to cross over the log, we have to take the long way across. We scale down the sloping cliff, carefully clinging to the wall to avoid slipping off the side.

The trek is arduous, the path coated in slick ice. I go behind her, ready to catch her if she begins to slip. As we take our final tentative steps off the incline, Willow loses her footing on a divot in the ice. I throw my arm out, slamming against her side to stop her from falling. She instead lurches to the left, tumbling into the cliff wall and righting herself.

"I'm glad to see your instincts are as quick as ever," she says, an awkward laugh bubbling out of her. "Thanks."

"Of course," I say.

We are quiet again. Whatever initial comfort we had found in her home last night seems to have dissipated with the rising sun. I have never had to navigate friendship after romance, and I feel entirely like a fish out of water.

It isn't until we've made it across the water and back onto Battlewood soil that I finally crack.

"This is weird. Is this weird?"

"It's weird," Willow confirms, and it breaks the forming ice between us. We laugh, shaking our heads. "I'm sorry I didn't warn you about Briar."

"There's nothing to warn me about, Willow," I say, offering her a hand to pull her up the scraggly rocks. She takes it, grabbing her skirts in the other hand and hopping up the rocks beside me. "You don't owe me anything. Honestly, it's probably me who owes you an apology, a proper one."

"What do you mean?"

"I was in a bad place when you left, and in true Jace fashion, I handled it poorly. I didn't want to admit that I had slipped again," I say. "I'm so happy to see that you've found happiness in someone, truly. You deserve the world."

Willow is silent, unmoving for the briefest of moments before she flings her arms around me and squeezes so hard that my breath comes out in a wheezy whoosh. As she steps back, I massage my chest to recirculate the airflow.

"Sorry," she says sheepishly. "We're going to be okay, aren't we?"

"We are," I say firmly, nodding. For once, I believe the optimism that comes from me, and a weight lifts from my chest as we fall into easy conversation. Without the pressure to meet each other's unmeetable expectations, we have found ease between us again.

When we make it to the village, I leave Willow with Merrid's family, hoping that she will be able to help as I assured she would. She tucks her legs beneath her in a criss-cross on the floor beside Ellisana's mother while Merrid looks on from the corner. I nod my head at him once and take my leave. I will only get in the way if I stay in their home.

Back inside the castle, I take a seat at my desk, where a small pile of rolled missives sits. They each bear a seal of sorts; one has the feather of a griffon vulture pressed deep into the maroon wax. I break it out of the wax carefully and add it to my collection of quills; fitted with the right nib, it will make a lovely quill. I unroll the letter to find a note accepting my invitation to the Spring Equinox festival and the flowery signature of Grand Chancellor Omarose of Dezaiyr, the desert lands of our small Nautilus of Courts. Setting that aside, I break the clay-colored seal of the next letter to find a note of acceptance from Grand Chancellor Aytac and his husband, Kaleth. I grin with excitement at the success of the invitations.

Beneath the letters rests the leather journal from Lilith. The pages inside are blank, waiting to be filled. I cannot understand how writing my thoughts would clear my mind. Wouldn't it just end up providing an easier route to perseverate on them? In spite of myself, I pick up a quill and dip it in ink. The nib hovers over the first page of the book, poised and ready to write. A droplet of black ink drips off the quill; it seeps into the paper, spreading like a spider's web in the fibers of the page. A second drip follows. I press the tip of my finger into it and drag it downward, curving and splitting into two trails. The paper rips from the force of it. With a sigh, I drop my quill down, paying no mind to the angry splatter it creates.

I rise, restless. My feet carry me out of the office, out of the castle itself. Before I know it, I am at the training grounds. I stand at the fence, watching the initiate warriors as they run through their exercises. I climb up and over the paddock fencing and into the yard. When they see my arrival, the warriors all stop and stand at attention. Despite the icy chill, there is a sheen of sweat on their faces. The thick leather helmets they wear to protect their heads from wayward blows are stained with sweat.

"At ease," I instruct them. Their stances relax, though several remain more upright and alert than the rest. I'd put money on them being the newest recruits. "Do you have room for one more?"

"Commander," Linota says, handing me a wooden sword and headgear. She and Galter clap their hands, the noise muffled by the thick gloves they wear to protect their fingers from frostbite. "Alright, kiddies, back to it!"

This breaks them from their trance, and they drop back into their formation. I join up with one of the older warriors, facing her down. She gives me a run for my money, cutting under when I least expect it, jabbing left when I think she will go right. At the very end of the run, I sweep her feet from under her, and she falls to the ground, flat on her back. I am panting and sweating from effort. I have not worked so hard in a long time, and it feels wonderful to be out here.

Stripping off my gloves, I press one hand to a stitch forming in my left rib. I offer my other hand to the warrior with a grin. She grabs hold of it, giving me her own wide grin. The leather gloves covering her hand are damp from sweat.

"Very impressive," I tell her. She sweeps her helmet off her head and shakes out a long mane of blonde. It is sweat-soaked, much like my own silver locks. I watch as the hair tumbles down to the small of her back.

"Not so bad yourself, Commander," she says, tucking the helmet under her arm and extending a hand; I shake it, and we both tug our hands back quickly, staring with wide eyes at one another. My skin tingles where hers met mine, and I notice that she surreptitiously kneads her hand with the fingers of her other hand. She drops both hands when she catches me looking.

We head back to gather in front of Linota and Galter. I doubletake when I realize that there is a Staff Sergeant insignia pinned to his left shoulder. Jealousy rips through me as sharp and quick as a lightning strike. As the jealousy wanes, it is replaced by guilt. I am happy for Galter; he works hard for his place within the warrior ranks and deserves to have been promoted.

Galter and I started at the same time, climbed the ranks of

initiate warriors together. Even so, I cannot help but think that if I hadn't gotten myself into the position I'm in now, that could have been me. The power I have now is a power I never wanted. Disappointment tastes like bitter ash in my mouth. I flash a quick smile as Linota catches my eyes, but by the pity in her eyes, I know that I have poorly disguised my feelings.

The initiates all listen to Galter talk with rapt attention. I find my gaze continuing to meander back toward the warrior I sparred with, and more than once, I catch her eye. We both look away quickly, though not before I see her cheeks turn pink. The initiates are dismissed, and they scatter in different directions. The girl I sparred with waves goodbye to me with a cheery grin.

"Staff Sergeant, huh?" I ask, nodding at the insignia on his shoulder. He flushes pink, pleased. "Congrats, Galter. It's a great move for you." I help him and Linota gather the training weapons and load them in the rolling cart.

"How's life in the castle?" he asks me. I sigh. "That good, huh?"

"I miss this," I say, motioning around me. "And I have a feeling that there is something dark around the corner. I can't explain it, but it's there."

"Intuition is always important to listen to," Linota says. We exit the training field and walk to the storage shed. The hinges whine as the door swings open. I tuck the cart in the corner of the shed, looking around at the hay-filled dummies and weapons. I feel like I am back in my training days again. I take a deep breath in through my nose and exhale slowly, trying to direct my thoughts away from regret and nostalgia.

"You're welcome to join us any time you'd like," Galter offers as we walk toward the village. "I know the initiates would be thrilled. I'm glad to see someone giving Harlow a run for her money."

"Harlow is the initiate I sparred with?" I guess. Linota nods with a quirked smile.

"Harlow Brokahl. A force to be reckoned with, in every way," she says. "In honesty, she reminds me of you, Jace. She's a bit older than you, joined up later than most, but she's got a penchant for getting herself into trouble and leaving a trail of broken hearts in her wake."

"She's cute," I say with an offhanded shrug. "I'm not surprised."

"Cut your losses, Commander, she won't let anyone closer than a sword's length," Linota says.

"Wha—all I said was that she's cute!" I exclaim, indignant. Linota and Galter exchange a knowing grin and shake their heads at me. An image of sparkling brown eyes and golden hair floats through my mind unbidden, and I force my attention elsewhere.

We enter the village and slow our pace to more of a meandering stride. I make it a point to stop and speak with each person we come across, however brief it may be. Their responses range from lukewarm to entirely ignoring me. When one person turns away from me without a word, I roll my eyes at his retreating back.

"There's growth for you," Galter says as we reach the pub. "A year ago, you would have kicked rocks at him and called him something colorful."

"I'm an almost-respected figurehead, Galter," I say with mock gravity. "I can't be kicking rocks at people now."

"I notice you didn't mention the name-calling," Linota says wryly.

"I'm allowed my own thoughts," I say with a shrug. Galter laughs, clapping me on the back.

"Please think about coming to our training sessions," he says.

"I will. Listen, make sure they're keeping up on their exercises in observation and quick action," I say. "I want to make sure that there is no room for clandestine violence against our guests. I'm—we're hosting a celebration of the Spring Equinox. I suppose I should announce that," I add thoughtfully. "I've already gotten some yesses from the neighboring Courts, and I'm hoping to hear from more soon."

Linota raises her eyebrows, nodding her head in surprise and approval. We part ways with a promise to help in any way they can. I hesitate, standing in the middle of the walkway while I try to figure out where to go. I don't want to go back to the castle, where I am alone. I wonder briefly if Willow has finished with Merrid's family and whether I should go check on them.

Instead, I march back up to the training field, pulling out a dummy from the equipment shed. The sparring today has lit a fire in me, and I am anxious to get back onto the field. I draw my own sword from its sheath on my hip, the diamond blade glinting iridescent in the sun.

I cut across, bringing the blade down from my shoulder to the opposite hip, and repeat. Switching, I practice cutting under and over. My body burns in a way that it hasn't in some time. The dummy stands in tatters, hay spilling out across the snowy ground. Breathing hard, I sheath my sword.

"Do you miss it?" a smoky, resonant voice calls. I look toward the source and find Harlow leaning over the paddock, hands clasped and draped lazily in front of her. She's tied her hair into a loose braid that hangs over her left shoulder and has changed out of her sparring uniform into a formfitting tunic and breeches. Even without the padding and protective gear, she's tall and broad in a way I could never achieve.

"Yes," I say truthfully. I tug the demolished dummy back over to the shed to be reclothed and stuffed.

"You're good," she tells me, joining in step next to me as I leave the field. Her familiarity with me is a welcome switch from the fearful reverence I've received from most people, and I grin at her easy nature. "You knocked me on my ass earlier. I've never seen that—" she shimmies her shoulders and jabs her arm forward, "—move before."

I appreciate the rippling of her muscles beneath her tunic, ignoring the ball of guilt that situates itself in my throat. Willow is only yards away, doing a favor for me, while I am making eyes at an initiate I've only just met today. Am I fickle, or is this just how things progress when you've split amicably from someone? I have no comparison for relationships which have ended well.

"You weren't an easy opponent, yourself," I reply. I stick my cold hands in my pockets, balling my fingers into fists to warm quicker. The cold has begun to lay claim at the tips of my fingers, and if I do not stymie the iciness, it will wind its way around my bones and it will be ages before I can warm again.

"Will you teach me?" Harlow asks, turning and stopping in front of me. Not expecting the abrupt stop, I smack into her. She doesn't waiver, but I stumble back; running into her is akin to running into the broadside of a wall. She reaches out to grab my forearm, steadying me.

"A little warning next time, yeah? I feel like I just got walloped," I complain, but there is no bite in it. She flashes an amused but rueful sort of look at me.

Standing this close together, Harlow is nearly a head taller than me, brawny and confident. She stares down at me with determined chestnut eyes. Compared to her, I feel suddenly small and insignificant.

"Teach you what?" I ask, confused.

"Sword fighting!" she cries, as if it's the most obvious thing in the world. "I mean, I know I'm good, but you're good. You don't have to make a decision now, but think about it, would you? I live in a small house off the main road here, there's a poorly carved wooden cat out front. I went through a woodworking phase—well, it doesn't really matter. If you're willing, just come find me."

I search her face, my own face screwed up in confused skepticism. I relent and make a noncommittal nod, half-shrugging. I don't know what to do with this request. The idea of being able to spar with someone again is tantalizing, a release I didn't realize I was looking for. This could be mutually beneficial for both of us.

"Alright," I say hesitantly. "Understanding, of course, that my duty to this Court comes before anything else. You'll need to wake early, though," I add warningly. "Mornings are the only time I can guarantee I'm free."

Harlow's face splits into a grin and she pumps her fist in the air, victorious. I see at once what Linota meant about seeing me in her. I know that smile; it's one that promises nothing but mischief and trouble looming on the horizon.

SIX

The door to the calligrapher's shop opens with a tinkling of bells. The scent of parchment and ink fills my nose. I inhale deeply. The smell is comforting. It reminds me of my father, whose fingers were always stained with dark ink. My father was a frequent customer at this shop, which led to many afternoons spent playing marbles on the floor while he discussed the differences between squid, berry, and pine ink. The proprietor, Faris, is stooped over a desk, his nose nearly pressed to the parchment he is working on. A triple lens is clipped onto the arm of his glasses, magnifying his work to a dizzying degree. In the silence of the store, all that can be heard is the crackling of his lanterns and the scratching of his metal-tipped quill.

When it is clear he has not heard me, I knock carefully on the counter that separates us. He jumps slightly and looks over his shoulder at me. Noticing me at last, he rushes to get to his feet. Not for the first time, guilt eats at me; I loathe the fact that people have had such a fear response engrained into them by this Court.

"What can I do for you, Commander?" he asks.

"Jace," I correct. "No need for the title, Faris. You've known me since I was in diapers. I was wondering if I might task you with creating announcements."

"Of course, of course," he replies. This time, he rises with purpose instead of fear. Pulling fresh parchment out, he flattens it on the counter and looks at me. "What are you looking for?"

"I'm hosting a celebration for the Spring Equinox," I say. "To be held in 30 days. There will be a ball on the evening of the Spring Equinox, during which time our people will have an opportunity to meet. We will have a grand feast, at which there will be dining, dancing, and a speech about where Battlewood's future will lead us. All are welcome to this celebration."

Faris writes quickly and messily, the nib splashing ink onto his face and hands as he goes.

"How many copies of this invitation do you need?" he asks me, looking up. The magnifying lens is still attached to his glasses, and he stares at me with a distorted and massive brown eye.

"Twelve should be fine," I say. "I intend to have some warriors dispatched to read the announcement out. Not all of our citizens can read, and I will not have them excluded because of it."

"I'll have them finished within the day," he promises me. I place a small pouch of coins on the counter for him. "My many thanks."

"Likewise," I assure him. I watch as he pockets the money and then hobbles back over to his desk to resume his work. When the scratching of the quill fills the air again, I leave and make my way to Merrid's home. It has been three days since Willow first tended to the family, and I'm curious to see how they are doing.

The village is busy today, the promise of the changing of seasons in the air. The sun hangs high and warm in the sky, melting the piles of snow and ice into rivulets along the stone walkways. Small displays of items have been set outside of shops to lure people in. One of the biggest issues I've seen in the short time I've held my title is that there is a disparity in wealth between those in the castle and those in the villages. There are plenty of wares to buy, if you can afford them. If you can't, you're left depending on the graciousness of those around you. The ones with money continue to flourish while the ones without continue to suffer.

It was never something I needed to think about when I was younger. My father, an academic, held a high job in teaching and my mother, a warrior, was provided for by the Court. I didn't know that I should have been grateful for the family I had until it was taken away from me and I was left entirely alone in my Court. Even now, despite my lack of human connection, I want for nothing else. I have begun to carry a small bag of coins with me whenever I leave the castle in order to give back to my people as best I can. To the smaller villages on the outskirts of the Court, I dispatch warriors to bring a small boon regularly. It's not a permanent solution, but it's a start.

Merrid answers the door after my first knock. The change in his demeanor is night and day from our first interaction. He greets me now with a wide smile, welcoming me into his home with a sweeping gesture. Ellisana sits before the fire, carefully brushing out delicate strands of cornsilk hair of her doll made of corn husk. She smiles widely at me, showing off a gap where she's lost a second tooth. It's so reminiscent of Aleca when she was that age that I have to fight a sudden urge to sweep Ellisana into a hug.

"Commander," Merrid greets.

"Good afternoon, Merrid. I wanted to see how you and your family were doing."

"Wonderful, ma'am. I don't know what your friend there did for my Blythe, but I sure am grateful." He indicates at a closed door, where I assume his wife lays just beyond. There is a fond sort of light in his gaze as he looks from the closed door over to his playing child. "I couldn't contemplate a life where we would go on without her."

"Was she so ill?" I question, eyes widening. Merrid bows his head, pressing a hand to his stomach.

"I feared we'd lose her by winter's end. I cannot thank you enough for saving her life, Commander."

"Think nothing of it, Merrid," I say, shaking my head. "Healer Willow is to thank. I merely brought her here."

He clasps my hands in thanks anyway, dropping them when Ellisana calls him to her side. I bid them goodbye before stepping out of their home and into the bright sun.

After I've left Merrid's home, there is little for me to do until the announcements have been finished and I can send people off. Not for the first time, I wish that my father's library had not been turned into ash with the rest of my home. I know he had books about the history of Battlewood, and I suspect that he kept books in secret about the history of Islilja before it. It seems my parents knew there was more than met the eye when it came to the Razniks and our Court at large; if they had been meeting with Syiera in secret, what other secrets were they keeping?

I resist the urge to go through the cinders of my home again. By now, the wind and snow have reduced the building to nothingness, a stone square the only indicator that anything ever stood there. The only thing I have of my former life is that box I removed, locked by chains and entirely untouched by the scorching, destructive flames. There is nothing I can find there. If I want answers, I will have to finally bring myself to go through Raznik's quarters.

By the time I have gotten back to the castle, I have lost my resolve to climb that staircase to his quarters. I haven't been able to bring myself to take that first step, always with nervous reservation. I don't want to go in there alone. Every time I think I'm ready to go in there, a feeling of disquiet overtakes me, and I talk myself into not going in. Instead, I wander aimlessly back to my quarters. An insistent reminder waits on my desk for me when I enter. The journal, as beautiful as ever, rests in the center of my desk, a quill lying next to it. I am positive that I did not leave that on my desk when I left. I place my hands on my hips and narrow my eyes.

"Now, what are you doing here?" I ask it, slowly walking to my desk. "You seem to have a mind of your own, don't you?"

The journal, as expected, remains silent and motionless. I wave my hands at it in annoyance and turn away, hanging my snow-flecked cloak in front of the fireplace. I stack some logs, throw in some paper, and set it alight.

When I turn back around, the journal is no longer in its place on my desk. Rather, it is floating at eye level and opened to a blank page. The quill hovers beside it, ready to be held. I freeze, eyes wide. I am acutely aware of the way my breath begins to exhale in trembles.

"No," I scold it, pointing a finger. "This is unacceptable—what am I doing?" I ask myself, disbelief rife in my voice. I am talking to a magic journal like it can hear me. Maybe I've gone insane after all.

I stomp away from the journal and make it only a few steps before the fluttering of pages sounds behind me. The journal has followed me. I turn slowly to face it; I can feel my nostrils flaring in irritation.

"Write." The words appear on the page in an elegant script. "It is the only way to heal."

"Am I supposed to just ignore the fact that you're a magical journal that can fly around and annoy me into submission?" I ask. I am entirely grateful to be alone right now. If anyone saw me having a conversation with a floating book, my tenuous credibility with the Court would go entirely out the window. There is no logic in this world that can explain away what is happening, and I squeeze my eyes shut in vain. When I open them again, the journal is still bobbing in the air.

The page remains blank for a few moments before new words appear.

"All is not as it appears in Battlewood, Commander. There is magic all around you, if you know where to look."

"And here I was worried you'd be vague, magic journal," I quip. This must be Lilith's doing. I snatch the journal out of the air. The moment the spell is broken, the quill falls to the floor, falling on the tip of the metal nib and sticking upright. I yank it out of the floor and march over to my desk, dropping into my seat with a pointed huff.

The journal lands on my desk with an unceremonious thud and I jam the quill into the inkpot with more force than is necessary. The metal knocks into the glass rim with a sharp clink.

I do not know what to write, and instead I write a list of the things that I have to figure out. One after the other, with no concern for priority, I write,

"Rune circle. Box. Quarters for guests. Festival. Tally. Sword lessons. Raznik's quarters. Cottage in woods. Battle magic. Magic journal? Magic in Court?"

Seeing the words written down does nothing to help me. The list is overwhelming. These are not tasks I can assign to my warriors to figure out. If there is additional magic in this land that has been hidden for all these years, then that leaves me with the additional task of bringing those who have hidden their magic into light and unifying those who fear magic with those who have magic. I drop my head onto the journal with a groan.

Willow finds me like this only minutes later. I hear the soft snapping of the closing door and sit up in my seat to find her entering as gingerly as she can, tiptoeing so that she does not make noise.

"I'm not asleep," I tell her. She startles and then laughs.

"You scared me! Are you okay?" she asks, coming over. "You have marks on your forehead."

I pull a small mirror from a drawer and hold it up, taking in my appearance. There is a large red oval on my forehead from where it rested on the hard journal. The ink must not have been completely dry when I leaned on it, and my forehead reads, "Tally. Sword lessons."

"Oh, perfect," I mutter, scrubbing at the marks. They smear some, but the backwards imprint remains. "Were you with the family?"

"Yes," she replies. "Ellisana's mother is in much better health. I left them with instructions and some medicine that should help her through the rest of it. I suppose I should return to my village; they've been without a healer for nearly a week now." She traces the engraving along the edge of my desk with a distracted finger.

"I can't thank you enough for helping, Willow," I say. "If you ever have interest in selling some of your wares, I'd be more than happy to compensate you."

"I'll think about it," she says, nodding thoughtfully. We lapse into silence. I glance back down at the page with my list on it, unsure what else to do. The silence now is an awkward one, tentative and fragile. Never one to handle uncomfortable situations well, I doodle absently at the bottom of the page. "Is it always going to be like this?" Willow's soft voice finally breaks the quiet.

"Like what?" I ask, though I know what she means. Silence, once comfortable, is now nearly unbearable. Too much has happened between us since last year, but not enough to keep us together. Another image of Harlow swims in my vision and I swallow a sudden surge of acidic guilt.

"Like we're strangers instead of two people who once loved each other," she responds. She stops tracing my desk and I can feel her eyes on me. I look up reluctantly, knowing that I'll find a pool of emotions that I cannot handle. My worry is confirmed when I see the way her dappled hazel eyes glitter with unshed tears. I swallow hard, not able to fully suppress a wince in response.

"I want you to be happy, Jace," Willow says. "I want you to find happiness with someone who can love you better and more thoroughly than I think I ever could have."

"I want the same for you, Willow," I say, and am surprised at how much I mean it. She deserves better than I would ever be able to offer, and for once, the acknowledgment of my own flaws does not cause my stomach to curdle. "Whether that be with Briar, or someone else."

Willow smiles ruefully at the mention of Briar, and I know that she is smitten with the healer. It does some to abate my guilt over my initial attraction to the ever-compelling Harlow.

When she leaves, I pull my journal back over to me and add one final item to the list I've crafted.

"Moving on."

......†......

By mid-afternoon the following day, I bid farewell to Willow at the edge of Garyn. When I have made it back across the log into Battlewood, I turn to face her. We are separated now by land and water. A pit forms in my stomach, the same as it did the last time we parted. She raises a hand above her head, waving with a small, sad smile. I lift my own hand in response, giving one short wave before we turn and walk away.

I almost wish for Tally's ghost to appear, to give me any reason not to think about loss and gain, power and sacrifice. Though, I suppose that wouldn't be fair either; more than once, she's told me that she isn't supposed to leave the woods. The cottage must be tied to it somehow. Why would she have brought me there otherwise? If I were braver, I would return to that place. Perhaps when Aleca and Syiera arrive for the festival, I can lean on their help to try to solve that particular mystery. The more time I spend trying to find answers, the more questions I'm left with in their place. If Raznik also had this many mysteries on his plate, it's no wonder he went spare in the end.

Of course, becoming addicted to corrupted magic had a hand in that as well. His descent into madness was ultimately why I chose to give my own addiction up for good. As much as I enjoy my vices, I fear madness more. The idea of losing control, of losing my entire being to the power of something else is my greatest fear. Vulnerability scares me in a way worse than death. Which, I suppose, is how I've arrived here, crying in the woods and haunted by ghosts and a journal intent on forcing me to make space for my thoughts and emotions.

I allow myself only a few moments before I turn my attention away from the empty border of Garyn and continue my way home, intent on spending the rest of the chilly evening wrapped beneath layers of blankets. I make only one stop on my way to my room, grabbing my journal and travel quill set. Once I've settled in my room, I open the book, dip my quill in its ink, and write until all the oil has burned from my lantern.

SEVEN

"You're cutting too high," I tell Harlow. She drops her arms to her side with a frustrated huff, letting the tip of her sword scrape across the padded floor. We are in the indoor training grounds at the castle; I agreed to train her in swordsmanship, but I did not agree to freeze my fingers off while I trained her. It is still dark out, the setting moon hovering just above the mountains. We stand across from each other in stockinged feet. It's the same way my mother taught me my footwork. The lack of shoes forces you to learn to move quickly, and by the time you add your shoes back in, you've mastered the art of it. It also teaches you quickly how to be nimble—you cannot win a swordfight if you've fallen flat on your back.

"Still?" she groans.

"If you start way up here, you're going to give me too much time to get out of your way, and you're going to exhaust yourself in the process." I bring my sword up over my head and cut down at her. She jumps away from me just as the tip catches the leather tie on the neck of her sleeveless tunic. The tie comes apart in two and the top eyelets flop open to reveal her jugular notch—a vulnerable space in a sword fight.

"You're shorter than me, though," she counters, lifting her sword again. "Shouldn't we account for that?"

"It's your responsibility to be able to fight smoothly and equally despite your opponent's height," I tell her. I sheath my sword and go behind her. Grabbing hold of her biceps, slick with sweat beneath my fingers, I tug down a couple of inches. Her sword, while still over her head, is now at a lower and more direct angle. Resuming my position and drawing my sword, I say, "Try again."

The speed with which she brings her blade down is alarming and impressive. Metal against diamond screeches, a spark flying from the point of contact. My arms shake as I hold off the force of the attack. She lifts her weapon away and mine falls back. The sudden lack of weight sends me back a couple of steps. I nod in satisfaction, and she allows a triumphant grin.

We pause to take drinks from our skeins. I lift my tunic to wipe sweat from my forehead. I feel more alive and on fire than I have in weeks. My hands, peppered with shallow scrapes from contact with Harlow's blade, burn from the salty sheen of perspiration that covers me. Harlow is not much better, her hair plastered tight against her neck. I take a moment to wipe down my blade, though it needs no maintenance.

"Where did you get that thing?" she asks me. She wipes at her face with a rag as she walks over to me.

"It was a gift," I tell her, which is not a lie. I do, however, choose to omit the fact that it was a gift made of and from magic, gifted to me by the Goddess of Fate. "Given to me last year when I was trying to find my sister."

"Some gift," she says, appreciation gleaming in her eyes. I offer the blade to her, and she takes it with reverent hands, trading it for her sword. I take it and the weight of it pulls my shoulder down. "I'd expect it to be a lot heavier." I watch as she adopts a stance and lunges forward, thrusting the sword into an invisible enemy.

"Loosen the tension in your grip and twist down," I instruct her, stepping into the space beside her. I press my fingertip against the straining ligaments in her forearm and the sword falls out of her hand and to the ground with a dull clang. "You just gave me an easy kill. If I sliced there, you'd be bleeding out right now." Harlow grimaces at me and I shrug, unbothered. She bends to scoop my blade up; her long fingers wrap and rewrap themselves around the hilt, but she cannot lose the tightness in her grip. I make a beckoning motion with my hand, and she comes closer to me.

Her eyes are sharp as she watches me. I adopt a stance, holding her weapon straight out in front of me. Several times, I twist my wrist to show her the way she held it, wrist up, and the way it should be held, wrist angled inward. She makes the motion with her empty hand, mimicking me, and then narrows her eyes and nods.

"I think I've got it," she says. I hand her weapon back to her and she repeats what I've just shown her.

"Much better but try to keep this part of your wrist facing down," I tell her, tapping my hand against her arm. "If you're ever caught in a situation where you don't have the proper gauntlets on, it could be your death."

From the distance, a large bell tolls its first call of the day. I look out the large windows at the misty morning. The rising sun gilds the tops of trees and smaller hills as it takes its space in the sky. My day will begin properly soon, and I'll have to put a pin in the lessons until another day.

For just a moment, I could swear a large, winged creature comes soaring out of the woods where the cottage ruins sit. I let out a sound somewhere between a shout and a curse and rush toward the window. As quickly as the creature was there, though, it is gone, and I am left to question if my eyes were seeing things in the distorted morning light. A rustle at my side lets me know that Harlow has joined me. She looks out the window intently, trying to follow my line of sight. I let out a big sigh and turn my back to the window. There is no need to drag another person into the dark mystery that is Battlewood.

......†......

That evening, I dip out of the castle. My head is throbbing from the day spent checking over food orders, invitations, and spaces for the festival. My desk is littered with forms I've filled out to request construction for an outdoors stage, permits for building, and additional yesses from Syiera and Felix. Tomorrow, I will need to speak with our innkeeper to request accommodations for the overflow of guests who will not fit in the castle. Besides themselves, the heads of each Court will be bringing one or two guards for their own protection, as well as their own personal maids. Housing for the maids will not be a problem, as they will sleep in the lower quarters with the rest of the castle workers.

I will need to speak with my own warriors about taking up extra shifts as safety detail. We are down several of our senior warriors—when I took over, I made quick work of firing Ocin, as well as several other warriors who had accepted corrupt deals with Raznik. There is no room for cruelty, corruption, and underhanded dealings under my watch. I make a note to meet with Linota, who oversees enforcement warriors, and Ceylan, who oversees the leadership warriors, in the next couple of days for their recommendations of who would be the best choices. I want to ensure that any chance for trouble is eliminated before it can appear.

Through history, there have been isolated incidents of concern. Twenty years ago, shortly after my mother became a warrior, there had been a breach in the Maelos Mountains by a group of vagabonds with a history of arson. One year later, another group of well-armored vagabonds from an outlying island north of us tried to attack the castle, resulting in a bitter and violent end. It was silent for six more years, until that same outlying island, famed for its brutality, sent a full military outfit to attempt to overtake Battlewood.

Our Court, which sits at the northernmost part of our Nautilus, tends to be an easy target for attacks. Historically, Battlewood had never had a military of its own. The military for the entire Nautilus is housed in Apaiji, near to the Empress and her leaders under her. Upon cessation from the rest of the Nautilus, Eambroch attempted to create his own. Pulled in too many different directions of where Eambroch wanted to wield his ruling, the military remained small and fairly powerless. At that time, it was little more than a glorified security regiment, a step above standard law enforcing protection.

Upon Eambroch's death, which was widely suspected to be patricide, his son Cygnes took over. With time and new leadership under Cygnes, the military grew in numbers, launching its own attempt at a coup on Garyn. The Council of Elders, having heard rumblings of the coup, deployed the warriors from the heart of Apaiji, nipping the overthrow in the bud before it could grow teeth. Cygnes ruled with an authoritarian fist and dreamed of creating a military that could rival Apaiji's.

Toward the end of Cygnes's rule, he became ill with a growth in his brain. In his final years, Cygnes became convinced that a massive attack was being planned against Battlewood. All other work came to a halt as he poured himself into creating the largest military he could, including mass draft orders which left no room for negotiation. His son Sepyphyr, the final Raznik of the Dynasty, took up the mantle and continued forward, unwilling to betray the wish of a dying man. It was under the third and final wave of the military that my mother joined.

Our military became too big to dismantle without subsequently wrecking the economy of our Court. Unfortunately, the Raznik Dynasty was a power-hungry one, and they used the military to their unfair advantage, often at the expense of their own people. If I had not stepped in when I did, I shudder to think of the state Battlewood would be in today. Raznik, much like his father, was beginning a descent into madness and grand ideation, something that never bodes well for the people at their mercy.

······†······

"Come on, Harlow, ten more!" I call, clapping my hands. She glares up at me from the floor, panting. Her palms are pressed against the ground in a push-up position, but she lays with her stomach flat against the floor.

"My arms are about to fall off," she says, breathless.

"Short military career," I cluck sympathetically. "What a shame."

"Augh!" she cries, pushing up with great difficulty. Her arms quiver from the effort. She cannot maintain the position and her arms give out, dropping her to the ground. She lays there with her face pressed against the slate, her torso rising and fall-ing quickly. I take pity on her and crouch, handing her a skein of water. She rolls over, sitting up and grabbing it. Water drib-bles down her chin as she drinks greedily.

"Alright?" I ask. She nods tiredly, and I clap her on the shoulder before rising again. She struggles to her feet, lifting her shirt to wipe her forehead and cheeks.

"Why weren't you ever an officer?" she asks, watching me closely. "You're really good at teaching."

"I wasn't in long enough," I say. "Is that something you're working toward?"

"I dunno," she says, pausing to drink more water. Her breathing has evened out. "I don't really know what I want."

"You're in good company," I say with a huffed laugh.

"What do you mean?" she asks, and I answer before I can stop myself. I do not like to share personal information with people, but the answer comes from me as if I am compelled.

"Just…this isn't quite what I'd pictured for myself," I say, gesturing at the room and, by extension, the castle.

"What did you picture?"

I pause before answering. The truth of it is that I didn't picture anything; I expected to be dead by now. It isn't a casual answer, though, and I pivot.

"I pictured myself with a good cup of coffee and a home on the sea. Maybe with a dog and a wife for company," I say instead. Harlow's gaze sharpens on me with interest, and it makes my stomach flip. Before she can call me on it, I issue a directive. "C'mon, on your back. I'm going to hold your feet, and you're going to do crunches until you're ready to throw up."

"Looking forward to it," she mutters, getting down on the ground. I laugh at her cheek, and she smiles in spite of herself. Once she has gotten into position, I place my knees on the tops of her feet and wrap my hands around her ankles.

Her tendons tighten and shift against my hold, and then she lurches herself upward. Our faces are only inches apart when she sits up, and our eyes lock for only a moment before she moves backward. We repeat this until she cannot sit up anymore, and she flings an arm across her forehead, body heaving where she lay.

"Your turn," she pants, propping herself up on her elbows.

"No, I—"

"Turnabout is fair play," she tells me, and I find myself lying on the ground, Harlow's hands and knees locking me in place. "Come on, Commander, let's see if you still have it."

I curl my body upward, coming face-to-face with Harlow's sly smile. With effort, I shift focus to keeping my breathing under control.

"One," she says. "Fifty-nine to go."

I swear at her as I sit up again, and I am rewarded with a rich, smoky laughter that works its way down my body and under my skin.

······†······

Three days after I've asked Linota about extra shifts for the celebration, I am called down to the training fields. It is an unseasonably warm day, and the snow has begun to melt away; tiny strips of mud and rock start to reappear beneath the dirty snow. The ground is slippery, and I take care while walking down the slope. The last thing I need is to fall on my backside in front of the people I'm meant to be leading. I think I'd die of mortification if I'm being perfectly honest.

Waiting for me in the fields is Linota and a group of warriors. I am surprised to see how many there are—I was prepared to bribe and promise my way into finding people to assist during the celebration. It isn't only fresh recruits, either. Among the first- and second-year warriors are some senior warriors, people I went through my own training with. I catch Harlow among their numbers and my heart flips in my chest. She smiles a secret sort of smile at me, and I feel my face burn.

"Not a bad turnout, Commander, eh?" Linota asks with a grin.

"Not bad at all," I agree. There are nearly two dozen in all, gathered and waiting to hear what comes next. With this many eyes on me at once, I suddenly feel self-conscious. I can feel heat creeping up my neck. I clear my throat and begin to speak.

"Erm, well, thank you, all for stepping up. We only have about ten days before our first guests begin to arrive. I think it goes without saying that this is one of the most important things to happen to Battlewood in a hundred years."

"Second only to you taking Raznik out," someone mutters. Laughter follows, and I narrow my eyes at the snarky warrior. Quickly, he adds, "Which I'm in full support of, Commander, ma'am."

"What's your name?" I ask.

"Markann," he replies nervously.

"Warrior Markann has just shown us a wonderful example of exactly how you are not going to behave. I don't want to hear any sideways comments, any muttering under your breath, and for the love of the gods, do not discuss politics with our guests. You're all smart enough to understand that Battlewood is in a delicate position right now. The wrong comment made to the wrong person could burn us to the ground. You have chosen to step up as representatives of this Court, and I expect you to do well by this Court, or step aside for someone to take your role. Am I understood?"

"Yes, Commander," comes the many-voiced response.

I go over the different roles that need to be filled, the various stations each person will need to run throughout the week the guests will be here. After some argument about who would best be served where, the vacant positions are claimed. I've done my best to set the newer warriors with the more seasoned ones, knowing that they will take them under their wings.

As the group disperses, I grab hold of Harlow by the elbow and drag her off to the side. Linota and Galter cast a long look at me before following the warriors out of the field. I ignore the suspicious, knowing arch of Linota's eyebrow.

"Everything okay, Commander?" she asks, confused.

"Yes," I reply. "I just wanted to go over your role. I've put you in charge of keeping my sister safe because I trust you. There may be more animosity toward her than anyone else since she was sort of the catalyst the resulted in Raznik's death. Please take care of her. I know she's strong and capable, but she's still my baby sister, and the only family I have left."

"No pressure, then," Harlow jokes weakly.

"If you want me to reassign you—" I begin.

"No, no, I've got this," she says quickly. "I promise, I won't let anything happen to her. Thank you for trusting me."

Her face is earnest, and I give a short nod, hopeful that she is up to the task Aleca will undoubtedly prove to be. It would not be the first time I've ruled with my heart instead of my head, but I cannot take this away from Harlow now.

"D'you want dinner?" Harlow asks, pulling me from my thoughts. "I'm headed to the pub, maybe you can come with me and we can talk a bit more about my assignment?"

I battle with myself for only a moment before giving in. If I were wiser, I would turn her down. I am not wise, however, and I am too curious to get to know her better.

We walk down the hill together, entering into the warm and raucous eatery. The bartender calls a greeting to Harlow. His wide grin falters when he notices me, but then he greets me as well. Harlow notices and looks at me curiously.

"People are unsure about my leadership," I say, shrugging as if it does not chap me in the least.

"That's stupid," Harlow says flatly. She jerks her head at an empty booth near the back of the tavern and we wade through the diners to reach it. "Raznik was a nightmare. I considered dropping out of the ranks for a while because of him."

She slides across the wooden bench into the booth, and I follow suit. The candle in the center of the table is burned low; the high, thin wax threatens to collapse in on itself. I poke at the soft wax, reshaping it to give the candle a little more life. A barmaid approaches our table, and she smiles at Harlow shyly.

"Harlow," she greets, dipping her head. "It's so lovely to see you again." It's as if I am not present, and I watch curiously.

"You're always a sight for sore eyes, Winnie," Harlow says cheerfully. She leans across the table, getting closer to Winnie. "Would you be willing to bring me a mug of your best? Maybe something for our commander, here, too?"

Noticing me for the first time, she straightens, wiping her hands on her aproned skirt.

"Commander, I'm sorry! I didn't see—"

"No worries," I say, shaking my head. "Please, Jace works just as well."

"Yes, ma'am," she responds. I suppress a smile. "Ale for you both?"

"Hot cider, if you have it," I say. When Winnie nods, Harlow winks at her in thanks. Winnie turns away quickly, fumbling with her skirt as she scurries through the crowd toward the bar. Harlow leans back in the booth again, running her fingers absently down her long braid. "You realize that girl is infatuated with you?" I ask mildly.

"Winnie? Nah," Harlow says, waving it away. I raise an eyebrow, cocking my head to the side, and Harlow pauses. "Really? Ah, hell."

I make a non-committal sound, instead pulling an ale-stained menu toward me. The parchment is ripped and wrinkled from overuse. Winnie returns with a tankard of ale and a smaller mug of steaming cider. The foamy ale sloshes over the rim a bit and Harlow sips from the tankard without lifting it.

"Why cider?" Harlow asks when Winnie has taken our orders and left again. "I feel like if any job deserves ale, it's yours."

"I don't drink," I say. "Not anymore. I relied on it a bit too much. Speaking of jobs, you wanted to discuss your assignment?"

Harlow accepts the subject change graciously, pulling out a well-loved journal, quill, and ink from her side satchel. I am impressed with her diligence and tell her such. She flushes, pleased with the compliment, and bows her head over her journal. Her nose nearly touches the paper as she writes in minuscule letters.

She fires question after question at me, not even stopping when Winnie delivers our food to us. I spare a smile at Winnie before answering another one of Harlow's questions.

What's Aleca like? What does Harlow need to know? Are Aleca and I close? How is Aleca responsible—in part—for Raznik's death? Are there any personality quirks she should know about? Do Aleca and I ever fight, and if yes, how do we resolve them?

She fills several pages of her journal with cramped writing before I reach over to stay her hand with mine. She looks up, and I notice there are flecks of ink along her nose and cheeks from the scratching of the nib against the paper, midnight blue freckles across pale skin.

"Your food is growing cold," I say. "Why don't you take a break and eat?"

She sets aside the journal and pulls her bowl toward her, ripping a small loaf of bread into pieces and dunking them into the creamy broth.

"Sorry for the interrogation," she says, sipping her ale. "I just want to make sure I'm prepared for this. This is the first real responsibility I've gotten since joining the warriors."

"When did you join?" I ask, cracking the top crust of my meat pie open. Steam erupts, newly freed, and moisture collects beneath my chin for a moment before wicking away.

"About ten months ago," Harlow says, "shortly before my twentieth. I know I'm a little older than most, but I couldn't figure out what I wanted to do with my life. I think already mentioned my botched attempt at being a woodworker?"

"The misshapen cat outside your house, yes," I recall. She points a finger at me to indicate I've remembered correctly.

"I was seeking stability, and the warrior life offered that for me. I'm still trying to figure out the real structure of our military, though."

"Our military relies on both branches to maintain order; our boots-on-the-ground enforcement officers are just as important as our leadership officers who orchestrate every minute detail of the military," I tell her, falling easily into the explanation. "In recent years, there has been less call for deployment of warriors to other places, but it's an important institution anyway."

As Raznik descended further and further into his madness, he became so focused on isolating his people that deployment of warriors became more about policing and punishing his Court than about security outside of our borders. I choose to keep that to myself.

She picks apart an already torn piece of bread with deft fingers and then says,

"Can I ask you a sort of personal question?"

"Fire away, but I can't guarantee an answer," I say.

"Can I see your warrior marks?"

It is not what I'm expecting, and it takes me by surprise. I run my tongue along the ridges of my molars as I contemplate her request. After a moment, I roll my sleeves up to my elbows, baring the ink on my arms. I am not nearly as tattooed as many of the other warriors of higher ranks: some of them are tat-tooed to the point that there is no visible skin. Despite this, there are enough marks there that I still carry a burden of guilt.

Harlow reaches out, twisting my arm in her hand to look at them. She's too familiar with me by half, but I let her conduct her silent assessment anyway, curious for her thoughts. She runs a finger along the moonflower on my thumb and then moves up to my wrist where she traces a finger along the shape of lilies with a half circle on the top left and bottom right of the stem and flowers. It's the one I received from Diviner Eloway in Apaiji, the one I only understood after the death of Raznik: the old symbol of my Court.

She moves up and follows the belladonna, tracing the scar that cuts through it from my fall in Garyn.

"You have a lot of flowers," she comments. "Unusual for warrior marks."

"None of those are," I say. "The flower is for a goddess, Karishua. The lilies are from a blind diviner in Apaiji, and the belladonna is to honor the life and death of my ex-girlfriend."

Harlow's hand stills for only a moment before she continues her assessment.

"Which one is from Raznik?" she asks. I point at a small black circle just beneath the crook of my elbow. Above it are thin lines, nearly like rays of sun; beneath it is one sharp, black line running horizontally. "Like his death meant new begin-nings," she says. I stare at her, and she feels the weight of my gaze on her. She meets my eye, and I shake my head.

"You're the only person who has picked up on that," I say. "I see you're honing your observation skills nicely."

"You're not what I expected," Harlow says. I tip my head to the side, my brow furrowing in confusion. Worried she's insulted me, she quickly adds, "I mean, I just never expected to find myself chatting with the commander of the entire Court in the back booth of a pub, you know? People should give you more of a chance to prove that you actually care about getting to know everyone."

I do not know how to respond, and instead I roll my sleeves back down. Harlow pulls her hands back, finishing her soup which has surely gone cold by now.

Conversation continues well into the night, past the closing of the pub. We find ourselves meandering down the mostly deserted roads of the village, and we do not part ways until the moon hangs high in the sky. When I am tucked beneath my blankets at last, I find my thoughts drifting back to her, and I wonder if she is thinking of me, too.

EIGHT

A new morning finds Harlow and I back in the training room. My heart thunders in my chest from exertion, and I hold a hand up, raising my arms over my head to catch my breath. The room is blazing hot from the fire, and we are both dripping with sweat. The window is resolutely stuck shut, offering no relief.

Harlow sheds her tunic, baring her beige breastband and a torso ridged with muscle. I allow myself an appreciative glance before dropping my arms to my side and turning away. I lift the bottom of my tunic to wipe at my face. This is doing nothing to deter my burgeoning crush on a very off-limits Harlow. I had a fairly sleepless night; any time I closed my eyes, all I could think of was her, our conversation, and the persistent desire to know her better.

"All right?" she asks from behind me. I lift a hand in a show of assent, and then turn with a steadying breath. I press my lips together in an attempt to keep a straight face. I don't know if I succeed, catching myself giving her another appraising glance.

"How are you with throwing off attacks?" I ask, sending a

prayer of thanks that my voice remains steady. I feel as if my body is reaching one thousand degrees. Sweat rolls in beads down my back.

"I'm…could use some work," Harlow admits, changing course mid-sentence. I nod, planting my hands on my hips as I consider next steps for training. I cannot concentrate between the heat of the room, the very fit Harlow in front of me, and the need to remain a consummate professional. Swiping at my face again, I finally give in.

"Do you mind if I follow suit?" I ask, motioning with the bottom of my shirt. "I know it's not exactly practical or appropriate, but I'm absolutely roasting." Harlow shakes her head and I make quick work of shedding my tunic and yanking up the legs of my breeches until they're somewhere closer to shorts. I tug at the shoulder straps of my breastband to make sure that it's securely in place and let out a sigh of relief. "Thank you," I say, already less overheated.

Harlow scrutinizes me, eyes trailing from my hands up to my shoulders where my warrior tattoos are on full view for the first time. Her own arms are bare, and I feel a sudden need to justify the ink that paints my skin. She does not comment though. Instead, she rolls her neck, eliciting a pop.

"So, attacks?" she prompts. She stands across from me, waiting for instruction.

"Right," I say. "Obviously, you have the basics down. I won't insult your ability as a warrior and make you go over those again. That said, you need to be able to throw someone off, or disrupt an attack if it happens."

"Do you seriously think someone will attack your sister?" Harlow asks, curious.

"I have no idea," I say. "Multiple people tried to attack me when I first took over, though, and Aleca has absolutely no training behind her. I barely made it out of the last attack."

Harlow stares at my arms again and I point at my newest tattoo, indicating Ocin's death. Her eyebrows raise, intrigued, but she does not ask any more questions. I suppose the proof of death is enough of an answer.

"Alright, then where do we start?" she asks.

"It's all about balance and using momentum to your advantage," I say. "If you understand those two things, you'll be able to take out someone twice your size. Though I'd hate for you to have to go up against a twelve-foot-tall person," I add, eyeing her long body. Harlow stares at me skeptically, and I move across the space, standing in front of her with my back to her. "Put your arm around my neck with the crook of your elbow."

I feel her raise her arm and then hesitate. Rolling my eyes, I reach back and grab her arm, bringing it around my neck.

"Relax, Harlow, you're not the first person to choke me." Harlow's muscles flex on instinct, and I realize the insinuation there. "I mean in battle! In practice! In—not, not—just hold your arm there."

With a breathy sort of laugh, Harlow closes the space between us and situates her arm as instructed. I wrack my brain, trying to refocus on the lesson—made infinitely harder by sudden feeling of her skin on mine.

Get it together, Grimme! I scold silently.

"Now what?" she asks; her smoky voice reverberates through my chest.

"Um," I say. "Um, now it's about knocking off balance." Without warning, I bring my hips forward and then slam back against Harlow. She is not expecting it and crumples at the waist, hinging forward and draping across my back. Harlow lets go of me and I go reeling forward, tripping and falling flat on my stomach against the floor mats.

"Oh gods, I'm sorry!" Harlow cries. I am yanked upward into a standing position, feeling for all the world like a ragdoll. We get back into position again.

"Now that you know what that feels like, I'm going to actually go for a flip," I warn her. Her abdomen tightens against my back and I feel her forearm flex on my trachea. I situate both of my hands on her arm, one in the crook of her elbow and one in the center of her forearm.

"Do it," she demands. I split my feet into a sturdier stance, one foot forward and one back. I bring my hips out again, further than before, and then career backward into Harlow with as much force as I can muster. She hinges forward again, and her weight falls across my body. I turn my torso into a ball, bringing her sliding over my shoulders and onto the floor.

Unfortunately, I forget to let go of her arm, and I'm flipped on top of her, rendering the attack entirely useless. Harlow lands with a thump on her back, her hair fanning out behind her head like an oversized halo. I am still clutching her forearm above her head as we lock eyes. Heat spreads from the crown of

my head into my toes, entirely unrelated to the fire crackling
merrily in the hearth.

"Okay, well, typically your victim would let go of you," I
say, awkward laughter bubbling out of me.

"So, who won in this particular scenario?" Harlow asks.
"Because you completely laid me out, but you went with me, so
I think my attack would be considered successful."

Neither of us has moved from our position, and she shifts
her body beneath mine. I release her arm, pressing a hand
against the ground on either side of her head and pushing into
a plank position above her. Her eyes darken as she watches me,
and as she parts her lips to inhale, my mouth goes dry.

I hastily roll to the side, leaping to my feet before the
moment can get away from us. I offer a hand and pull her into
a standing position.

"I think we call that I tie," I say. My voice is shaky and I
wipe my hands on my breeches. I can still feel her touch on my
skin, and I clench and unclench my hands to stop myself from
reaching back out for her. "Why don't we try again? I'll attack
you this time."

I throw an arm around her neck, rising onto my tiptoes to
efficiently hold her in a choke. She flips me easily and I fall onto
my back, letting out a whoosh of air.

"Good," I say from the floor. She pulls me up, dropping her
hold on me the moment I am on my feet. "Again."

······†······

"You may sleep when you are dead, Commander!"

I leap out of my bed, grabbing for my sword beneath my

125

pillow. Light suddenly pours into my room as the curtains are yanked open and I throw a hand up, shielding my burning eyes. My sword is still held aloft in front of me to ward off an attack that has not yet come. Slowly, I adjust to the assault on my vision and, eyes watering, I lower my hand.

He wears his dark hair looped into a loose bun on top of his head, and his face has been overtaken by a curly beard. Several small blue-black symbols have been tattooed onto his fingers in the time he's been gone. Despite these changes, the trickster smile remains ever-present.

"Aureus Thane, aren't you a sight for sore eyes," I say, dropping my sword on the bed again. I wrap my arms around him tightly, grateful to have him back so soon. The sun is shining brightly again; melting icicles from above pebble the windows and leave streaks as the droplets descend. Winter has found its end, and for that, I am grateful. I do not thrive in the damp and cold.

"I thought you might need my assistance as you gear up for your party," he says. "Get dressed, and we'll meet in your office. I've already asked for breakfast to be sent up."

Before I can scold him for taking over my command, he is out the door. I shake my head, a small laugh rising as I gather my clothes for the day. When I arrive at my office, Aureus is already sitting and serving himself a plate of food. Across from the seat beside him is a long black garment bag, tied tightly in a knot at the bottom.

"I'd tell you to make yourself at home, but that doesn't seem to be a problem for you," I say drily, grabbing myself a plate and filling it with eggs, hot fruit, and oats. A steaming mug of coffee waits for me on the small table, colored caramel by a gracious serving of milk.

"Home is not a place, but a feeling," Aureus says sagely, popping a slice of fruit in his mouth.

"How very philosophical of you, Majesty," I say. "You shall make a fine ruler someday." His face darkens for the briefest of moments, but he does not rearrange his features back to neutral quickly enough. I tilt my head to the side, curious.

"I don't intend to be a ruler," he says with a note of finality. It is rare that I hear such seriousness in his tone, and my hand pauses as I begin to spoon some oats.

"Forgive me for being so glib," I say. "I hadn't realized—"

"It's nothing you would have known," he tells me, waving it off. "However, it's nothing we need discuss further right now. I'm here to talk about you."

I take the hint and resume eating my breakfast. I've always known that there was something lurking beneath his carefree and jovial façade, something wounding and private. I know how it feels to carry secrets and the way they lace you open from within, and after a few moments' consideration, I say gently,

"I will not push but know that you are not alone in this world."

He says nothing, but he reaches over and squeezes my knee in a silent thanks. I stare out the window behind my desk while we eat, watching as the first sparrows of the season fly past. I always loved watching the birds with my father, and we spent many days sitting near the trees, throwing seeds, fruits, and nuts to them. Seeing them now fills me with a feeling of newness and hope.

"By the way, I've informed your student that you will be unable to make it to your lesson today," Aureus says. His emphasis on 'student' forces me to turn my attention back on him. He stares at me expectantly, as if he's found out a secret he wasn't meant to.

"Harlow?" I ask, knowing exactly who he's talking about.

"Is that the name of Lady Cornsilk?" I make a face at him. "She's cute."

"She's a student," I respond. "Nothing more, nothing less. I know what you're trying to insinuate, Aureus, and it's not true." I pray my face does not betray me.

"You may think that there is nothing happening there, but you're the only one who does," Aureus says. "Students don't look that crestfallen when they learn their private lesson has been canceled for the day."

I snort, knowing how much pressure I've placed on her by assigning her to my sister. If there is anything to be crestfallen about, it's out of fear of failure. Still, I cannot quell the traitorous flush from painting my cheeks.

"Harlow has a lot on her; I assigned her to guard Aleca, and I worry I may have made her nervous. Unfortunately, she's the only one I trust with my sister." Aureus raises his eyebrows at me as if I've just proven his point and I throw my hands up, exasperated. "Oh, honestly, Aureus! I assigned her to Aleca because I can trust firsthand that she can wield a sword properly if necessary!"

"Because of the private lessons," Aureus predicates. "How many other warriors are receiving private lessons, Commander?"

Ignoring him and his smug look, I consider for a moment whether his words might be true—and how I feel about it. For the briefest of moments, I allow myself to appreciate how pretty she is. She's attractive in an unconventional way, the sharp planes of her face standing in contrast to her broad shoulders and well-defined musculature, a stature I've never been able to achieve myself. I shake my head, breaking the train of thought.

He does not believe me, that much is clear. He stares at me with an appraising eye, chewing thoughtfully on a piece of sausage as if he knows where my mind has just gone. Abruptly, he points the sausage at me and I jump.

"That may be your truth, Commander, but it is not her truth. I know a girl in love when I see one, having been on the receiving end of moony eyes more than once."

"Interesting, you strike me more as the type of person who prefers to keep company with your own sex," I reply in a teasing tone. He shrugs, unbothered.

"I am a man of many facets, and find love in whomever I may find it," Aureus says, gesturing grandly. "Providing, of course, they are of age and consenting. Regardless, we talk not of my love life, but of yours."

"I have no love life," I say flatly. "May we please discuss

something else? Anything else?" Looking around the room, I try to find a different subject, and my eyes land on the forgotten black bag draped across the chair.

I point at the garment bag, and he takes the bait. His face splits into a delighted grin, and he all but throws his plate aside in favor of the bag. He loosens the knot at the bottom, and begins to pull whatever is inside out, and then pauses.

"I know what you've done, and we will return to this conversation. Now, turn away from me," he commands. "I want this to be a surprise when you see it."

"Okay…," I say hesitantly, turning my face away and closing my eyes. The bag rustles behind me, and I hear what sounds like tiny pieces of glass clacking together. Aureus makes small busy sounds, tutting and muttering *okay, alright, there we go,* and then,

"Alright! You may look, Commander."

I turn around again, and my mouth falls open. Aureus holds up a light blue, gauzy gown. It looks as if it is made of air. There is little embellishment on the front besides sporadically placed crystals. He turns it around for me, and that's where the real art is. Showing off the open back draping with crystals, he twists it to allow the gathering of beads to glint in the light. The crystals fall like droplets of water.

"This is incredible," I say, staring.

"And it's yours!" Aureus says. "Try it on. I'll be here when you're ready. No, don't fight me," he cuts me off as I open my mouth. "I had our seamstress whip up a few different gowns for you, and it would be an incredible insult to turn her work away. Go, dress!"

I take hold of the gown gingerly, terrified of damaging it. I have never held something so fine and delicate in all my life. Back in my room, I shimmy out of my pants and shirt, so plain in comparison to the garment hanging beside me. As I slip into the gown, the cold glass beads against my back send goosebumps up and down my arms. The material is feather-light and swishes in a satisfying way around me as I take a few steps in it. It fits like a glove, somehow. I lift the skirts so that I do not step on them and make my way back to my office.

"How do I look?" I say as I enter. I do a twirl for him and then come to a stop.

"You're an absolute vision," Aureus declares. "I knew that silver hair with these crystals would be perfect."

"How does this fit me so perfectly?" I ask.

"I stole a pair of your breeches and a tunic when I left," he says without remorse. "Our royal seamstress, Wyntras, could spin gold out of garbage. I asked her to make some gowns befitting a fierce but ever-softening Commander, and she made good on her promise."

"'Some?'" I repeat. "Aureus, one is too many!" Secretly, I am enamored by the gown and enthralled to know that there may be more where this came from. In my younger days, I rejected any and all dresses brought my way, convinced that no one would take me seriously if I was dressed like a girl. My time in Garyn and Apaiji changed that for me, proving that there was more than one way to effuse strength.

"Consider it a royal gift as you step into your new power," he says. "The rest should arrive with my parents and sister."

I thank him again as I slip back into my room to change. The dress I had planned to wear looks like a tattered potato sack compared to the new gown I tuck into my long armoire. The blue wisps of fabric remind me that I am no longer so alone in this world, and as I close the doors to the armoire, I sigh in contentment.

......†......

For the first time since I can remember, things are going well for me. Things are falling into place where they need to, and I am finding support in unexpected corners. I cannot shake the feeling that it is all about to go awry, but I try to ignore it and focus on the positive instead. There have been too many times in the past that, convinced the worst would happen, it did. Aleca calls it a self-fulfilling prophecy.

She arrives within a day and a half of Aureus. My sister and I greet one another with loud shrieks, throwing our arms around each other. I turn my attention to Bronwyn and shake her hand firmly. We came to a begrudging understanding of one another during my time in Apaiji, fleeting though it was.

We settle into finalizing the decorating of the area. I have tried to use the money left from my parents, as well as from my own warrior stipend, for as many repairs as possible. It feels selfish to be using the hard-earned money of my people for extravagances. We were certainly never rich, by any means, but I'm able to recognize that we lived in privilege anyway. When they died, the entirety of their estate went to me; unfortunately, there was little beside money to claim by the time Raznik was finished with their legacy and my home.

The grand ballroom has been kept entirely a secret, except to those who worked to restore it. However, the rest of the castle begins to come together as banners of silver and cobalt are hung on either side of the main entry. Similar swaths of fabric are looped between the pillars of the entrance hall, and a cobalt carpet has been laid out, replacing the worn red carpet from before.

Silver and brass fixtures gleam under the candlelight, polished within an inch of themselves. Years of gloom and neglect have been painstakingly undone and the castle looks more beautiful than I have ever seen it. Outside is much the same. The flora has been cultivated and shaped, and broken stones repaired. Near the center of town, a maypole has been erected, a tradition of centuries past. On the day before the final celebration, it will be decorated with wildflowers.

I have had to dive deep into our archival history to find the ways in which Battlewood once celebrated the arrival of Spring and the continuation of allyship with other Courts. The Raznik family was thorough in their erasure of our history. It took nearly a week before I was able to find a single book mentioning Battlewood as it once was, and it was hidden deep within the shelves of the office, rebound to look like another book entirely. The Razniks were men of mystery and lies until their final days.

......†......

"Are you going to tell me why we have a shadow, or do I just have to guess?" Aleca whispers to me as we walk through the castle. The sun hangs high and bright in the sky, drying up the sodden ground. We dressed to go for a walk outside. Her cloak of iridescent turquoise shimmers under the flickering lights of the sconces.

Harlow walks closely beside us, one hand surreptitiously resting on the hilt of the blade I know she has hidden on her hip. She has tied her cornsilk hair up and out of her face, tight braids on either side of her head and the rest pulled into a tail situated high on the back of her head. At the nape of her neck, the symbol for Linota's squad has been freshly shaved into her hair.

"Harlow," she says, reaching in front of me to shake Aleca's hand.

"Aleca," my sister responds, shaking the outstretched hand hesitantly. She scans Harlow's bare arms, no doubt looking for tattoos denoting any lives she may have taken. A look of relief washes over her as she sees that there are no marks of any kind on Harlow's arms. I do not remind her of the marks I wear, nor the marks our mother bore.

"You have a shadow because you're a menace," I say, tweaking Aleca's arm. She glowers at me and pulls her arm away.

"I am not a menace," she says with as much imperiousness as a 16-year-old can manage. I raise an eyebrow at her, pressing my lips together to hide a smile.

"Al, you broke out of prison and ran away to a magical

academy. I don't think there's a much clearer definition of menace than that," I say. "And," I add in a more serious tone, "the people of Battlewood are not always quick to forgive. Many see you as the reason why Raznik died, and I can't guarantee your safety when I'm not around."

"You're the one who stabbed him!" she cries. A servant pauses in her dusting before continuing again. "Oops, sorry," she says in a quieter tone.

"And I paid dearly for it. Just humor me, please," I say. Aleca rolls her eyes at me. I know she thinks that I'm being an overprotective sister, but she hasn't heard the things that I've heard. She doesn't know that there is still much anger and betrayal simmering in the Court. Flipping her cloak at me, Aleca walks a few steps ahead of me, as if trying to prove her strength and independence. I sigh, and Harlow gives my arm a squeeze.

"I've got her, Jace," Harlow promises.

I smile weakly and watch Aleca as she flounces ahead, her cloak billowing like a cloud behind her. It is hard to put my trust and faith in others, especially when so many have been taken away from me by someone I thought I could trust. It is something Lilith continues to point out to me in our mind healing sessions, that I've learned to be self-sufficient not out of want, but out of need. In doing so, I've stunted my ability to allow others into my life.

We lapse into quiet as we exit the castle and walk down the slope. Instead of heading toward town, though, I veer right to where the Pyre and the path into the woods sit. In the bright daylight, with my sister and Harlow alongside me, I feel more equipped to explore the place where Tally's ghost first found me. I haven't told either of them about this experience for fear of them refusing to go with me, and frankly, I'm not brave enough to go back into those woods alone.

As we near the entrance to the trees and the forest beyond, I can feel my hands start to sweat. What happens if Tally appears again? Will anyone else be able to see her? What if I've made this all up and am slowly going mad? Suddenly, I realize how little thought I've given to this venture, and I begin to back away from the copse of trees, shaking my head. I come up against something solid. Hands grab hold of my upper arms, stabilizing me as I wobble from the impact.

"Hey, are you okay?" Harlow's smoky voice asks. I turn and see her and Aleca staring at me, concerned. I feel my own eyes wild with panic and I blink several times, trying to regulate. Harlow ducks her head to meet my gaze directly. She scans my face, and her hands find my arms again; the pressure grounds me and I take in a shaky breath, exhaling slowly through my nose.

"Tell them," Tally whispers. Her breath is cool on my neck, and I whip around so quickly that my neck pops. There is no one there, nothing. "Go on, Jay. Tell them."

I spin again, trying to find where Tally is hiding. There is no one except Harlow and Aleca, who both stare at me in uneasy concern. I grab each of them by the hand and drag them into the trees, hidden from sight. I do not say a word as we march through the trees. The snapping of branches echoes sharply as we step on them. A cluster of birds takes flight out of a tree near us, screeching through the air. Vaguely, I am aware of Aleca protesting at how roughly we are moving through the woods, but I ignore it.

When we come to the clearing where the cottage is, I finally stop. My breathing is labored, and I drop their hands to clutch at a stitch in my ribs. The cottage is still in ruins; whatever magic caused the glamour the first time has apparently been dispelled. New vines have begun to climb the broken rocks of the foundation, eating away at what little stability was left to ruin. The clearing is still except for a gentle breeze.

"What is this place?" Harlow finally asks. Relief fills me despite my fear—if they see it too, it must be real.

"I think there are spirits trapped here," I say. A sudden gust of wind rocks through the trees, whipping Harlow's hair free of her braid. Aleca's headscarf goes flying high into the air, landing on a sharply jutting piece of wooden framing. She chases after it before I can tell her not to. As her hand lands on the silk, she lets out a high scream and falls backward, the silk tearing into two strips.

Harlow and I sprint forward. Harlow manages to catch Aleca before she lands on the ground. Aleca is white, shaken. Her eyes are wide and frightened as she stares at something in front of her.

"Father?" she whispers.

NINE

There is no time for me to puzzle over the mystery of my father appearing before Aleca in the clearing, nor why I was unable to see him. By that evening, the Grand Chancellor of Kydier, Aytac, arrives with his husband and their two servants. There is no fanfare to signal their arrival—I have decided that there will be no fanfare for any of the leaders. Relations between the Courts are weak and mistrustful, not something seen as a celebration.

I take supper with the men in the little-used dining hall. The room is much larger than three people need, and it is another reminder of how this Court once played host to gatherings and feasts. The chandeliers, hanging high above the mahogany table, cast a warm glow over us all. The walls are newly baren, having once been home to tapestries bearing violent depictions of our history.

Conversation is uncomfortable and stilted, none of us sure how to engage—or what to discuss. We land on surface discussions of our lands, the harvests, and our families. I defer to them, listening as they talk about their children, whom they've left with their nursemaid for the week. Once we've finished, I show them to their quarters and introduce them to the warrior who has been assigned their safety while they are here. The men retreat and I make my way to find Aleca.

I find her in the library with Bronwyn, their heads bowed together as they talk quietly. Harlow hovers in the corner, out of earshot but still within eyeshot of my sister. I take a seat next to her, watching my sister closely. She's been quiet since we left the forest earlier, and it worries me.

"How is she?" I whisper to Harlow. She looks over at me with a grimace. "That bad, huh?"

"You can't blame her," Harlow responds. She turns in her seat to face me. Fiddling with the fraying ends of her braid, she adds, "She just saw the ghost of her father—your father—in the middle of a forest. That's not exactly an everyday experience."

"Speak for yourself," I mutter, slouching down in my seat and crossing my arms over my chest. My knees fall open, and I can almost hear Aleca scolding me for how boyish the position is.

"Do you see him too?" she asks. Her voice is unsure, as if she is crossing a line with a too-personal question. I shake my head. Still staring at my sister, I say,

"I see my ex-girlfriend." Harlow shifts in her seat as I reveal my ghost, sitting up straighter. "Raznik murdered her a few years ago and made it look like an accident."

Harlow lets out a low whistle. I quirk my eyebrows in agreement and look over at her. In the dim gloom of the library, her face is cast into shadows that soften the sharp edge of her jaw. Her braid reflects the flickering firelight of the lanterns.

"I had no idea that there were other ghosts there. She kept saying, 'help us,' but I didn't think about who 'us' could mean." I run a hand over my face, sudden exhaustion settling over me like a shroud. My eyes close of their own volition and I do my best to smother a yawn. If I do not stand up, I'm going to fall asleep in this seat.

"You look dead on your feet," Harlow says, and then winces. "Sorry, that was poor timing." I wave it off with a half-smile. I clap my hands to my knees, willing myself to rise. As I rise, I swear I can hear my joints creaking like old trees in the wind. Bidding Harlow a good night, I drag myself back to my room.

The weight of the day and the celebration ahead has finally caught up to me. I've been sleeping poorly, and my body is paying the price for it. I draw my heavy comforter tightly around me, nesting in the center of the bed. My head has barely hit my pillow by the time I fall asleep.

······†······

I awaken to the sound of someone shouting at me. In the darkness, my senses are dulled and slow to sharpen. The fire has gone out in my hearth, and my room is icy. I fumble around as I try to untangle myself from my sheets. Another shout sounds from directly beside me, though it sounds as if it is underwater. Tally appears, shimmering champagne-gold in the darkness. Her face is terrified.

Adrenaline spikes in me, and all at once, my senses rush back to me. Tally shouts again, and this time I can understand her.

"You need to get Aleca! She's left the castle," she cries. I race around my room, grabbing a pair of breeches and a tunic from a pile on the ground. I shove my feet into my boots and jam my heavy cloak on. I fasten my sword belt around my waist and sheath my sword.

"Where is she?" I demand, throwing my door open. I sprint down the dark hallway, using the light cast by Tally to see my way. I slip as I round the stairs, slamming my hip painfully into the corner post. A limp slows my gait as I burst through the doors. The moon hangs high and bright in the sky, casting a low light over the land.

I pause as I try to gather my bearings, trying to use the elevation of the castle as a lookout for my sister. Even with the light of the moon, it is difficult to make out details of what is below me. Hip throbbing, I start down the hillside. Tally remains beside me as I go.

"Tally, where is she?" I ask again once I have finished my descent. Tally worries her hands as she says,

"The cottage, the cottage!"

A litany of curses streams from me as I pick up my sprint. Plunging into the darkness of the forest, I have to rely on Tally to guide me through. Focused on Tally, I catch my foot on a root and go sprawling to the ground. I smack my temple into a rock and stars burst in my vision. Groaning, I rise, wobbling as I try to regain my stability. Tally's hands flutter around me, as if she wants to help but knows she can't—the glamour breaks the moment she makes contact with me, and neither of us can handle her true form right now.

Motioning with my hand, we continue forward. We are close to the clearing, and the moonlight begins to stream through the thinning treetops. I hold a hand to my throbbing temple and approach my sister. She is sitting with her legs criss-crossed, staring up at the cottage. I press a hand to my mouth to silence a sob of relief. She is safe but entirely alone, no Harlow or Bronwyn to be found. Aleca does not move as I near her.

I sit beside her, silent. Relief gives way to rage as I sit there. Any number of things could have happened to my sister on her trek to the cottage, and it is not a position she should have been in. I notice at once that the wrist blades I purchased for her in Apaiji are nowhere to be found, and I want to shake her for being so foolish.

"Do you think Mom is trapped here, too?"

Her voice is hoarse. She has been crying, I realize. My anger washes out of me at the sight of my little sister in such a state. I scoot closer to Aleca until our hips are touching. Wrapping an arm around her, I say,

"If she is, we'll free them all." I squeeze her arm and she rests her head against me. She shudder-sighs as her breathing regulates. Tally hovers by the cottage, watching, and I mouth my thanks to her. She nods, and then disappears inside the cottage, nothing more than glimmering vapors. I cannot deny that this is real, anymore.

......†......

Harlow slumbers outside Aleca's door. I hear a roaring in my ears and I shake her roughly. She does not wake, and I shake her again.

"Jace!" Aleca protests. She places a hand on Harlow's shoulder, shaking gently. Harlow comes to, looking around blearily. When she sees me and Aleca standing in front of her, she jumps out of her seat.

"What—?"

"Come with me. Now," I say, pointing down the hall. We make our way to my office in tense silence. They both enter before me. I close the door behind me slowly, not allowing it to slam like I want to. Turning to face them, I lock eyes first with Aleca and then with Harlow. "Would anyone like to take a crack at explaining?"

No one speaks; I didn't expect them to. They exchange a glance with one another and I snap my fingers, bringing their attention back to me.

"I'll go, then, shall I?" I ask. "I was peacefully asleep, and then imagine my surprise when Tally shows up begging me to get outside!"

"Tally?" Aleca asks, jaw dropping. "How—?"

"We all have ghosts," I snap. "And it's because of Tally that I found you, so don't go running your mouth on how much you hated her." I turn my attention to Harlow, who has been silent thus far. I draw closer to her until I am less than an arm's length away from her. "I trusted you," I say. My voice is low, my words precise. "I asked you if you could handle this, and you said yes."

"I can!" Harlow says. "I don't—I mean, I can't remember—"

"Jace, it's not her fault," Aleca begins.

"Out," I say, pointing at my door. "Aleca, you and I will talk about this later, but right now, I need to speak with Harlow. Get back to your room, and do not leave it until I come get you, am I understood?"

"I hate when you pull rank over me," she says. She storms out of the room. I wait for the doors to click shut and then bear down on Harlow. Her eyes land on my face.

"You've been hurt," she says. It's the wrong thing to say.

"Yes, because of you!" I shout. "If you had done your job, I wouldn't have needed to chase my little sister through a pitch-black forest! Where the hell were you, Harlow, huh?"

"I—"

"I asked you if you could handle this! I told you how important it was to keep my sister safe, how slippery she could be, and you decided to sleep on the job anyway? If you were that tired, you should have asked for relief!"

"That's not what happened!" Harlow shouts back. "I swear, Jace—"

"You may call me Commander Grimme or nothing at all," I interrupt icily. Harlow swallows hard before continuing.

"Commander, I swear, I was awake. I even drank a mushroom tonic to keep myself ready for the night watch. I don't remember falling asleep!"

"Well, sometime between your tonic and me finding my sister alone in the forest, you did fall asleep," I snap. "If you couldn't handle it, you should have told me. I shouldn't be able to rely on the ghost of my dead girlfriend more than my own warrior!" My words rise into a shout again. I begin to pace, clasping my hands tightly behind my back. For the first time in weeks, I feel the charge of staticky magic in my fingertips, and now is not the time to have an emotional burst.

"Then why did you assign me to Aleca?" Harlow asks. Her voice matches mine in volume.

"I have been giving you lessons for weeks, Harlow! I needed you, not another warrior!" The moment the words are out, I want to take them back. It feels like an admission of something, though I can't tell of what.

"You still have me!" she cries, frustrated. She grips her braid tightly in her hand and tugs it over her shoulder running her hands along it several times. It's something I've noticed she does when she is in high states of emotions. I stop my pacing to face her.

"Do I?" I challenge her. My voice drops from a shout, but it carries no less anger. "Or do I have a warrior who can't uphold her promises?"

"That's not fair," she says, her voice soft and wounded.

Instantly, the tension shifts into something quieter and more fragile. We stare at one another, aware that we are on the precipice of true damage. I inhale slowly and deeply, exhaling through my mouth. In this moment, standing across from Harlow, I am aware of the power imbalance between us. I hold all of the power over Harlow and her position. In a different life, it was me who stood at the mercy of those above me, and I was offered a second chance.

"You're dismissed for the night," I finally say. All of the fire has gone out of me. "I will find you in the daylight, and we can talk then."

Harlow hangs her head, nodding, and leaves. I close my eyes tightly, steeling myself for another sleepless night, and then make my way to Aleca's room to stand guard for the rest of the night.

Alone with just my thoughts, I replay my argument with Harlow over and over in my head. There was an undercurrent of something unsaid, as if we were both on the verge of confession. Have I relied too heavily on Harlow, unfairly placed burdens on her shoulders? Was I duped into believing that I could place trust in her?

With a burn of shame, I remember that there was a third person involved in all of this: Aleca. She has pulled the wool over the eyes of those much more trained than Harlow, and I cast her out before she could explain herself. Blinded by my fear, my anger, my feelings of displaced betrayal and disappointment, I took it out on Harlow. I hang my head in my hands, rubbing at my aching and tender temple and eye socket. Pain blossoms beneath my fingertips.

Away from the intensity of the room, I can think more clearly. I do not pretend that this fight was about only my sister. That was the catalyst, but not the entirety. The betrayal I felt when I realized Harlow had fallen asleep on the watch was more personal than professional; I recognize that now. Have I been approaching our lessons with too much familiarity? I enjoy the way I feel when we are together, but I worry now that I've blurred lines and allowed myself to think less with my head and more with my heart than is my norm. Chagrin burns like acid in my throat.

Even in the aftermath, I still trust Harlow above all others. Perhaps I have placed too much on her, so desperate to share the burden of responsibility I have been crushed beneath.

With a sigh, I lean back in my chair, prop my right ankle on my left knee, and wait for the morning to come.

......†......

By the time the sun rises, I am miserly. My face has swollen, my neck aches from sitting all night, and I am filled to the brim with emotions. I feel a tightness in my chest that will not go away. I decide that Aleca has had enough opportunity to sleep, and I rise, entering her room. She is still fast asleep, tiny snores rising and falling from her half-open mouth. Here, with whisps of purple-and-blue hair strewn across her rosy cheeks, she is every bit of the young girl she pretends not to be. The fire burns out of me and I sigh.

Settling myself on the other side of her bed, I run a hand along her hair, brushing it out of her face. Aleca breathes softly and turns on her side, curling into me. We haven't laid together like this since we were children. If I close my eyes, I can almost believe that we are safe in our home, that none of this has happened.

I allow my eyes to flutter shut, finding comfort for the first time since last night. Before long, I am drifting in and out of sleep. The next time I am conscious, Aleca has gotten out of bed and dressed. She sits at the small vanity, fiddling with small glass jars of something. I wipe at my eyes, clearing the sleep from them. She catches my movements in her mirror and comes over to me with a small jar.

"Here," she says, uncapping it. She dips two fingers into the cream and swipes it along my temple and eye socket. The cream is minty and cool against my skin, and the swelling subsides almost immediately. "I haven't figured out how to get rid of bruises yet, but this will help with the swelling, at least. I've been practicing with healing magic."

"Thank you," I say. I flex my hands, sore from the impact of the forest floor last night. "Aleca—"

"I know," she says, cutting me off. She sighs and sits next to me on the bed. "You told me not to go off on my own, and I did anyway."

"I didn't tell you that because I'm being overbearing," I say. "There's something weird happening here, and I can't figure it out. It's unpredictable, potentially dangerous. Besides that, there is so much riding on this week going well. If I hadn't found you last night…" I trail off, unsure what to say, but Aleca understands the implication anyway.

"Did Tally really tell you where I was?" she asks. She tries her best to keep the contempt out of her voice but does not quite manage. I compose myself before answering.

"Yes. I first saw her a few months ago, and up until last night, I thought I might be hallucinating it."

"Months?" Aleca repeats. "Jace, why didn't you tell me before now?"

"What would your response have been if I had told you, 'Hey, Al, nothing serious but I think I'm being haunted by the ghost of my ex-girlfriend, who also happens to be giving me really cryptic messages?'" I ask. Aleca presses her lips together.

"Fair enough," she concedes. She loosens a leather string from her wrist and ties her wavy tresses up and out of her face. "I'm sorry I snuck out last night."

It is silent, and then Aleca confesses in a whisper,

"I spiked Harlow's drink with sleeping powder. You won't fire her, will you?" Her voice drips with guilt. My jaw drops open and I snap it shut, seething.

"Aleca Grimme, you didn't!" I cry. She looks away from me. "How could you do something so vile? You drugged the person I entrusted your care to? You should be ashamed of yourself!"

"I am," she asserts. "I like Harlow, I really do, and I didn't mean for her to get into trouble. I just…I haven't seen Father in so long. I miss him."

"That's not Father, Aleca, not really. Don't let yourself get caught up in illusions. Whatever this is, I think that's what it wants. Prey is always easier when its guard is let down." Aleca makes a face, no doubt taking issue with my likening her to prey. I consider telling her about the glamour spell cast over Tally, and which I assume is cast on our father, but I refrain. Something tells me that she is not ready for that information. I hesitate, tracing images into the velvet comforter and then wiping them away again.

"I swear, Aleca, if you do this again, I'm handcuffing you and your guard together for the rest of your trip, am I understood? I know you think you're tough and independent, but you're my baby sister, and that comes first." I grab her around her waist and tug her into my arms, wrapping my legs around her when she begins to squirm. I hold tightly until she squeaks a relenting cry.

"You're such a grump!" she says as she rights herself, but her cheeks are tinged pink with contentment. "Syiera and Obsidian will be arriving tomorrow. What do I tell her?"

"Nothing, for now," I say. Rising from the bed, I walk to the door and then turn back around. "I meant what I said, Al. You may go nowhere without me or Harlow. I expect you to apologize to her, today and not a moment later."

"I will, I promise," Aleca says. I nod and leave, shutting her door behind me. Guilt burns me from the inside out, and I hurry from the castle, intent on providing an apology of my own.

After a short walk, I stand outside of Harlow's home, staring at the dark blue door as I try to bring myself to knock. An oddly gnarled wooden cat sits on a stump beside the door like some sort of guardian, and I run a finger along the top of its head. Smoke rises from her chimney and I watch it disappear into the sky, steadying myself before raising my hand. I knock hard twice and wait.

The door opens and Harlow stands there, a fluffy grey cat in her arms. I wonder momentarily if this cat was the muse behind the wooden one outside. The cat chirps at me pleasantly.

"Oh, it's you," she says dully. The emotionless greeting makes me grimace with regret. She steps back, jerking her head to invite me in. She is in her sleeping clothes still, a ratty pair of breeches and a sleeveless top which reveals her smooth, muscular arms. Her hair has been tied up and out of her face in a messy knot at the top of her head. It's the first time I've ever seen her so unkempt, and it drives home just how human she is beneath the hard warrior exterior. It's endearing in an unexpected way, and the guilt rests heavier on me still. I wish now that I had covered up the bruise that paints my eye and temple, left visible in a fit of passive aggressiveness.

I nod at her, entering the small but comfortable home. It's a one-room home, broken into separate spaces by a linen changing screen, a tall bookshelf, and a long table. A loaf of bread cools on the table, steam still rising from it. Her sword sits atop her uniform, which has been piled in a corner near her bed. I trace my finger along the warped wood grain of her table before turning to face her. She stands near the door, still clutching the cat.

"He's cute," I say by way of icebreaker. "What's his name?"

"Beans," Harlow responds. "He's an escape artist, is what he is. I've chased this stupid cat more times than I can count." She pauses and then holds him out to me. "Would you like to hold him?"

"Sure," I say, taking him from Harlow. He's a big cat, heavier than I expected. My arms drop with the sudden weight of him, and Harlow snickers despite the awkward tension. I scratch him behind the ears, eliciting a purr from him. "Speaking of escape artists, I…need to apologize. May I sit?"

Harlow indicates to the long log bench at the table and I swing a leg over it, still petting Beans as I do. She takes a seat at the other end of the bench, putting space between us. I suck my bottom lip between my teeth, chewing as I work out my words.

"I'm sorry, Harlow. I was out of line last night, and I owe

you an apology. My sister will be finding you later to provide one of her own, as well. It seems she spiked your coffee with sleeping powder so that she could sneak past you and find our father again."

Harlow's brows snap together, and she works her jaw for a moment, unsure how to respond. It's a betrayal of the highest order to be drugged by one close to you, and I cannot begin to imagine what's running through her mind. I take advantage of the silence to continue.

"I'd like you to stay on as Aleca's primary guard, if you're still willing," I finally say. "You're a good warrior, and I cannot entirely fault you for being bested by my sister. She pulled one over on our last Commander and…well, you know how that ended.

"Anyway, all I'm trying to say is that she is good at what she does, and it wasn't fair for me to take that out on you. I got scared, and I took your willingness to help me out for granted. I can ask someone to take shifts to relieve you of the burden, if you're willing to give me and my sister a second chance. You may feel free to give Aleca a piece of your mind, if you so desire. She more than deserves it."

"I'd be honored to stay on, Commander," Harlow says, and suddenly, I miss hearing my name fall from her smoky voice.

"Now that you know just how talented Aleca is at escaping on you, I need to know that you're prepared to fully take her on. I don't say this to make you feel bad, but she's incredibly difficult when she wants something. You've gotten a taste of what she can be like."

"I can keep my promise, I…well, I promise." Her eyes are wide and earnest. Guilt pools in my stomach.

"I shouldn't have said that last night, Harlow. I know you can," I say. "I was angry and frightened, and I tend to swing for the low-hanging fruit when I feel backed into a corner. Have you rested enough that you feel ready to take your spot back up today?"

"Yes, ma'am," Harlow says. She looks down at her ratty clothes, and then adds, "Well, I can be in short order." She rises from the bench, grabbing her wrinkled uniform from the ground and dipping behind a changing screen.

She throws her sleeping clothes over the top of it, and her shirt lands by my feet. I stare at it, the back of my neck getting hot.

"Why is his name Beans?" I ask, looking back at the cat and resolutely trying to ignore the sounds of Harlow dressing. I roll my eyes at myself; there are far bigger fish to fry than this right now.

"Found him stuck in a bag of beans when he was a kitten," she says, stepping back around from behind the screen. She deftly ties her hair in a braid and sheaths her sword. "The cat is a menace, but he's a good boy, aren't you, Beansy?" she coos, leaning down to smother her face in his fluffy belly. He squirms in my arms, trying to get away from the onslaught of affection. In his attempt, my hand flings free and smacks Harlow on the cheek. Her head knocks to the side.

"I'm so sorry!" I gasp, dropping Beans and grabbing hold of her face to steady her. I run my thumb along the cheekbone

I just assaulted and then drop my grip on her. I point at Beans, who licks his haunches haughtily on the ground. "That was very rude of you, Beans."

"If you're waiting for an apology from him, you won't get one, Commander," Harlow says, rolling her eyes. She douses the fire in her hearth with a bucket of water. "Thanks for letting me try again," she adds. "I won't let you down this time."

Harlow grabs her sword and sheath, tying it around her waist. She shoos Beans with her foot as we leave her home, and she has to back out very artfully to prevent the grey cat from escaping. She is locking her door when I speak again.

"Harlow, if it's all the same to you…will you please call me by my name again?"

Harlow pauses, still bent over her lock as she considers my question. When she rises, she turns to face me with a wide, sunny smile that sends my heart racing.

"I'd very much like that, Jace," she says, and I decide that there is no better sound in the world than my name on her lips.

······†······

The sun is finishing its descent behind the mountains when the final delegation from the Nautilus and the Crescent Isles have arrived. We gather in the lesser dining hall. The table nearly groans under the weight of the food and drink that has been prepared. Our kitchen has outdone itself.

I have never felt more like a child than I do as I sit surrounded by these leaders. The youngest still boasts ten years of age more than my own nineteen. I can feel my knees knocking together as I rise to stand at the head of the table, staring at a sea

of strange faces. I have barely had a chance to greet them inde-
pendently of one another, and now here they all are before me.

I send up a silent prayer to my goddess, asking that I not
completely botch this. Taking a deep breath in, I begin to
speak.

"Thank you all for coming here. I cannot tell you how
excited I am to begin to forge new alliances with you all. I look
forward to meeting with each and every one of you tomorrow.
I'm sure much has changed in the last hundred years." A
chuckle ripples around the table and, bolstered by the reception
of my words, I continue.

"Battlewood has much work ahead to undo the damage that
has been done, but it's my promise to all of you that I am com-
mitted to the work. For now, though, let this serve as welcome
enough. I'm sure you're all hungry and ready for me to stop
talking. Eat, drink, and enjoy one another's company!"

Unexpectedly, Empress Syiera begins to clap. The others
follow suit, and my face prickles with sudden heat. I press a cold
hand to my cheeks as I sit. Aleca beams at me from her seat
and I throw a weak smile her way. She is drawn into conversation with Obsidian, and I am left to my own thoughts.

The room is filled with the scraping of silverware against the
plates, the clinking of glasses together, the voices of those around
me as they converse openly and easily. For many, this is more a
reunion than an introductory meal. I find relief in the fact that
the King and Queen of Alymere are only familiar with Syiera;
in some way, it feels like an evening of the playing ground.

This is where I truly feel what Lilith calls my social anxiety.

I have no idea how to open conversation with strangers, nor do I feel comfortable. My parents always said that Aleca had enough social alacrity for the both of us, often taking charge in new situations. I have made a habit of deferring to others until I've found some form of comfort with those around me.

It's one of the things that drew me into the life of a warrior: you find comradery with a small group of people, and they become your family. There's no bumping of the elbows or schmoozing to be found when you're one artful sword fight away from death. I fear my days of quiet deferment are over, however, and I have no choice but to leap headfirst into discomfort. Lilith would be so proud of me.

I am seated nowhere near the few people with whom I feel comfortable. I pep myself up three times in my head before I open my mouth to speak.

Grand Chancellor Omarose of Dezaiyr is seated beside me, and she, I've observed, is also on the quieter side. I rack my brain for something to say, anything, and settle on,

"The feather you gifted me was beautiful. I have had it made into a quill."

"I'm so glad," she responds, her words heavily accented. "I must admit, I nearly turned your invitation away."

"I'm grateful you changed your mind," I respond. "May I ask what your hesitation was?"

"Your predecessors were violent men," Omarose says lightly, taking a sip of wine. "They made many threats to me and my people throughout the years. I have been Grand Chancellor for a long time now, and I have seen many things. I must admit, I hoped the downfall of Battlewood would be among them."

I cannot fault her for saying it. She is not alone in hoping for Battlewood to receive its due. I push the vegetables around on my plate with my fork as I calculate my answer.

"I hope that with time, I can repair what Battlewood has done," I say at last. Omarose grants me a smile, her teeth shimmering like pearls against her dark lips. I smile weakly; there is still much work to do.

After everyone has finished their meals and nightcaps, they part ways. It has been a long day for many, and they need the rest. Aureus takes hold of my elbow and pulls me aside to ask that I meet him in my office. I nod, and he disappears into the crowd of guests.

I do not leave until the room is empty except for the servants. I take a moment to thank each of them for their work, slipping them each a coin for their service. The halls are quiet when I leave. I trail my fingers along the smooth wood of the banister as I walk up the curving staircase toward my office. The surface is shiny and reflects firelight off it.

When I arrive at my office, Aureus sits there with my sister, Harlow, and another girl who looks to be my age. There is no mistaking who she is: except for the tattoos and beard, she and Aureus could be twins. Her thick black hair has been tied into a braided chignon at the nape of her neck, and she holds her hands clasped behind her back, looking around my space.

"Ah, Lady Commander," Aureus says. "Your first event went well."

"Thank you," I sigh. "I hope none of you will be offended if I become one with this couch right now." I drop myself onto the couch, tired. Aleca takes a seat beside me, rubbing my shoulder blades softly.

"Jace, I want you to meet my sister, Nesryn. Nesryn, this is Jace, Commander of Battlewood," Aureus says.

"It's a pleasure to meet you, Your Royal Highness," I greet, rising to hold a hand out. Nesryn shakes it with a firm grip. Her fingers, much like Aureus', are decorated with rings of silver and gold.

"Commander," Nesryn greets me. Her voice has a higher, sweeter lilt than I expected from her. "I hope you'll pardon my candor, but I must tell you…you live among many ghosts. What on earth is happening in your lands?"

TEN

I lay in bed with my eyes wide open, staring at the ceiling. It is pitch black in my room, the sun long since set on Nesryn's cryptic words. I cannot afford to lose sleep, but it seems that I will not find it tonight. Many ghosts, she said. How many of those ghosts are in the castle? In my room? I look around, as if one will suddenly make itself known to me. Nothing happens. I punch my pillow with a grumble and flop to my side, willing sleep to come.

It never does. By the time my eyes become heavy, the sun has begun to paint the sky gold. There will be no sleep for me. I toss my covers aside, yawning widely. I slide into my soft slippers and pad my way down the stairs to the kitchen. The staff are already at work, the din of bakeware and cutlery loud and lively. They all stop when I enter, and I wave a tired hand.

"Please, don't stop because of me. I'm just here for co-cof-coffee," I say through a yawn. "Extra caffeine, if you have it," I add with an embarrassed laugh. A woman near me hands me a silver carafe and a mug.

"Espresso," she tells me. "Extra caffeine, just like you asked. It'll put hair on your chest and a pep in your step."

"I suppose if hair on my chest is the price I pay, I shall pay it," I say. To my amazement, a tinkling laugh cycles through the room. I am unused to being met with appreciative laughter, and I feel myself preen beneath it; it is a small sign that attitudes are changing. There used to be little laughter in the castle.

Instead of going back to my room, I step outside to breathe in the cool, fresh air. I do not move from the top of the stairs, unwilling to get my slippers soggy. I take a seat on the wide flat railing of the stone steps, staring out over the land as it begins to wake. The dew catches the rising sunlight and refracts it back, like tiny flames in the grass. Movement to my left catches my attention, and I squint to make the image clearer. There is someone in the training fields, practicing with the cloth dummies.

A flash of bright blue hair causes me to double-take. It is my sister, hunched over with a blanket pulled tightly around her shoulders. That must mean that the person practicing is Harlow. I envision Aleca grumbling and complaining colorfully as she sits on the ground with her back against the fence. I cannot believe that Harlow has managed to get Aleca out of her bed so early. When we lived together, it nearly took a blood sacrifice to get her out of bed.

A stab of regret pulls taut in my chest as I watch Harlow parry. I miss our morning lessons, and, though we made some form of amends, guilt still gnaws from the way my temper bested me. It brings me comfort knowing that she took the conversation to heart, but I should never have let myself speak to her that way.

Pouring myself a second cup of coffee, I watch as Aleca points at the dummy Harlow is stabbing at. It bursts open with a bright spark, sending feathers and hay flying into the air. My mouth drops open at the blatant display of magic, impressed despite myself. Harlow's smoky laugh carries up the hillside. She sheaths her sword and offers a hand to Aleca, pulling her upright. They begin to trek toward the castle; I assume that was Aleca's way of telling Harlow that she was done sitting in the grass watching her swordfight a dummy.

I quickly swing my legs over the railing and scurry inside before they see me. It appears they are finally beginning to bond with one another, and I do not want to get in the way of that. I need Aleca to find some equal ground with Harlow if she is going to be on her best behavior.

I pass by Omarose, who is dressed in a golden skin-tight, sleeveless bodysuit. She has covered her shaved head with a colorful cloth. She nods at me as I pass.

"Good morning, Grand Chancellor," I say. "Out for a run this morning?"

"The cold air is good training for my lungs," she responds. "So different from the hot desert air of my own Court. Even now, at the end of winter, the sun is so very hot. Your lily-white skin would burn in a moment." She grins at me, and it is not entirely friendly. There is a commentary in there about my perceived weakness, I think.

"I suppose I shall take precautions when I visit your lands, then," I say, going for jovial and landing somewhere closer to a responding challenge. She raises an eyebrow at me before nodding. We bid each other goodbye, and I continue through the castle, rounding the corner just in time for me to hear Harlow and Aleca enter, laughing. I pause, torn between not wanting to eavesdrop but too curious to care.

"Oh, come on, Harlow! You don't want to be just the slightest bit rebellious here?" Aleca asks. She is using the voice she always uses when she's conspiring to break the rules.

"Not a chance! I don't ever want to do something to make your sister double-guess me again. You have no idea how much I look up to her, as a warrior, as a person, and as the Commander," Harlow says. Warmth pools in my belly and I press a hand to stem the blush from rising to my cheeks. There is a moment's silence and then Aleca asks,

"Do you like her?" Her tone has lost all mischief and transformed into one of gossip, if not a touch suspicious.

"Aleca!" Harlow exclaims.

"I'm just asking! I mean, it would…"

Their conversation grows fainter as they trail further away from me, and I find that I desperately wish I knew the answer to my little sister's question. I allow myself only the briefest of seconds to try to ground myself before I must dress and make my way down to the receiving room. Not for the first time, I remind myself of my position of power, my mission during this festival, anything to steer my mind clear of any romance, perceived or otherwise. Bless her for being a nosy little gossip, though—that kind of question is only one that a little sister can get away with asking.

In the receiving room of the castle, I am seated at a small table, a spread of tea and light pastries set out for my company. Today is the day that I meet one-on-one with each leader from the Courts to discuss our futures as allies. I am starting first with the Courts closest to Battlewood and making my way down the Nautilus.

Felix greets me pleasantly, and I respond in turn. We discuss the bridge once more, agreeing to break ground in the coming months. Wren offers education in the way of healing, including courses in tinctures, salves, and other homeopathic remedies that largely do not exist in Battlewood. It is a wonderful idea, and we set up an additional meeting once the festival has concluded.

As they leave, Aytac and Kaleth enter the room. They are imposing men, russet skin wrapping around large muscles that strain at their linen shirts. They both hover nearly six feet in height. Aytac's face breaks into a wide smile, the corners of his eyes crinkling, and the softening effect is immediate. His caramel eyes twinkle as he and his husband take a seat across from me.

"Commander Grimme," he greets. His voice is higher than I would expect from him, almost flute-like. "It's wonderful to truly meet at last. My husband, Kaleth," he introduces, nodding at his husband. Kaleth raises a hand, the gold-and-ruby wedding band around his finger bright under the light cast from the candelabra on the table.

"Commander," he greets. His voice is so low that I feel its rumble reverberate in my chest. Kaleth does not regard me with the same open interest that his husband does.

"A pleasure to meet you both," I say. "I'm so pleased that you've accepted my invitation. I know that our lands have a history between them—"

"It does not help that you, yourself, took a life in them," Kaleth cuts me off. My mouth snaps shut, shame and surprise painting my face crimson. Aytac reaches over, resting a hand atop Kaleth's. He settles back in his seat, staring at me with something between suspicion and curiosity.

"I…did," I begin slowly, measuring my words carefully. "I am not proud to have, and I did not take it lightly. Unfortunately, there was very little else I could do at that moment. I regret having to have interceded in such a way, but I will not apologize for protecting someone important to me. I'm sure you can understand what it's like to want to keep someone you love safe."

I hold Kaleth's hard gaze for a moment. His eyes, a bright cerulean that are made brighter yet by his dark skin, narrow in scrutiny. After a moment, he relents with a nod and a glance sideways at his husband.

"You were saying, Commander?" Aytac encourages.

"Yes," I say, bringing my attention back to Aytac. "At one time, Battlewood had a wonderous trade with your lands. The mosaics our Court boasts are created by materials from your land. When the Pact was created, it ceased all communication with any outsiders. I'm sure you've noticed that Battlewood is distinctly grey in comparison to the many colors of Kydier."

"I had, I'm afraid," Aytac agrees. "I have to wonder how your people find peace and beauty in so severe a land." I nod, pressing my lips together.

"An excellent question," I say. "The answer is that they don't. Battlewood has made a name out of austerity."

Aytac hums his agreement, resting his chin in his hand and drumming his fingers on the tabletop. He considers my words; beside him, Kaleth seems to communicate something to him with nothing more than an eyebrow and a tip of his head.

"What would you offer in return for opening lines of trade again?" Aytac asks me. "After all, the word trade makes one think that it's something for something."

"Historically, we traded meats, furs, and mountain flora," I say. "If this would continue to be of interest to you. I understand that cultures may have changed in the last century; ours certainly did."

It turns out that the offer to trade arts for goods is an amenable one; Aytac and I part our conversation with a firm handshake and a hesitant, though still suspicious, smile from Kaleth.

Omarose enters shortly after lunch, and her face promises to make this conversation a difficult one. I swallow hard as she takes a seat across from me. The many-layered chains of gold and beads draping down her neck clack together as she shifts in the seat, crossing her right leg tightly over her left.

"Chancellor Omarose," I say, my hands fluttering around my glass of water and my quill before settling in my lap. Omarose makes me nervous, and I do not quite know what to do with myself when I am around her. Omarose adjusts the rings on her fingers, watching me with a sharp, raised eyebrow.

"Commander," she says.

"Thank you for taking the time to speak with me," I say. I run my hands down the tops of my thighs, trying to wick the moisture that has gathered on them. She tracks the movement; a not-entirely kind smile pulls her pointed lips upward. "I must admit, of all the Courts here, yours is the one I know least about."

"That's for a reason, Commander," she tells me. I wait for her to continue, but it becomes clear quickly that I am going to be the one to carry this conversation.

"I'm sorry, I'm afraid I don't know what you mean," I confess.

"I am not surprised," she says. "There seems to be a distinct air of…chaos around your Court. Poor communication. False promises. Theft."

I narrow my eyes at Omarose. Her face has adopted a hard quality to it. I can almost feel the air crackle between us with enmity. I can understand where the Courts are coming from, to a degree, but I refuse to be blamed for the sins of those who came before me. I tap a finger against my glass of water, measuring my words before I speak.

"Grand Chancellor, I'd ask that you speak openly and honestly with me. I do not like to rely on information gleaned through the lines."

"You want honesty, Commander?" Omarose asks, leaning forward. Her dark lips are pulled back in a sneer, her walnut-brown eyes gleaming with something akin to feral distaste. "Your precious Raznik stole something of mine, corrupted her beyond recognition. I offered him use of her service as a sign of good faith, and instead, he kept her for himself."

"You keep saying, 'her,' Chancellor. Who are you referring to?" I ask, puzzled.

"You know her now as Elouned," Omarose said, the name dripping off her tongue with vitriol. "When she lived in our lands, her name was Ifoké."

My face contorts in confused shock, and I sit up straighter in my seat. Omarose watches me as I process her proclamation, trying to put together loose pieces. I have never known Battlewood to be without Elouned, our one and only Valkyrie. I've never stopped to consider the fact that she was the only one in our lands, another blind acceptance of how things have always been.

"It may be of help to know that Elouned, or Ifoké, as she was, appears to have been loyal to Raznik alone. She disappeared around his death and has not been seen since. That said, I'd be happy to aid in returning her to your lands to atone for whatever may have happened," I offer.

"She betrayed her sisterhood and her land," Omarose says. "Her atonement will come in the form of death alone."

Omarose levels me with a gaze, as if issuing a challenge. I

force myself not to look away from those hard eyes. I press my lips together, discomfort filling my chest. I fear that Omarose, and Dezaiyr by extension, will prove to be a complication for some time to come.

······†······

"I know you've had a long day, Commander, but I was wondering if I may have a moment of your time?" Nesryn asks. She leans in the doorway to my office, where I've just finished another entry into Lilith's journal. Though I was loathe to admit it at first, I have found merit in her method of dumping my thoughts onto paper; I find I'm able to streamline my mind in a much more efficient way than before.

"Yes, of course, Your Royal Highness," I say, beckoning her in. She enters, closing the door behind her softly.

"Just Nesryn will do," she replies.

"As will Jace," I say. She nods with a small smile and looks around the office.

"This office doesn't seem to reflect you." She wanders around the perimeter, taking in the lack of personal effects. She pauses at the carpet in front of the hearth and stares at it, cocking her head to the side with a scrutinizing look. "May I?"

"Uh, sure," I say, joining her. Together, we tug the loveseat and ottoman out of the way and roll the carpet up. There, as vibrant as ever, stares back the rune circle. Nesryn turns her face to cast me a look of disbelief. "Do…you know what this is?"

"Do you?" Nesryn asks. She rises and pulls me into a standing position. With a low whistle, she tugs a band of stretchy string off her wrist and twists her thick black hair up and out of her eyes.

"Not a whit," I reply. "It's just been sitting there, taunting me for months. I can't find any information about it, partially because I don't know what to ask for. I've been in a precarious situation: magic is incredibly contentious in Battlewood, and it would cause an uproar if those who still support Raznik knew that he was practicing magic. The most I've figured out is that it's some form of battle magic."

"It's more than that." Nesryn shakes her head and walks around it, the same path I've walked so many times before. "This is battle magic, yes, but also death magic."

I feel the horrified look wash over my face before I can control it. My brow furrows and my nose wrinkles with distaste. I've never heard of death magic before, but it sounds distinctly unpleasant. No wonder I couldn't figure out what to research.

Nesryn walks along a straight line carved through the circle and stands in the middle. Beneath her feet, the center rune flares to light, black and glittering. I watch with rapt attention as she moves about the next line of runes, bringing each one to life one at a time. They all flare a different color, and though it means nothing to me, it must mean something to Nesryn.

She treks around the next circle, and then the final outer circle, and then comes to a stop. The final rune flares a bright red, so bright that my eyes water. Nesryn leaps aside just as a spark shoots up from the rune; the cinders land on the bottom of her skirt and she stamps it out before it can catch.

"Huh," she says. I arch an eyebrow, dipping my head incredulously.

"All that, and it warrants only a, 'huh?'" I ask. I shove my hands into my pockets to quell my urge to pick at my cuticles.

"No, of course not," Nesryn says thoughtfully. She twirls a loose lock of hair around her finger, staring down at the puzzle before us. As if remembering herself, she shakes her head and looks back up at me. "This isn't why I came to find you, although it certainly lends credence to what I was coming to talk with you about. Do you have anything planned for this evening?"

"No, I had planned to settle in with a cup of tea and some light sword practice," I say.

"My, do you know how to relax," Nesryn says drily, a small smile quirking the left corner of her mouth. "Would you instead be willing to come for a walk with me?"

"Of course," I say, glancing out my window at the dusky blue sky; clouds hang heavy in it, promising a rainstorm. We stop by my quarters so that I can change into more weather-appropriate garb, and then we make our way outside. I let Nesryn guide me where she wants, though I begin to regret it as she brings us to the one place I've spent too much time at recently. Harlow and Aleca are already at the Pyre when we arrive. I turn a questioning eye up at Nesryn.

Instead of responding, she gingerly tugs the bottom of her long dress up, tying it into a knot at the middle of her shins. I get the feeling that this is not the first time she's done this, and I wonder what sort of trouble she gets herself into at home.

Being the sister of a veritable trickster, I do not believe for a moment that she does not follow in his rule-breaking footsteps. She tightens the band around her hair and then begins forward.

"What's this about?" I whisper to Aleca. She shrugs, making an *iunno* sound. I glance around Aleca to look at Harlow. She responds with a similar shrug. I chew on my lip, following Nesryn as she leads us into the forest. My stomach ties in knots as we approach what I know will be her destination: the cottage in the clearing. Aleca slips her hand into mine, clammy with nerves. Few things rattle her, but spirits and ghosts have always been a source of fear. I squeeze her hand in reassurance. For a moment, it is so reminiscent of the evening that we were marched to Raznik's office for her prison sentence that my breath hitches in my throat. Though the circumstances tonight are much different, I find myself sidling closer to Aleca.

The trees swallow us, and we follow closely behind Nesryn. She marches forward as if she has been to the cottage a hundred times before. Her footing is sure and straight, never stumbling once. Through the woods, I think I spot a whisp of a spirit, blue-and-white in the trees, but it is gone before I can tell. To Harlow's right, I see a similar whisp, gone again too quickly to make out detail. I am not the only one seeing them, though: Harlow lets out a gasp and whips her head around, trying to find the source of light.

"Um, Nesryn," I call carefully, "it may be helpful if you tell us what we're doing before we get there."

She stops in her path and turns to face us. This time, there is no mistaking it. Blue-and-white whisps float up and around Nesryn, circling her briefly before turning into mist. Aleca's hand trembles in mine, and I see her reach over for Harlow's hand as well.

"Your land is haunted," Nesryn says. "I believe I can help. Often, spirits become trapped by the need to complete a soul task."

The words are followed by a ringing silence, punctured only by the calling of a corvid in the distance. Aleca jumps, nerves near to snapping. Harlow leans around Aleca and whispers to me,

"I mean, you seem them too, yeah? I'm not just imagining things?"

I stare forward as she speaks but turn to catch her gaze as she asks her question. I rove my eyes over her face for the briefest of moments, looking first at her eyes before dipping down to the lip she has begun to worry between her teeth and then back up.

"I see them," I confirm. We resume our spots, flanking Aleca once more. More whisps have joined Nesryn, and she appears to be in conversation with one that hovers near her left ear. I watch in complete consternation, wishing fervently that just once, I could have a normal day in this blasted Court. A branch snaps somewhere to my right, and Aleca startles again.

"I want to leave," she demands, but her voice is shaky.

Nesryn finishes her conversation and turns her attention back onto us, shaking her head softly.

"You need to see first what I see."

We step out of the trees and into the clearing where the cottage sits. It has degraded some since I last saw it. Several stones have fallen out of the foundation, and a window is broken which was not broken before. I steel myself for the appearance of Tally, but she does not show; in fact, no spirits are revealed. Nesryn withdraws a small pouch from beneath the bodice of her dress and pulls the drawstrings open.

She reaches in, taking a pinch of something and sprinkling it into her outstretched palm. Softly, she blows on it, dispersing whatever it is across the entryway of the cottage. The substance sparks as it leaves her hand, winking out almost as quickly as it flared. For a moment, nothing happens. Then, the earth rumbles beneath our feet. Aleca's hold on my hand tightens so sharply that I feel my bones crunch together.

Slowly, the earth shudders to a stop and the door of the cottage creaks open. There is nothing but shadowy darkness inside. The three of us remain rooted where we stand; I can feel the cool prickle of fear begin at the nape of my neck and run down my spine. My breathing comes more quickly now, my chest rising and falling with anticipation.

"You may come out," Nesryn calls softly. There is another moment's pause before a champagne-colored shimmer begins to form. It's diaphanous at first but gradually becomes more solid. The spirit is a young man, no older than twenty. His hair, flaxen waves, reflects the shimmer that surrounds him. He wears a look of total terror as he steps out of the doorway. He is no one I recognize, but from my right, Harlow lets out a sound like a wounded animal. "You all may come out."

Behind him steps out Tally, followed by my father. His left arm is extended behind him, and then my mother steps into view, clutching tightly to his hand. Spirit after spirit pours out of the house, more than the small cobblestone cottage would ever be capable of holding. They all wear the same look of fright, their eyes darting between Nesryn and the three of us.

"My girls," my mother whispers. She breaks away from the group and walks toward us, raising a hand to her mouth. She is dressed in her warrior uniform, the same outfit she was burned in. The medals of honor clink against one another as she moves. I ease my hand out of Aleca's iron grip and step forward slowly.

"Mother," I reply. A lump the size of a peach pit has lodged itself in my throat as I stare at her, drinking in her silver hair and pale blue eyes; if I didn't know what lay hidden beneath the glamour, I would swear she was alive again. We reach out to one another, but do not let our fingertips touch. Both of our hands tremble. I watch as her eyes trace the beginnings of my belladonna tattoo until the design disappears beneath my shirt sleeve.

Father finds his way over to her, and I drag my gaze away from my mother to look at him. As in life, his salt-and-pepper hair is neatly coifed, and his green eyes are magnified behind a pair of simple wire glasses. He looks every bit the academic that he's always been. I stick an arm out behind me, encouraging Aleca to come forward with a wiggle of my fingers.

Small, soft fingers wrap themselves around my own coarse and calloused ones. Beside me, Aleca openly sobs as she looks at our parents. She reaches out to our father, nearly touching him, and I jerk her back just before she makes contact.

"Don't," I warn. "You don't want to know what is hidden from us."

"What are you talking about?" Aleca asks, trying to move towards him again.

"Show her, love," Mother says. I've never heard her sound so sad and tired. I bring my gaze to her, feeling my face pucker and then crumple with emotion. She holds a hand out, open and welcoming. I take a deep breath and place my hand in hers.

The glamour drops in an instant; I am vaguely aware of the shout that sounds from Aleca as I stare at our mother. Her hair, which had been tied tightly in warrior braids, becomes straw-like and frayed. Her skin turns waxy, stretched tightly over the sharp planes of her face. Her eyes, milky blue, are sunken, and a large gash on her cheek shows a line of teeth. Her hand becomes nothing more than bones beneath mine and a thin golden bracelet slides down her skeletal wrist, catching on the pisiform bone of it. It is the same exact bracelet that I've seen on Tally so many times before.

Mother smiles sadly at me, and I bring her hand to my lips, pressing a kiss to it. She presses her other hand to my cheek, and the tenderness behind it brings me to my knees. All of the feelings I've suppressed since her death come ripping out of me and I let myself cry for her death for the first time. I can feel her running a hand over my hair as I do, my face buried into my hands.

I collect myself as quickly as I am able, wiping at my eyes

and nose with the sleeve of my shirt as I rise. Aleca has not touched Father, has not allowed the glamour to be stripped of him. She speaks spiritedly with him, informing him of her near brush with death and subsequent apprenticeship with Syiera.

This jostles a memory of a conversation we had with Syiera shortly before our departure, and I turn my attention back to Mother.

"You and Father went to Apaiji," I say. "You died because you were trying to save us."

"Yes," she replies. "Jace, you must understand that we thought we were doing the right thing. You and your sister were so young and vulnerable. Aleca showed signs of magic from a very young age, before she could even speak. She's always favored your father in that way."

She casts a sidelong look at my father and Aleca, who sit with their heads nearly together, deep in conversation. I look past them to find Harlow clutching the hands of the man who first left the cottage. He is more exposed bone than skin, hidden beneath baggy and tattered clothing.

"What happened?" I ask, already knowing how the story will end.

"He caught your father first. Your father died from illness, but it was not organic; Raznik slowly poisoned him over time, and by the time we realized, it was too late. The poison was clever—it mimicked the symptoms of Black Cat Flu almost exactly. Bad luck, memory loss, weakening physical strength, all of it. Then, one day, your father walked in to see Raznik sprinkling something in his tea. When he confronted him, Raznik tripled the dose and forced the tea on your father." She inhales sharply, shakily. "I found him on the floor of his office that night. He'd stopped breathing hours before."

She gazes over at Father again, a soft and sad smile playing at her blue lips.

"How did it happen for you, Mother?" I ask. I push the sleeves up her arms as best as possible; the material is tight and stops midway up her forearm. Despite it, I can see the faded ink of her warrior marks, the tattoos signifying her journey through the ranks.

"What was the official ruling?" she asks, and I realize that she wouldn't have known what was said postmortem.

"That you died in battle," I say, "but that doesn't make sense, because there was no battle at that time."

She nods slowly, absorbing the information with a thoughtful look in her eye.

"I suppose I should be grateful that my death was not so slow as your father's," she says. "It was very quick. I was in the forest, trying to plan our escape route along the foot of Maelos Mountains. There was a noise behind me, and then everything went black. I know now that it was Raznik."

"I killed him," I say. The satisfaction at his death washes over me anew, filling me with a fiery anger that I haven't felt in months. "Why isn't he here with you all?"

"They're here for a different reason," Nesryn responds. I jump; I hadn't heard her approach.

"What does that mean?" I ask. "Al, c'mere," I call, waving my sister and father over. They join us, and for a moment, I relish the reunification of my family, however temporary and numinous it may be. My father, still in his glamour, smiles warmly at me. I quell the urge to wrap my arms around him.

"Your old Commander was immersed in battle and death magics. I suspect that he got in over his head; his magic became corrupted," Nesryn says. "You recall the runes in your quarters?"

"Vividly," I say.

"The ley lines of the castle have become corrupted by improper magic." Nesryn picks a stick up and draws a rough approximation of the rune circle in the soft dirt. Pointing with the tip of the stick, she says, "The beginning of this circle, here in the center, that's fine. As he devolved, though, it became more erratic."

"What is it supposed to mean?" Mother asks, tilting her head to the side as she examines it. For the first time, I hear my father speak.

"If I may?" he asks Nesryn. She nods, motioning for him to go ahead. "If my knowledge and memory serve me correctly—which I have faith in, given my dashing intellect—," he adds, winking at Aleca, "these marks are the combination of two separate rituals. What started off as a bid for power turned into a bid for immortality."

ELEVEN

A metallic screech fills the air just as Father finishes speaking. It's the one I've heard multiple times before, and I'm fairly confident that whoever that screech belongs to is directly involved in this. Collectively, all of the spirits who fill the clearing look up to the sky, their initial fear overtaking them again. One by one, they race back into the cottage, disappearing as the darkness consumes them. Soon, just our parents and Harlow's spirit remain. I see Tally appear again, gently taking hold of his arm and tugging him away from Harlow. They vanish into the cottage and Harlow stares after them, cheeks streaked with tears.

"We have to go for now," Mother says. She and Father grab hold of one another, backing away from me and my sister. "Get out of here, all of you, now." Her tone is commanding, the warrior in her coming out. Our parents disappear on the spot, turning into vaporous light. Not needing to be told twice, we turn and run. Harlow has not moved from her spot, and I shove Aleca toward the forest and race back over to her. I grab her beneath her arms, heaving her to her feet.

"Harlow, please," I beg. She still cannot bring herself to move. Shifting my weight to my right leg, I stick it between her legs. I take hold of her right hand with my left and drape it around my shoulder; bending, I wrap my arm around the back of her knee, squat, and pull her body around my shoulders. I press her right hand to my chest with my hand, keeping my left hand free, and begin to trek toward the trees as quickly as I can. It's been some time since I've had to do a warrior carry, and I am grateful for muscle memory.

Aleca and Nesryn stare at me with concern as we join them. The screech sounds again, closer and more violent sounding. I shake my head.

"Don't worry about it, just move," I say. I shift Harlow's weight around me and press on, not stopping until we break free of the trees. The sky is like black velvet, heavy storm clouds obscuring the moon and stars. A droplet of rain falls onto my face, and then another, and suddenly it's as if the sky opens wide. A deluge of rain pours down on us, making the ground slick and muddy.

A strike of skeletal lighting jackknifes through the sky, and almost immediately, a roar of thunder follows. I pick up my pace, nearly running now. Another strike of lightning lights the sky up for a brief moment, followed by two more strikes. Thunder fills the sky, vibrating against my chest. We are nearly to the castle; by this point, I am fueled by adrenaline alone.

As we enter, I command my sister and Nesryn back to their quarters and then carry Harlow to mine. She has not moved a single muscle since the clearing, and I do not want to leave her alone tonight. I will have to trust that Aleca understands the gravity of the situation and will keep herself safe for the night without Harlow standing guard.

I deposit Harlow onto my bed. We are both soaked to the bone. I move to my hearth, struggling to strike a match as my hands shake from the chill that has begun to wrap itself around me. Slowly, the flames begin to splutter and spark as they try to catch the wood. I poke at the logs until there is a gap for airflow and the flames capture the wood at last.

Harlow is motionless atop my thick comforter, her blonde hair plastered to her forehead and cheeks. She is staring up at the ceiling and in the darkness, I can see the reflection of fire in glassy eyes. Her clothing clings tightly to her body, and when I gaze closer, I realize that her teeth are chattering together. I gnaw on my lip, and then go over to my armoire, pulling out my roomiest and coziest clothing.

"Harlow, can I help you change into dry clothes?" I ask, brushing her hair from her face. She nods slowly, still staring up at the ceiling. With some effort, I pull her into a sitting position. "Can you help me?" She shakes her head, and I sigh. "Okay, um…then I guess…" I stare down at the pile of clothes and the near-catatonic person beside them. "I'm going to undo your breastplate, okay?"

Slowly, I undress her, walking her through every part of it so that she does not feel vulnerable to me. I leave her underthings on, and after a few long minutes, she is redressed in a fleece-lined shirt and soft pants. I deftly tie her hair up in a plait and pull the covers over her. She rolls onto her side, and I watch her for a moment, unsure if I should speak.

Instead, I dig my bedroll out of the chest at the foot of the bed and unroll it, along with a pillow and thin blanket. Exhaustion overtakes me and, aided by the dry heat thrown by the fire, my eyes flutter shut moments later.

I jolt awake the next morning, and it takes me a moment to realize that I'm safely on my floor instead of catapulting off the side of a cliff. My chest rises and falls as I try to regulate my breathing. Stiffly, I push the blanket aside and rise; sleeping on a slate floor is unforgiving.

The fire has long since extinguished and the room is chilly in the early hours of the morning. From the window, I can make out the very beginnings of the sunrise, the rays of light made murky by a heavy fog hanging between the mountains. As I roll my neck to loosen the kinks that have found their way there, I realize that my bed is empty. Harlow's belongings are gone, as well. She must have woken in the night. After some deliberation, I tie the top layer of my hair in a topknot and steal away from the castle, down to her small home in the village.

I haven't even raised a hand to knock when the door swings open. No one is in the doorway and I look down to find Beans wrapping himself around my ankles, chirping a greeting to me. I bend down to scoop him up, scratching him behind his ears as I enter the home.

Harlow is seated at the small table before her hearth, playing with a spoon in a wooden bowl. She brings the spoon up, watching the liquid spill from the head of the spoon back into the bowl.

"I saw you coming," she says. Her voice is entirely devoid of emotion, and I frown.

"When did you get back?" I ask. Beans nips at my hand, and I dump him out of my arms. He lands on the ground with a dull thud and trots away, tail held aloft. Harlow sticks the cutlery in the bowl and pushes it away, rising from the table.

"A few hours ago," she says. "I'll wash these and get them back to you." She motions at herself, and I realize that she is still wearing the clothes I changed her into. In the daylight, I can see that they fit her poorly. Several inches of ankle and wrist are exposed by clothing made for someone far shorter than she.

Harlow runs her hands along the plait I twisted her hair into, her telltale sign that she is overwhelmed. I do not know what to say now that I've verified that Harlow is safe, the relationship between us still fragile.

"Thank you for helping me last night, Commander," she finally says. Her eyes are focused on the ends of her hair jutting out between her fingers.

"Please call me Jace," I say. "I don't like whatever…this…is." I motion at the space between us, hoping that she'll understand what I mean. The unfortunate thing about us both is that we struggle to find the right words when it counts.

She pauses in her ministrations over her braid, looking up at me. I chew on the inside of my cheek, staring back at her. My eyes are wide with anticipation, as if I can read her mind if I stare hard enough. The braid drops from her hands, and she nods carefully. Tension bleeds out of me, my shoulders drooping with relief.

"Well, I'll let you get on with the morning," I say. "I just wanted to make sure you were okay."

I am two steps from the door when Harlow's voice stops me.

"It was my brother," she says. I turn around to find her leaning against her table, fiddling with the cuff of her sleeve.

"I didn't know you had a brother."

Harlow jerks her head at her bed and walks over, taking a seat on the edge of it. She pats the space next to her and I perch gingerly there. Beans hops up, kneading the fuzzy blanket beneath his paws and purring. Harlow pets him absently, staring off into nothingness.

"Yeah, he pretty much raised me. My mom was a real shit-bag—oh, sorry," she says, covering her mouth.

"I've said worse," I tell her drily. "Don't censor yourself on my account."

"She disappeared when I was still in diapers, and Fallon was left to take care of me. He was a lot older than me, nearly eight years. I recognize now that leaving a ten-year-old to raise a two-year-old is insane, but Fallon was already used to parenting our mom, so we kept to ourselves and didn't let anyone know she'd left us."

"What about your father?" I ask. Harlow shrugs.

"Never met him," she says. "Neither did Fallon. Then, Fallon disappeared one day, and I assumed that he'd had enough of being my parent and left as well. I was twelve, so that was…" She pauses, counting on her fingers. "Eight years ago, now."

I hadn't realized that Harlow was older than me. I do some calculations in my head quickly, trying to figure out the timeline between then and now.

"You only joined the ranks of warriors in the last year, right?" I ask. She certainly wasn't enlisted when I was under Linota; I would have remembered her, absolutely.

"Yes," she says. "I know I am a lot older than most everyone else, at nineteen—well, twenty, now—, but I had become something of a nomad once Fallon disappeared. I lived with an aunt in a few villages over from here for a year, and then at an orphanage when my aunt got sick of me. Well, that was a nightmare, and I ran away shortly after my fifteenth birthday, bent on finding Fallon.

"I never did find him, and I've spent the last eight years of my life believing that he abandoned me, when in all reality, he's been dead. I think…I think Raznik killed him. He couldn't remember what happened, but he didn't die from natural causes."

Her eyes are glassy with emotion, and she swipes at her nose with her sleeved arm. Never having been one to deal well with emotions, my hand flutters between us before landing just above her knee. She meets my gaze.

"I'm so sorry, Harlow," I say. "That's…you didn't deserve any of that."

Harlow places her hand on top of mine, a feeble smile curving her sad mouth. She hesitates and then laces her fingers into mine. Her hand dwarfs mine; my entire hand nearly fits into her palm. Her nails are short, dirt still collected beneath them from the night before. The skin of her palm is tender, but calloused against the soft skin on the top of my hand. She sighs, relaxing her body and leaning on me. Her head comes to rest on my shoulder.

My first reaction is relief; that Harlow feels safe and comfortable enough to lean into my touch means that whatever awkward and unspoken tension has lingered between us is no longer there. It's difficult to experience something like we did last night and not come out closer because of it.

My second, and more insistent reaction, is an awareness that we are close to crossing into uncharted territory. I'm not foolish enough to deny the fact that there is a spark between Harlow and me. I didn't need Aureus for that. I'm also not foolish enough to pretend that in the deep, dark nights when sleep evades me, I haven't considered the idea of what it would be like to lead Battlewood with Harlow at my side. Despite this, I know that the discrepancy of power and vulnerability is too great a chasm to bridge.

A sigh escapes my lips, more wistful than I would have preferred. Harlow lifts her head off my shoulder and I feel her gaze on my face. Slowly, I turn to face her. Her eyes, whiskey in the firelight, hold an emotion I haven't the ability to identify. There is something fragile and unspoken between our gazes. I can feel my lips part, and before I can further dissect the moment, Harlow leans in to close the space between us. Almost as if my body moves of its own accord, I lean in. Her lips meet mine, soft and measured. Her free hand lifts, cupping my jaw. Realizing what is happening, we both pull apart and put space between us. We leap to our feet, taking several large steps back from one another.

Even after she has pulled her hand from my jaw, my skin buzzes. I have never seen her so flushed, and I know my face reflects the same color, the color of crushed berries. Harlow's home suddenly seems infinitely smaller, like we are giants in a space built for people much tinier than us. I can feel my eyes wild and frenzied.

"Um, I—well, I—that was—"

"I'm so—I mean, we—"

We speak at the same time, our words tumbling out of us and warping together in an unintelligible stream.

"You go first," I say with a shaky laugh. I wipe my clammy hands along the thighs of my pants, but it does no good. Heat prickles along the back of my neck. I ball my hands into fists, fighting the urge to draw Harlow back into a kiss. The dam, poorly cobbled together after the near-incident during our lessons, has broken entirely and my resolve is at an all-time low. When there was space between us, I could keep my heart and mind separate from one another. Now that it has been breached, I know it will be twice as hard to keep the flood at bay.

"I'm—I didn't mean to…I know that we can't…do this," she motions between us, "and I didn't mean to pressure you or, or put you in a bad position. I don't know what came over me," she says. Her voice is husky with emotion, and she plays with the ends of her braid frenetically—her constant tell when she's anxious.

"No, it's okay," I say, shaking my head. "I also didn't mean to…well, you know. I don't want you to feel like I'm leveraging vulnerability or power against you. Things happen, I suppose." Not things like accidentally-on-purpose kissing your student-slash-warrior after whom you've been secretly pining, but I do not feel the need to delve into the nuances with Harlow. "We don't have to…I mean, this doesn't have to mean anything."

A micro-expression ripples across Harlow's face, gone before I can further analyze it. She nods, still worrying the ends of her braid between her nimble fingers.

"Right," she agrees. "Sure, yeah, you're right."

"I should—"

"Of course," she cuts me off. "You've got a lot to do. You should go."

I nod, rooted to my spot. Beans takes the opportunity to reach up my legs for me to hold him. I bend, scratching behind his ears before shooing him toward Harlow. She watches us closely, abandoning her anxious fiddling when Beans vies for her attention.

"I'll see you later," I say, moving toward the door. "Take the day to recuperate, and we can talk more tonight. The feast begins around nightfall."

The moment the door to her home snaps behind me, I take off, sprinting until I cannot focus on anything but the bright, sharp stitch in my chest and the screaming burn of fatigue in my legs.

······†······

The kitchen is abuzz with activity, chefs and sous chefs
shouting to one another as workers race around. When I check
to see if they need anything, I am assured that it is under control and am shooed from their workspace.

My warriors are suited in their best armor, ready to aid and
protect as needed. For the first time in recent history, the people
of Battlewood have been invited to the castle en masse, and I
do not know what behavior to expect. My only comparison is
that of their behavior in the amphitheater, a space built for
punishment and riots. The last time I was there, my death was
demanded. I fervently hope that the same cannot be said for
the ballroom.

Aureus and Nesryn arrive at my room an hour before the
ball, a small bag swaying from Nesryn's arm. They are already
dressed, looking every bit the royalty they are.

Aureus wears a pair of tight white pants and an emerald
jacket, the lapels embroidered with golden curlicues. A thin
leather belt crisscrosses around his waist, a golden chain dangling from one side to the other. Beneath the jacket is a white
shirt with a large bow of similar emerald fixed at his neck. Finishing his look is a fur-trimmed cloak of gold-and-green velvet.
His tall boots clack against the slate tiles, and I realize that there
are jeweled chains draped along the tops of his boots. He has
pulled his hair into a sleek, high tail.

Beside him, Nesryn wears a gown of the same emerald
green. It is made of many layers of chiffon, with an intricate
corset around her waist made of golden beading, coming to rest

just below her chest. A golden collar boasting emeralds and dia-monds is wrapped around her neck like a choker, draping down to her shoulders where a chiffon cloak is affixed. Her hair has been left down in waves of black curls. They both wear a single golden circlet on their head, unadorned except for a pear-shaped emerald.

Staring at them, I don't know how I will ever be able to compete for the stage with them. I have never worn anything half as fine as their outfits, not even when I took a meeting with Syiera last year.

"Wow," I manage. I try to quell the feeling of jealousy in my throat at the sight of them. As if reading my thoughts, Aureus says,

"We look good, but don't let that trick you into thinking we're anything other than troublemakers at heart. Plus," he adds, grabbing hold of Nesryn's arm and tugging it aloft, "we're here to assist." The bag dangles from her arm, stopped by the thick bangles around her wrist. "Have you your gown, Commander?"

I take it from the armoire, untying the garment bag and sliding the gown out from inside it. I had forgotten what a work of art the gown was, and seeing it now brings a temporary relief to the jealousy. I step behind a dressing screen to disrobe and put the gown on. The cold glass beads against my skin send gooseflesh up and down my body.

Nesryn had pulled her items out of her bag and spread them across the top of my vanity which, except for my brush and hairpins, is typically bare. Now, an assortment of brushes sits beside small glass pots of colored creams. A comb with a sharp metal tip sits next to my wire brush, and I eye it warily. In the wrong hands, that comb would make a good weapon.

She beckons me over, and I sit atop the velvet stool, taking great care not to snag the delicate beading and tulle of my gown. She combs through my chin-length hair, humming to herself as she does so. Deftly, she ties two tight braids on either side of my head. Along the crown of my head, she braids a thicker section of hair, tying a third small one into it on either side. A number of strands fall loose from them, unwilling to remain part of the twists.

From his pocket, Aureus withdraws a black velvet pouch drawn tightly shut. He pulls the strings open and dumps the contents of the bag into his other hand. From the bag falls what look like several pieces of jewelry. He sorts through them and then holds up an elaborate ear cuff and matching cuff bracelet. Both are studded with diamonds and an aquamarine-colored gem. I gasp at the sight of them.

"I cannot accept diamonds from you!" I insist. "These would feed the Court for weeks."

"Then sell them once the feast has ended," he says with a shrug. Aureus motions for me to hold my wrist out, which I do. He fits the cuff snugly around it, and then moves to my side to fix the other cuff to my left ear. A chain dangles from it, sporting an aquamarine stone. Nesryn waves Aureus from her space and stands before me with a thin brush and a pot of kohl.

"Close your eyes, Commander," she tells me. I do so, starting when the brush makes contact with my eyelid. I struggle to keep my eyes shut at the foreign feeling, and Nesryn scolds me twice. She pauses and then a fluffier brush is brought against my cheekbones. Finally, she swipes at my mouth, hums her satisfaction, and instructs me to open my eyes. When I catch my reflection, my mouth drops open. I look like a proper ruler, regal and imposing. The youthful angles of my face have been sharpened with a dark powder, and the black kohl lining my eyes makes them look like an even brighter silver than usual. My mouth is stained the color of plums. The sleeveless gown puts my warrior marks on full display, and I look powerful.

I barely register a knock on my door as I stare at myself in the mirror. Behind me, Nesryn drops into view. She places her hands on my shoulders and flashes me a wide smile. I smile back, more grateful than ever that the universe saw fit to bring Aureus and Nesryn into my life.

"Good evening, Commander. I was on—" The words die on Harlow's tongue as we lock eyes across the room. She stands frozen just inside the doorway. Heat blooms on my face and I'm grateful for the rouge which Nesryn has swiped across my cheeks. Harlow stares openly, her mouth falling open. "Wow."

Aureus' mouth also falls open, his expression morphing from intrigue to delighted mischief, much like the cat who got the canary. He looks between us, a devilish smile forming.

"Wow, indeed," he says, his voice nearly a purr. I shoot a glare at him, which only makes his smile wider.

"I, erm, was on my way to get Aleca and I thought you may want an accompaniment as well." Harlow's voice is higher than usual, and there are two bright spots of pink high on her cheek-bones. Her eyes catch mine, dart away, and catch me again.

"That would be lovely," I say. "Thank you for the offer. Nesryn, Aureus, thank you for your assistance this evening. I shall see you once you've entered alongside your parents."

My message is read between the lines, and Aureus bows to me before linking arms with Nesryn.

"We shall see you shortly," he affirms. "Lady Cornsilk," he adds in a greeting to Harlow, tossing one final look of glee over his shoulder at me as he bounces out with his sister. She glances at me, confused, and I roll my eyes with a shake of my head. As I rise to join her, the glass beads clack together, filling the stilted silence.

"You look incredible, Jace—Commander," she corrects. Dressed in her formal warrior uniform, we cannot be on a first-name basis. I have never seen her in her formal uniform, and my mouth goes dry. Formal uniforms are as different from battle uniforms as they come. In place of chainmail-and-armor breastplates, the female warriors wear a thick leather breast-plate, embossed with silver and gold flowers and leaves. Three small chains connect across the torso.

A similarly embossed metal collar is fastened around the neck, a sharp spike on either side to deter sneak attacks from behind. A silvery-grey cloak is fastened to the left shoulder, draping down and around to connect on the right hip. Tying the outfit together is a leather belt with surreptitious sheaths for the warrior's weapon of choice, hidden cleverly by the long cloak.

Harlow has pulled her long blonde locks out of her face,

twisted up into a high bun with silver strands wound through-out. A thin black line has been drawn across her eyes, a thicker black line drawn beneath stretching from her hairline to the center of each eye. It is the traditional paint of a warrior, worn only during a celebration or event. She looks as powerful as I feel, standing at her imposing height and carrying herself with the ferocity of a hundred warriors.

"You, as well," I finally manage. I glance behind her at the open door, running through considerations in my head. It would take nothing for her to close that door behind us and shield us from anyone's eyes. It would also be unwise to close that door; my hold on my resolve is tenuous and threatens to slip at the slightest provocation. She follows my gaze, looking over at the door before stepping back slowly and closing it. She does not break eye contact with me as she does so. The door snaps shut with a determined sort of snick, making my heart lurch with anticipation.

I drum my fingers against the side of my leg anxiously and then step forward, crossing to Harlow. She steps backward, her back coming up against the door, and then we are locked together. Her fingers take hold of my waist in a bruising grip, and my own hand snakes up to clutch the back of her neck. Between kisses, we give up any pretense that there is not some-thing between us.

I have to force myself to break away and I do so breath-lessly. Some of my lip stain has transferred to Harlow's mouth. I swallow hard, a sheepish grin stealing over me as I go to my vanity to grab a cloth for her mouth. She takes it, wiping her mouth as I reapply the stain carefully to my own lips.

"No more," I say sternly, but the effect is dampened by how breathy I still am.

"Yes, ma'am," she says, a wicked gleam in her eye. I take a deep breath and instruct her to open the door, remembering shoes at the last moment. I tear my gaze away from Harlow long enough to dig through my armoire for an appropriate pair of shoes and realize that Aureus placed a pair of matching high-heeled shoes there at some point while I was dressing. I stare at the heels with apprehension before slipping them on.

I wobble like a colt on the heels, unused to the added height. Harlow offers me her arm, and I take it gingerly, praying that she cannot feel the way my pulse lurches beneath my skin as we exit my room. I trace the shape of the tiny dagger she has tied to the inside of her gauntlet as we walk down the hall toward Aleca's room. The tapping of my shoes against the slate floors rises, echoing in the high rafters of the hall.

The thin heel of my shoe catches in a divot in the floor and I tip forward, stumbling as I try not to tear the tulle of my skirts. Harlow's elbow tightens against my arm, her other hand shooting forward to catch me. The force of it sends me spinning until I am face-to-face with her. We are both motionless as we stare at one another; my breath hitches in my throat, and I know she hears it.

"All right?" she asks softly. The moment stretches between us until the sound of someone shouting a greeting meets our ears. It breaks our gaze and I step back, righting my skirts and brushing off imaginary lint.

"Yes," I say. "Thank you for catching me."

"Any time, Commander."

I take Harlow's arm again, trying this time to take more care as I walk. Heat courses through my body and I will myself to cool down in the wintry halls.

Aleca meets us at her door, eyes widening at the sight of my dress. She, herself, is done up in a gauzy, glittering lavender gown, unadorned except for shimmering constellations made of silvery beads along her bodice. A silver crescent moon is fixed in her hair, one lone raw piece of quartz crystal dangling in the center.

"Where on earth did you get that?" she asks, motioning for me to twirl. I comply, and she whistles in appreciation. "Jace, you look like a real leader!"

"I am a real leader, weasel," I say, reaching forward to pinch Aleca's side. She sidesteps it and sticks her tongue out at me. "It was a gift from Alymere. More specifically, a gift from Aureus. I think he knew that I would likely show up in breeches and a tunic if he didn't intercede."

"Do you think they could find another gift for me in there, somewhere?" Aleca asks. She takes hold of Harlow's other arm, and Harlow becomes sandwiched between the Grimme sisters.

"Your gown is nothing to turn your nose up at," Harlow says. "You look beautiful."

"You have to say that," she whines.

"She does not have to say that," I refute. "I am paying her to protect you, not tell you lies to soothe your vanity."

"I am not vain!" Aleca says, tossing her long, colorful locks with a sniff.

"Say that again without the flourish, and perhaps I'll believe you." In a stage whisper, I lean in and comment to Harlow, "She's always pranced about like a show pony. Never met a mirror she didn't love."

"Jace!"

"It's an older sister's right to use whatever ammunition she can," I say. "If you don't like it, you should have been born first."

"I had absolutely no control over that," Aleca says.

"Accept your lot in life, then," I instruct her. We are at the top of the stairs now. Once I begin my descent, there is truly no going back from the forward march of progress. Harlow releases her hold on me to take her leave with Aleca, leaving me to make the descent alone. She squeezes my arm reassuringly, and Aleca whispers,

"You've got this, Jace." More loudly, she says to Harlow, "You have a bit of lipstick there." She points at the corner of her own mouth, and Harlow lifts a hand to wipe. Aleca's eyes go wide. "I knew it! You two kissed! There was no lipstick."

Harlow's mouth drops open, indignant.

"You little—!" she says, poking Aleca in the ribs. Aleca laughs, curving her body away to avoid Harlow's finger. I watch them as they go down the stairs, snickering together like old friends. It does much to steady my anxiety.

I nod to myself, taking a deep breath in to steel my nerves. One by one, I take the steps down and then, hands trembling, I push the doors open to the Grand Hall, opening them to the world for the first time in a century.

TWELVE

The hall is resplendent under the light of the chandeliers and wall sconces. The mosaic on the floor has been painstakingly restored and looks bright and new. On either side of the room, the tables and chairs have been set upright and dressed with new linens and boast pewter place settings. The band has already begun playing soft music in anticipation of our first guests.

A guard on either side of the double doors takes a door in hand, holding it open to welcome feast-goers, much like the entry doors. Between the two entryways, a pocket of cool air fills the entrance hall, and I fight off a shiver borne of nerves and chill. I stand in the center of the space, ready to begin greeting people as they arrive—and praying that they will arrive. I have had nightmares of opening the castle to a lavish feast with no attendees but myself.

These fears are soon allayed, however. A small group of people has begun their ascent from the village to the castle, and as they draw nearer, I see that it is led by Merrid and his wife Blythe, Ellisana clasping both their hands between them. The group enters, eyes widening as they take the castle in. Historically, very few citizens have ever been allowed in the castle, and most people go their entire lives without setting foot in or near it.

"Merrid, Blythe, Ellisana," I greet, holding a hand out. Merrid shakes it, a genuine smile on his face. Ellisana has donned her finest dress, a red A-line gown with hand-embroidered flowers along the bottom of the skirt. She breaks free of her parents to show me how the skirt twirls around her, and I make a great show of adoration.

"Commander, I cannot thank you enough for your assistance in my recovery," Blythe says. She takes my hand between hers, a look of earnest gratitude on her face. I smile.

"I'm pleased to see you're well," I say. "Grand Chancellor Felix of Garyn will be here tonight; I'd love to introduce you to him. It is from his lands where your healer came."

They nod, and then a guard leads them away, into the ballroom.

For nearly half an hour, I greet guest after guest, delighted to see their open curiosity at the castle. It is far better than the animosity I had anticipated. Battlewood has had very little reason to dress in their finest and come together in recent times, but it seems people are willing to set aside suspicion in lieu of curiosity.

Once the final guest has been greeted and shepherded into the Grand Hall, the leaders of the other Courts line up to enter, one after the other. I enter first, leading the charge, and the other Grand Chancellors follow, along with the royal family of Alymere.

Empress Syiera enters last, and the room becomes hushed with reverence. I do not believe that there was ever a time when the Empress had entered our lands, even long before Syiera took over. A ripple of whispers moves through the room, and Syiera graces the people with an indulgent smile.

At the front of the room, the head table has been stretched horizontally, overlooking the feast-goers from the stage. Syiera and I are seated in the center, side-by-side. A table set nearby seats the additional delegates from the Courts; this is where my sister sits, in full view of me. She flashes me a wide smile. Beside her, Harlow grins at me as well, the corners of her eyes crinkling with fondness. My heart flips in my throat, and I wonder if there is a way I could steal her for a dance tonight.

When the band plays the final note of their song, I rise, mouth going dry. Every single face turns up to face me, and I am entirely unused to the attention. The last time this many people were looking at me, it ended poorly. I clear my throat and suck in air, preparing to throw my voice the way I was trained to when I was an initiate.

"Good evening, all," I begin. The room murmurs a greeting back to me. "Welcome to what I hope is the first of many gatherings at Battlewood Castle. Our Court has experienced much pain, growth, and change in the last year, and while I cannot change our history, I can rewrite our future, with all of you. As someone born and raised here in this very village, I think it comes as no surprise that Battlewood remains my first and foremost priority.

"While I stand here, it's with the understanding that I am

only borrowing my space at the helm of our Court. It is you, and those who come after you, who will carry our legacy on. It is my earnest hope that we can come together as a Court and show our neighbors what it truly means to be a citizen of our land. Here and now, I am calling an end to the Pact of Silence. For too long, we have been at odds with the people who were once integral to the culture of our Court."

Another ripple of whispers breaks out, and there is a smattering of unsure applause. I'm nearly certain that I hear someone hiss at me. From my periphery, I see Linota nodding her head, proud. I inhale deeply and continue.

"Tonight, I hope you all have the chance to meet the leaders of our neighboring Courts. They have agreed to come together as a show of good faith to all of you. We have been led in darkness for long enough. As we rise together, I encourage you all to take time to introduce yourselves to one another and to our leaders from the south, west, and east of us.

"Furthermore, there will be a midnight celebration at the center of the village; I'm sure many of you saw the maypole as you made your way to the castle. I hope that you all can join us as we celebrate not only the Spring Equinox and the newness of growth, but the newness and growth of our Court, as well.

"I hand over the title 'Commander' for the title of my peers around me: 'Grand Chancellor.' Tonight, we return to our roots, to the Empire we once served. Tonight, we return to the land we once were: Islilja. We will no longer be known for ruling with an iron fist of brutality. We were once a land which valued trade, beauty, and individuality, and together, we will become that land again. So, to the citizens and guests of Islilja, please eat, dance, and renew your faith in our Court."

True applause swells as my words ring out over the room, and I am stunned when people rise to their feet, cheering. There are, as expected, shouts of dissent and booing, but those people are quickly led from the hall. A few people see themselves out quietly, muttering angrily to one another as they go.

I feel my heart pounding violently in my chest, the soft fabric of my dress lurching with each pulse. My face goes slack-jawed from relief at finally being done with my speech, and a circle rubbed on my back by Syiera brings me back to my senses. With a jolt of embarrassment, I realize that I've become teary-eyed by the response.

The band begins to play again, and the serving staff seem to appear out of thin air to begin serving food. Several children have gathered in the center of the room and begin to dance wildly with one another, more interested in showing off their party wear than eating. I laugh when I see Ellisana leading the group in a spirited version of a popular folk dance.

My stomach is in knots from the speech, and I poke around at the plate of small tomatoes and balls of cheese, willing my hunger to return. While my anxiety has abated since ending my speech, the frantic energy still has my hands shaking and my mind racing. I knew there would be anger at the changes, but knowing and seeing are two very different things.

"You did quite well, Grand Chancellor," Syiera says as she delicately spears a tomato and pops it into her mouth. "I knew you were destined for greatness, and I'm pleased to see the way you've accepted the challenge. Do not let the voices of dissent scare you away from leading."

"I suppose I owe this to you," I say. "If you had not answered our questions, shown us what was truly happening in our land, I would have been content to defect and never consider Battlewood again."

"I merely cultivated the seeds which had already begun to take root," Syiera refutes with a small shake of her head. "I look forward to what is to come under your guidance, Jace."

"May I ask you something, Empress?" I ask carefully, quietly. It would not do for prying ears to overhear our conversation. From my left, I watch as someone approaches the table, holding a hand out to Grand Chancellor Felix and introducing himself. I cannot hear his words.

"Of course," she responds. She places another tomato in her mouth, tipping her head expectantly as she looks at me. I do not know how she manages to eat with such grace. I would manage to squelch tomato seeds and balsamic glaze all over me the moment I tried to eat.

"Do you—I mean, can you—," I begin, unable to find the right words. I shake my head and try again. "Something has taken root in Battlewood, something dark and volatile. I know that it has something to do with corrupted magic, but I do not know how to disrupt it. Princess Nesryn has been instrumental in opening my eyes to how deep the corruption goes, but I fear that we cannot remedy it on our own."

Syiera goes still, closing her eyes. I can see her eyes darting back and forth beneath her lids, as if she is in a deep sleep. When she opens them again, they are drawn.

"Your answers lay in Sepyphyr's quarters," she says. "You must find a way inside. You have not entered them yet?"

"No," I say, shaking my head. "I haven't been able to bring myself to go alone."

"Begin there," she says. "Though you will find many questions, there too will you find many answers. I'm afraid there is little I could do to assist you."

I make a face, and she grants me an understanding smile. I hadn't expected that there would be some master spell she could cast to undo the corruption and the ghosts, but there had been a part of me that had hoped anyway.

The first plates are whisked away, and I watch my helping of tomatoes and cheese as they go, wishing I had taken even a single bite. In their place, a broth with vegetables is set down, and I begin to eat immediately. Syiera is drawn into conversation with Queen Maren, and their soft voices fade into the sounds of the feast.

Once the meal has finished, the music begins to play in earnest. Slowly, people make their way to the center of the room, dancing with one another. Others remain seated, drinking and conversing together. Though the leaders of the Court are regarded with uncertainty, several people introduce themselves to the Grand Chancellors before making their way over to me.

A shadow falls over me, and I look up to see Aureus standing there. He holds a hand out, jerking his head toward the dance floor. When I try to shake my head, he takes hold of me, pulling me out of my seat and down the steps of the stage.

We assume the position of the dance, our hands clasped tightly. His other hand rests on my waist, careful not to touch my exposed skin.

"You've done marvelously, Grand Chancellor," he says, moving us about effortlessly. "I'm proud of you."

His pride means the world to me, and I tell him so. His eyes twinkle in response. Lifting his arm, he twirls me, and I laugh. I feel the tension begin to melt out of me as he whisks me around, and I realize how nice it is not to be the one in control for once. In every other aspect of my life, I have been the one calling the shots, making the decisions, and leading the way.

We pass Obsidian and Bronwyn, who look as if they are together in a world of their own. Their foreheads are pressed against one another, and they share their own private smiles. As Aureus spins me, my eyes land on Aleca, who regards Obsidian and Bronwyn with open envy. I sigh; she must still be holding a candle for him. I had hoped, when Keiran had come to retrieve her, that she had moved on. Harlow leans in and whispers something to Aleca. I wonder if she also noticed.

"What's weighing on you, Jace?" Aureus asks.

"Nothing of matter," I say. "My little sister seems to have caught feelings for Obsidian, Syiera's right-hand man. I...may have threatened him when I was in Apaiji—don't look at me like that, my sister is a child and he is grown—and it appears that while he cares for another, she still cares for him. It's hard to watch my baby sister's heart be broken."

"Matters of the heart are a messy affair, and I've found that the young love with intensity," Aureus says. "Perhaps I should put her in the path of my cousin, who also studies at the Academy."

"I'd be much obliged," I say.

The song comes to an end, and Aureus releases me. Nodding at the table, he says,

"It appears you have someone who would like to speak with you. Perhaps I'll find you for another dance later."

"A leader's job is never done," I say drily. I nod at Aureus and make my way back to the table to shake hands with a woman who tells me that if I insist on making changes, I can step aside now for someone who "actually cares about the culture of our Court," and that I should "be ashamed of the heartless way I took the life of such a noble man." It is not the first time I've heard this sentiment tonight, and I've quite had enough.

Over her shoulder, I catch Harlow's eye. She raises an eyebrow and I press my lips together, hoping that I can silently convey the need for a rescue. She gets the hint and is by my side in a moment.

"Excuse me, I'm so sorry for interrupting," she says, the picture of remorse. "Com—Grand Chancellor, I mean, you're needed for an incident in the entrance hall."

"Please excuse me, madame," I say, taking the woman's hand in mine. She scowls as if I've doused my hands in mud before touching her. I hold back a laugh. "I'd be happy to continue this discussion once I can provide you my full attention."

We rush away before she can further make her opinion known and exit through the large doors into the hall.

"I assume there is no incident and you're an accomplished mind reader," I say.

"Accomplished eye reader, I would say," she replies, flashing me a bright smile.

"Your services are appreciated," I tell her. The cool air is refreshing against my warm skin.

"Any time, Grand Chancellor. I like to think I've become fairly proficient at reading your eyes."

I do not look at her, knowing both that she is correct and that she will find something I'm not ready to confess.

······†······

Beneath the bright, high moon, softened by liquor and good food, the partygoers amble excitedly down to the maypole at the center of the village. Some part from the crowd, starting for their homes. I feel my eyes fluttering with exhaustion, and I pinch the inside of my wrist to startle me awake. The maypole stands in waiting, torchlight illuminating the many-colored wildflowers that have been inserted into the mossy covering. A multitude of silken ribbons hang from the pole, rustling in the nighttime breeze.

I stand in front of the pole before the gathered crowd. I hold my hands up to claim their attention, and they go quiet. In my periphery, I see the band setting their instruments back up to play the music for our impending dance.

"We've made it to midnight," I say, "and now, we welcome change as we enter into a new season of life. In the olden days of Islilja, a dance about the maypole signified the ushering in of new life, prosperity, and growth for the coming days. Those who would like to participate, I invite you to circle around, and when the music begins, we dance."

I take a spot at the center, waiting for others to step up. There is a great clamoring as people move to a free spot, laughter and chatter filling the space. I nod at the musicians, who begin a waltz. I have been practicing the steps in secret, knowing that I will be looked to for leading the dance, and I step toward the ribbon, lifting it. I take several steps back, several forward, and several back again before stepping to the side and beginning the weave around the pole. The others pick the steps up quickly, and before long, we seamlessly wrap the ribbons around the pole.

When the ribbons have been wrapped to their entirety, we reverse the steps and unwrap them. I indicate for everyone to divide into two groups, and then we begin to bob and weave, plaiting the ribbons as we lift and drop our arms around one another. As the ribbons are plaited to completion, I come face-to-face with Harlow. She smiles widely at me, and I've never found her more beautiful than as she is now, illuminated by flickering firelight and alight with excitement. I know my thoughts are written across my face as we tip our heads toward each other before stepping back and reversing the ribbon weave.

As the dance comes to an end, the music swells and people begin to cheer and dance. A server has brought out more skeins of wine and glasses are passed around. Several children are huddled together, eating leftover pastries from the feast at the castle and giggling. I step away from the pole, allowing the silk ribbon to slip from my fingers and flutter away. Aleca is in conversation with Bronwyn and Obsidian, her eyes glancing as surreptitiously as they can at him while Bronwyn speaks. I look forward to her meeting Aureus' cousin.

"That was something," Harlow says, taking a space beside me. I jump, startled, and she laughs. "Sorry, I didn't mean to scare you."

I wave her apology away, pulling my gaze away from my sister to look at her. She has retied the braids in her hair and tightened the bun which had come loose during the dance. We stand in silence together, watching the revelers as they slowly begin to leave the party, exhaustion catching up with them in the wake of excitement and adrenaline. More than one of them will be nursing a nasty headache and sour stomach in the morning.

"I'm going to go get your sister," Harlow says. "She tried giving me the slip earlier to talk to that guy with the massive arms, but I've been keeping an eye on her anyway. Is he her—?"

"Not if he knows what's good for him, he isn't," I say darkly. "Aleca fancies herself an adult, but she's still a child and I threatened him once that I wouldn't allow him to take advantage of her vulnerability. I don't think he would, truthfully, and he is otherwise occupied with Bronwyn, but I'm sure you've learned by now that my sister is nothing if not persistent."

"Yes, I have noticed. That seems to be something of a

family trait," Harlow says with amusement. I nudge her hip with mine, smiling.

"Don't be cheeky," I say. "Why don't you go get some rest? I'll get Aleca and bring her back to the castle. You've more than fulfilled your duty for the evening."

"Are you sure?" Harlow asks. I nod, jerking my head in the direction of her home. "Thanks. I'll see you in the morning, then." She waves, setting off for her house, and I search through the crowd for my sister.

I find Bronwyn and Obsidian sitting at the foot of the maypole, chatting and drinking a glass of wine. Making my way over to them, I ask,

"Did you see where Aleca went?"

"She said she was coming to find you," Obsidian says. Annoyance tugs the corners of my mouth down. If she absconded again, I'm going to lock her in her room until the Apaiji delegation leaves. "Would you like us to help you find her?"

"No, no, that's okay," I say distractedly, looking around the area again. The crowd has thinned considerably, and her bright hair is nowhere to be seen. "I'll see you in a bit, I'm going to go find her."

I wander around, checking dark corners and trees for her. She is in none of those spaces and panic begins to set in. I send a warrior off to the castle to see if she's in her room while I continue my search for her. By the time the warrior returns, the village has nearly completely emptied; the band has left, and except for a few stragglers, I am alone.

"She's not there, Commander—I mean, Grand Chancellor," the warrior says apologetically. I curse, digging my toe into the soft dirt as I consider my next moves. I dismiss the warrior with a wave, chewing on my lip until it splits. The tang of iron blooms across the tip of my tongue and I spit it out.

Before I can make a decision, Harlow comes sprinting into my view, her hair loose and wild behind her in the wind. She no longer wears her dress uniform, and instead is in her sleeping clothes, a leather brigandine the only piece of armor she has on. Her sword has been sheathed in the leather waist strap and bangs against her leg as she moves.

"Jace!" she shouts, skidding to a stop in front of me. She pants, pressing a hand to her chest as she tries to catch her breath. "Aleca—Fallon told me—she's—oh my gods."

"Breathe," I tell her, grabbing her arms. "Breathe and try to tell me again. What about Aleca?"

"Whatever's got those spirits trapped has taken Aleca and trapped her, too," she says, hoarse with fright. My heart drops through to my toes and sweat prickles along my hairline and neck.

"Where?" I demand.

"Hidden away," Harlow pants. "We need Nesryn."

……†……

We sprint to the castle in record time, my heels cast aside somewhere near the maypole. Harlow has loaned me a pair of her flat-soled shoes, a size too big but better than the stilettos that left my feet cramping. I slam my fist against the solid wood of Nesryn's door incessantly until the door swings open to reveal Nesryn's very irritated lady-in-waiting.

"What on earth—oh, Grand Chancellor," Maple corrects, dropping into a curtsy when she realizes who is making all the noise.

"Forget about that right now," I say tugging Maple back into a standing position. "I need to speak to Nesryn immediately."

Maple steps back, allowing us into the room, and then scurries to the bed where Nesryn is still fast asleep. She shakes her carefully, and the princess rises, pulling wads of cotton from her ears. That explains why she wasn't able to hear our pounding.

"What is this?" she asks, taking in my gown and Harlow's sleeping clothes-cum-armor.

"Aleca's been taken by whatever is trapping those spirits," Harlow explains. "We don't know where." Nesryn slips from her bed quickly, tying her hair back and rummaging through a chest for something. She withdraws a mask adorned with leaves and a dark cloak. Fastening the cloak around her neck, she presses her feet into a pair of shoes and then reaches for a discarded pair of breeches.

"Maple, I shall be back shortly. If I am not back by sunrise, you may share only with my brother where I have gone. I will be in the forest near the burning Pyre. There is a clearing there, with an old cottage."

"Yes, Highness," Maple says, dropping into another curtsy. The propriety of it all makes me grit my teeth. We are wasting time on curtsies and flowery language.

"If we're ready?" I ask, motioning for our group to get a move on. Nesryn nods once, and we rush out her door.

"She's been taken by our spirit captor?" Nesryn asks as we pad down the steps and out the doors. "When you last saw her, she was alive and in her own right mind?"

"What do you mean, alive?" I ask sharply, fear sending my heart stuttering. "Of course she was alive, and she's still alive!"

"I only meant—"

My foot slips out of the shoe and I stoop to jam it back on, tying it as tightly as I can around my foot. I should have stopped by my room to get a pair of my own shoes when we were at the castle, but I didn't even think to do so.

The cottage is silent when we arrive, dark for the first time since I first uncovered it. I look at Harlow in the glow of a lantern, confused.

"I thought you said she was trapped?" I query.

"That's what Fallon told me…," Harlow says, trailing off. She stares at the empty clearing in front of her, tugging at the ends of her hair. Nesryn walks forward until she is an arm's length from the cottage. She presses a hand to the door, stepping back when a champagne-colored glow begins to undulate from beneath it. No spirits appear, but Nesryn begins to speak anyway.

"We do not have time for this," I hiss to Harlow. Adrenaline begins to wane as we wait for Nesryn, and I am shivering in my gauzy gown. The faintest beginnings of daylight begin to rise in the sky, turning it from navy-black to dusty lavender. "I can't believe this. I was prepared for every possibility, except this!"

"It's nothing you could have prepared for, Jace," Harlow says soothingly. I cross my arms tightly across my chest, trying to preserve what little body heat I have left. She notices and holds her arms open, and after a moment of hesitation, I step inside them.

She runs her hands along my bare arms, heating them with friction from her calloused hands. I sink into her touch, too tired to keep my carefully constructed walls up. I am exhausted in every sense of the word, and truthfully, I want nothing more than to bury myself in my blankets and have a good cry.

Harlow's arms tighten around me, and I press closer to her. I can feel myself beginning to drift off and I force my eyes open. They feel as if they are covered in sand, heavy and gritty. My makeup, which has slowly melted over the course of the night, burns as it begins to run into my eyes. I rub at them and my hand comes away streaked black with eye makeup.

"May I?" Harlow asks, holding her thumb beneath my eyes. I nod, and she slowly swipes at the makeup until it has been removed from my face. I stare up at her, my eyes hooded with sleeplessness, and she runs a soft hand along my jaw.

"We need to go elsewhere," Nesryn announces, rejoining us. I lift my head to look over at her, not abandoning the warm nook that's been made for me by Harlow's body.

"Where?" I ask tonelessly.

"Sepyphyr's quarters," she responds. I sigh, stepping away from Harlow to gather my skirts in my hand.

We make our way back to the castle in silence. The sun hangs low in the sky, painting the Court with the first strokes of daylight. Harlow offers to stop by the kitchens for coffee while I change out of my gown.

I gaze longingly at my bed, the thick down comforter still pulled taut and waiting to be turned down. I am sick of sleepless nights. Frankly, if Raznik was as sleep-deprived as I am, I can understand how he was driven to madness.

I splash ice-cold water from my wash basin on my face to wake me up and then plunge my hands in until my wrists are submerged. The iciness against the sensitive pressure point gives me a jolt and I withdraw them, shaking the excess water off where it splatters against the floor. Sheathing my sword, I exit my quarters again and find Harlow standing there with a large, steaming mug.

I take it from her gratefully and drink, not caring as the liquid scalds the roof of my mouth. She sips much more slowly from her own mug. At her side, a travel carafe has been hooked on her leather belt. Not for the first time, I send silent gratitude to the kitchen staff. I will have to bring them bonus wages when this has all settled.

Nesryn meets us in the hall, and together we make our way up a winding spiral staircase to the infrequently visited floor where Raznik once quartered. The hallway is dark and cold, the wall sconces unlit. When I hold the flame of our candle to the sconce nearest me, it flares to light, burning off the dust that has collected there since his death. We light the remaining sconces, and soon the hall is filled with illuminated dust motes that rise as we walk. Beside me, Harlow lets out three sneezes in a row.

At the end of the hall stands Raznik's door, locked tightly. A dark onyx stone has been pressed into the center of the door, surrounded by a starburst of rubies and topaz. I try the handle, knowing that it will not budge. I let out a noise of frustration anyway. Beneath the bronze handle is a keyhole, the shape of which I've never seen a key before. It looks like a rune of some sort, and I wonder if there is a corresponding one somewhere in the circle on my floor.

Harlow pulls a pin from my braid and kneels beside the lock, shimmying the pin to and fro as she tries to pick it. She shakes the doorknob, but it remains resolutely locked. Nesryn fares no better as she whispers some sort of spell at it. The keyhole blazes a sparkling black light briefly, but when she attempts to open it, the door does not budge.

I share my theory about the keyhole and the rune circle on my floor, and we trudge back down the staircase to my office. With great effort, I roll away the heavy rug for Nesryn to access the circle and then take a seat, refilling my mug with coffee from the carafe.

"What is that?" Harlow asks, watching Nesryn as she does whatever magic she does to make the runes spark.

"Excellent question," I respond. "All I know is that it has something to do with that cottage and Raznik's descent into madness. According to Nesryn, it's comprised of battle magic and death magic, which are two magics I didn't even know existed until recently."

As with the first time I watched Nesryn complete this ritual, the final rune shoots bright red sparks up, burning the wooden floor where they land. This time, though, Nesryn goes back around the circle, completing the ritual in reverse. She gives a final commanding shout, and the entire rune circle begins to glow the same sparkling black light as the door.

I stare expectantly at the floor, but nothing happens. The light continues to undulate around the rune circle. Nesryn cocks her head to the side, observing for a moment before beckoning me over with a finger. I rise from my seat with a groan, and Harlow gives a helpful push at the small of my back.

I can feel a coolness emanating from the black fire as I stand in front of it. Curiously, I reach a hand out to touch it and pull back with a startled shout as it sends a shock through me. My hand goes numb and I shake it to bring feeling back.

"You need to try to get to the center," she tells me. I stare at her incredulously, rubbing my still-numb hand with my fingers.

"Is that safe?" Harlow's concerned question comes from behind us.

"Mostly," Nesryn says. "It will not be without consequence, but only the Commander—or, Grand Chancellor, as it now is—can obtain what we need. Do you see there, in the center?"

I lean forward, squinting. In the center of the fire is a concentration of sparks, spitting upward over the circle. Nodding, I lean away again. Feeling is beginning to return to my hand, and it feels as if I am being stabbed with a thousand thin needles.

"That's where the key is, I believe. When Sepyphyr ruled, he was able to access the key on his own, as this ritual was of his own design. It recognizes only the one who holds power which, now, is you. I assume it was a safeguard against his successor ever gaining access to his space. However, in his ego, he never considered that another may be able to replicate his magic," Nesryn tells us. I eye the circles of fire, wondering if there is a way Nesryn can quell the flames if the attempt goes awry.

"You can stop the fire if it becomes unsafe?" Harlow voices the nervous question for both of us.

"I should be able to."

The words do nothing to make me feel better and I inhale sharply. I have no contingency plan for my Court if I die.

"Tell Aureus that he is to rule in my stead if I die," I say, feeling entirely too dramatic. It is the kind of statement I would expect from Aleca, and I laugh softly at myself. The thought of my sister reminds me why we are here—she needs me.

With a deep breath, I close my eyes and step forward into the fire.

THIRTEEN

Sharp shocks jolt through my feet, and I feel my legs begin to numb at once. The fire, which appears so mild from the outside, is a force to be reckoned with. The flames are cold and a battering wind sends me swaying like a ragdoll.

By the time I clear the first circle of runes, my body is numb to my waist. My steps have slowed immeasurably, and it's all that I can do to force myself forward against the wind. My hair is ripped from their braids and locks of it, glowing an ethereal silver in the fire, whip into my face, stinging my eyes. I reach a hand out, shielding my eyes as the fire burns brighter.

I've cleared the second circle, and I fall to my knees as I reach the center, all but my neck and head now buzzing with numbness. The sparks are impossibly bright, burning my eyes and making them water. I reach into the center of them, and though I cannot feel them, I know they are burning me.

I am screaming with exertion as my hand meets the floor. It gives way and I topple forward as my arm falls downward into a small, circular hole. The sparks are smothered by my torso, and I blindly wiggle my hand around, feeling for anything.

My fingers scrape against something small and thin, and it takes every ounce of concentration to get them to close around it. Twice, I drop the item just as I am about to pull out of the floor. At last, I extricate my arm and the small thin item. The fire rises and swells around me and then extinguishes, sending a shock of air outward.

I roll onto my back, staring up at my ceiling. I am paralyzed except for my eyes, which dart around wildly. When I try to speak, I find that I cannot move my mouth. Harlow's terrified face swims into view, and though she is speaking to me, I cannot hear her. She cups my face in her hands, then grabs my shoulders, my arms, and my hands. She speaks again, and it sounds as if she is under water.

Nesryn appears beside Harlow. She reaches forward to pluck something from my hand, holding up a key victoriously. As I lay there unable to move, all I can think about is how well she would have gotten along well with my father. He, too, was much more focused on the pursuit of knowledge and ritual than emotion and well-being.

Harlow says something to Nesryn, and I can tell from her face that it is not something kind. Nesryn's eyes narrow and she raises one eyebrow at Harlow before looking at me again.

As with my hand, the feeling of needles begins to prickle in my feet. It moves torturously slowly up my legs, into my sides and down my arms. I have no idea how long I lay on the ground while Harlow sits beside me. Nesryn has risen and disappeared out of my line of sight. By the way Harlow's glance darts up every so often, I know that she is at least still in the room.

I realize that Harlow is grasping my hand tightly in hers as the feeling returns. I give it a small, weak squeeze in reassurance and the relief on her face is palpable.

"Are you okay?" she asks. Her words are clearer now, and I nod my head. "Nesryn, she's mobile again!"

Nesryn comes back to my side, peering curiously at me. I raise my eyebrows in question, and she holds up a small brass key.

"It was worth it, then?" I rasp out. She nods, smiling with satisfaction. I clear my throat, closing my eyes. She's lucky. I would have been beyond irritated if that had been for nothing.

With effort, I sit up. My muscles scream in protest, and I catch a whiff of something burning. I look down and realize it's me. My tunic is peppered with burn marks and the fabric flakes away where it has been charred the worst. My right sleeve is equally burned, and the blackened fabric is stuck to my skin. I grit my teeth and pull it from the burns on my skin. I wish Willow would take me up on selling her healing balms and salves here.

"Alright, now what?" I ask. I hiss in pain as I tug the last of my sleeve from my arm. My torso is no better, and I begin to pull the fabric from the wounds there.

"Now, you sleep," Harlow says. I pull a face and she shakes her head. "Jace, you're exhausted, and you need to heal."

"No, what I need to do is find my sister," I argue. I lurch my body forward, propelling myself to my feet. As I stand, I tip forward unsteadily before I can gain my footing. Nesryn has one hand on the doorknob already, but Harlow grabs hold of my left wrist, stopping me from moving forward.

"Harlow—"

"No," she cuts me off. "I know that you're worried about your sister, but you're no use to her if you're ill or hurt." I try to pull my wrist free from Harlow's grip, but she tightens her hold.

"She's right," Nesryn relents in disappointment, dropping her hand from the door. "Between the three of us, I'm the only one who got any sleep last night. Why don't I call the healer, and then I'll go stand guard outside of Sepyphyr's room? If anything happens, I'll get you."

Their faces brook no arguments, and I give in with a groan. Nesryn ties the key around her neck and slips out the door, promising to return shortly with Healer Rex. Sighing deeply, Harlow and I leave my office and make our way down the hall to my room.

As she lights a fire in the hearth, I slowly remove my tunic; it's impossible for me to get my right arm out on my own without irritating the burns. Harlow offers help, and she carefully pulls the fabric from my arm as I hold still. She tugs it over my head and throws it into the fire, where it alights with a dull hiss, throwing high flames against the stone wall.

Harlow moves away from me to undo the straps of her brigandine and drops it onto the ground beside the couch stretched before the fire.

"Do you have an extra blanket?" she asks, taking a seat on the couch. "I'll kip here."

"Don't be stupid," I mumble tiredly. "My bed is plenty big for both of us, and more comfortable than that old thing."

I've already clambered into bed, shivering against the cold air on my bare torso. I haven't bothered to change into a sleep shirt, worried that the fabric will impede the healing. A breast band will have to do for now. When Harlow hasn't moved, I flop to my side with a huff and pat the open space beside me. I watch through half-closed eyes as she battles with herself before finally making her way over.

"Thanks," she whispers, slipping beneath the heavy comforter. As sleep overtakes me, I can't help but allow myself one small, contented smile.

At some point during our slumber, we have found ourselves wrapped around one another. My head rests on Harlow's chest, and her arm is curled around me, holding me close. My own arm is draped across her torso, my hand tucked beneath her. The ease with which we've found comfort in each other sends my mind racing. I know I was lying when I told her that our kiss didn't have to mean anything, but I wonder now if she was lying too. I lift my head, beginning to pull away, and her hold on me tightens.

"Please don't," she murmurs, her words slurred with sleep. Happy to stay where I am, I drop my head back down onto her chest, and she lets out a hum of contentment. I fall asleep again to dreams of blonde hair and soft touches.

When I wake again, Harlow has risen and is busying herself before my mirror, wrapping her hair up and out of her face. I watch her from my bed for a moment, fondness crinkling the corners of my eyes. It's too easy to play pretend when we're here in my room together, the world shut out around us. In another life, I wouldn't have to take my scraps of companionship where I could find them. She catches my gaze in the mirror and turns with a shy smile.

"Good evening," she says. "How are you feeling?"

"Much better," I admit.

"Healer Rex came while you were asleep," she tells me. "He asked me to tell you to put salve on your burns and keep them wrapped."

"Thanks," I say, realizing that I am, indeed, covered with wrappings. The thin strips of fabric have been fixed to me with some type of sticky glue. "I can't believe I slept through that. Did he tell you anything else?"

"'I've seen this girl more times in the past few months than I have in her entire life,'" she parrots. I smile sheepishly, nodding in affirmation. Oh, and Aureus has met with the Court heads on your behalf. He said something about a meeting this morning?"

"Oh, no!" I cry, smacking a hand to my forehead. "The goods trading meeting, I completely forgot."

Somehow, amid this all, having all of the leaders of the Courts gathered here in my castle has fallen to last place on my priorities list. I cannot forget their presence again.

Harlow hands me a stack of papers wrapped in protective leather. I leaf through them quickly, and realize that in my stead, Aureus has taken all of my notes and plans and has had magnificent luck in bargaining and landing on agreements. Gratitude burns warmly in my chest.

"Nesryn also stopped by to let us know that nothing has changed from inside the room, and to join her when we're ready."

"I'm ready," I say, leaping out of bed. I press a hand to my forehead for a moment as the room swims, and then my vision focuses again. I rummage through my armoire for clean clothing and then duck behind my folding screen to change. When I reemerge, Harlow gives me a hand pie and a mug of coffee. I eat the pie eagerly, washing down a mouthful of meat and vegetables with lukewarm coffee. I drain the mug and then set it on the edge of my vanity.

"Shoes and sword?" Harlow asks, pointing at my bare feet. I slap a hand to my forehead and rush back to my armoire, grabbing a pair of thick-soled shoes. I am in such a rush that I put them on the wrong feet and have to tug them off to try again. I grab my sword from my bedside table, jam it into its sheath, and then we are out the door and up the stairs.

Nesryn is speaking with Aureus when we arrive. Their conversation ceases as we join them, and Nesryn hands me the key from around her neck. Harlow withdraws two more pies wrapped in parchment paper from her pocket and hands them to the siblings.

While they eat, I insert the key into the keyhole. It makes a metallic click as it fits into its slot, and I turn it with ease. Trying the knob, it turns and the door swings away from us into the room. I cannot see anything past the doorframe, as if there is a black shroud hiding whatever is inside. I turn to ask Harlow for a lantern, but she places one in my hand before I can speak. I nod at her, grateful that she can read my mind.

Holding the lantern up at eye level, I peer through the thick gloom. The light provides no help. We are going to have to enter blindly. I wonder how many more safeguards Raznik put into place before his death. Curious, I shove the lantern through the doorframe. The blackness swallows both my hand and the light. I pull my hand back out, examining the brightly burning candle inside the glass walls.

"Interesting," I say. "There's nothing else to do but go in and hope for the best."

"I'm the warrior, here. I'll go first," Harlow says, pulling her sword from her sheath and holding it out. She does not allow us to argue with her before she steps forward, disappearing inside the room. It's quiet for a moment and then, sounding very far away, her voice calls, "It's safe!"

One after another, we step through the doorway. The darkness is thick as it envelopes us, and I'm reminded of the way my father once dropped his glasses into a bowl of custard, how they moved slowly through the gelatinous matter. I feel a gentle squeeze on all sides of me, and then I pop through the dark and into the room.

My mouth drops open as I take in the scene around me. There is no way that this room exists within the confines of the castle. The room opens into a massive expanse of space. Despite the multiple hanging chandeliers, the room is dark and dim. A gloom hovers over it as if it has never fully seen light.

One side a wall is completely lined with shelves, their contents varying sizes of cloche jars, bottles, and books. A long table is stretched beneath the shelves; it looks as if Raznik had been in the middle of creating something when his life was interrupted. An open jar filled with a dried substance that looks suspiciously like blood rests beside an unrolled piece of parchment. A larger jar filled with some sort of powder is still closed tightly and a set of measuring spoons rests atop the lid.

None of this catches our attention the way that a gigantic, sprawling table in the center of the room does. We move toward it in unison, as if we've all just noticed it at the same time.

"Holy hell," Harlow whispers.

"Is that the cottage?" I ask, peering more closely. It's a stupid question to ask—that's exactly what this table is. A miniature display shows off an exact replica of the cottage. If I move my head to one side, it looks like the perfect, cozy version. If I move my head to the other side, the façade shifts, and I am looking at the ruins. I make myself dizzy as I twist back and forth and look up at the ceiling to recenter my vision.

"I do not see your sister," Nesryn calls from across the room. My heart sinks, though I had not expected that we would find Aleca here. It would be too neat and easy. A flicker from the cottage miniature catches my attention and I look back over at it.

It is as if something—or someone—is trying to escape from it. I lean as close to it as possible, squinting to sharpen my vision. As I draw nearer, I hear whispers rising it; they are no louder than the sound of chittering mice. I cock my head to the side to discern what they are saying. At first, I think that I am imagining things when I hear my name. However, Harlow quashes that when she asks,

"Is someone trying to talk to you?"

Then, just beside the cottage, a minute ghost appears. She bores the same dark curls and sundress as the very real specter of Tally who has been haunting me. Her voice is tiny, barely intelligible in the massive room with its high-reaching ceilings.

"Destroy the tether, Jace," she says. "Destroy it before it's too late."

I pace back and forth, my hands clasped tightly before me. Whirling on my heel, I repeat the path until I am certain that I am wearing away the floor beneath me. Aureus and Nesryn sit on the couch in my office, Harlow perched on the arm of it. They all watch me silently as I try to solve the meaning of Tally's words. Finally, Aureus says,

"As fascinating a problem-solving method as this is, I fear it may be one of your less effective ones. Care to try a different one?"

I stop, turning to look at them. Nesryn is examining her fingernails, entirely disinterested in this. I get the feeling that she likes things a particular way and has little interest in the emotions of others. It is not necessarily a bad thing; I wish that I had the ability to better compartmentalize my own thoughts and feelings versus everyone else's.

"I'm open to suggestions," I say. I run my fingers through my hair, wincing when I catch a knot in the fine threads. I disentangle my fingers carefully, pulling at the snarled hairs. Harlow beckons me and situates me in front of her on the ottoman. She deftly works her fingers through my knotty hair, and I close my eyes, leaning against her legs.

"Remind me what Tally said?" Aureus asks.

"'Destroy the tether before it's too late,'" I say, repeating the cryptic message. It means no more to me now than it did when I first heard it. Harlow's fingers come to a stop and then she has a hand wrapped around either side of my head. She presses a kiss to the top of it. I crane my neck up to look back at her, a soft smile curving my lips. I push myself back into a standing position, but do not take back up my anxious pacing.

We bounce ideas around back and forth, each one as unlikely as the next. Is the tether the castle? The rune circle? Is there something inside the cottage which is the tether? So much time passes that I have to throw another log on the dwindling fire. As it flares to life, Nesryn speaks for the first time in a while.

"Are we not considering that the replica is the tether?"

I pause, considering her suggestion. I try to recreate the replica in my head, building the cottage with the surrounding trees and placing a mini-Tally in the center. There is something still missing, though, and I make a groan of frustration.

I wander over to my desk to pull out a piece of parchment and a quill. As quickly as possible, I draw a smudgy likeness of the replica and bring it over to the low table in front of the couch. Everyone bends over it, examining it closely.

"You're missing the border of items," Nesryn says, tracing a square around the cottage. "If I may?" She holds out her hand for the quill and I hand it to her. Her hand flits around the parchment. As she draws, I exchange a confused look with Harlow and Aureus. They look at each other and then back at me, shrugging. She pulls back to reveal a collection of items surrounding the cottage.

Her drawing is much better than mine, but the items there do not make sense to me. There is what appears to be a coin, a stack of parchment, a stuffed bear, and a pair of wire-rimmed glasses, among other things. My eyebrows snap together as I examine the paper, trying to figure out what any of these items may mean.

Harlow gets there before I do, and she points at the coin.

"This looks like my brother's," she says. "He carried this around with him everywhere he went. He found it buried by our house and thought it was pirate gold."

I lean in again, looking closer at the drawings and then my mouth goes dry.

"Those look like my father's glasses," I say, "and this bear…-Tally used to sleep with a ratty old bear, even though she pretended not to." I spin the parchment, looking at the other items. There are nearly a hundred items in total, each one different from the last. I pat at my pockets for the oddly shaped key and then am out the door, sprinting back to Raznik's quarters.

My hands are so shaky that I scrape the key against the lock several times before I am able to insert it properly. I throw the door open, diving into the viscous gloom that separates the room from the rest of the castle.

My foot sticks and I have to give it a good yank to get through the black cloud and into the room. It pulls my shoe off and I crouch to feel around blindly for it. From this vantage point, I notice for the first time an undulating glimmer beneath the table holding the diorama. Shoe in hand, I stalk over to the table and drop to my knees.

This close, I can make out a distinct shape to the glimmer. It is in the shape of a twining chains, slowly and consistently spinning from the bottom of the table to the floor. It never changes shape or length, but when I try to touch it, it flares and casts me several feet across the room. I shake my hand, trying to rid myself of the buzzing burn in my fingers. Whatever that is, it does not like to be disturbed.

I look around the room for something else that may be used in place of my hand, and I land on an old metal-tipped javelin. I yank it from the bracket holding it in place and stalk back over to the table, crouching down and adjusting the javelin in my hand.

Gripping tightly to the table, I swing the javelin through the chains. I regret it instantly; the metal tip acts as some sort of conduit and the swell of magic is stronger than before. I go soaring through the air, crashing against shelving and dropping to the ground. The javelin is still in my hand, smoke rising in curling tendrils from the blackened tip.

The impact of being thrown rocks jars and books free from the shelves and I drop the javelin to protect my head with my arms. I feel the glass shatter against my arms, nicking my hands as it breaks apart. With a pained groan, I rise unsteadily to my feet, shaking shattered glass from my hair and tunic. Shards of broken jars crunch under my feet as I move away from the crash site, and I press a hand to my throbbing spine.

From the doorway, the other three emerge, coming to a stop at the sight of the mess.

"I found the tether, I think," I say. My voice is strained from the pain radiating in my spine. I am entirely done with magic that wreaks havoc on my body. Just once, I'd like to see magic that pours me a good cup of coffee and brings me warmed slippers. "There, beneath the table. Do not touch it," I add warningly. I wipe the backs of my hands against my pants, vanishing the blood drawn from the glass into the soft fabric there.

"Not the items?" Aureus asks, approaching the table and bending over to examine the magic. He rises again, looking at the border of items. He lifts a child's shoe, peering at it before setting it down and moving onto the next item, a ring of some sort. Both times, the beginnings of a spirit begin to appear beside the cottage before vanishing again. "These all look very personal."

He's right. Looking at the perimeter of objects, I feel as if I am looking into someone's personal trunk. There are well-loved books, necklaces, brooches, a metal goblet, and buttons scattered throughout. I spot Tally's stuffed bear, and I reach for it. I run a finger along the worn and patchy fur and the scratched glass eyes, swallowing the thick emotion that has risen in my throat. Tally's spirit appears as I hold the bear, and it does not disappear until I set it down, patting it tenderly on the top of its head.

Curious, I pick up a tattered journal, holding tightly. A man's spirit appears, staring up at me expectantly until I set it down and he dematerializes. Each of these items is tied to a spirit in the cottage, tethered there by whatever chain is beneath the replica. I move around, looking for my father's glasses. Beside them sits my mother's locket, the only piece of jewelry she ever wore except for the thin golden band on her ring finger. I crack the locket open carefully and find the youthful faces of me and my sister peering back up at me.

Inside the diorama, my mother appears. I pick up father's glasses and he appears shortly after. They smile sadly at me, and my heart clenches, tightening in my chest. I smile back at them, my own sadness pulling at my eyes, as I set the items back down.

"What is this?" Harlow asks, and when I turn, she is tucked away in a corner beneath a tall stained-glass window. She has her back to us, peering down at a worktable of sorts. I leave the cottage to stand beside her. At first glance, it looks like a jeweler's table. There are loose stones and globs of metal, debris from whatever project was being worked on. A set of magnifying glasses sits beside it, along with a thin, sharp tool of some sort. A golden bracelet is on display, worn by a twisted metal hand. It looks familiar to me, and then I realize why.

"All of the spirits are wearing these," I say. The bracelet is entirely unremarkable, and I wonder about the presence of the stones. I cannot imagine that Raznik would waste precious materials like this on spirits. I reach gingerly for the bracelet, pulling it off its display and turning it over in my fingers. On the inside, I spot an engraving of some type. I cannot make it out in the dim light of the room, and I pull the magnifying glasses up, squinting one eye shut and manipulating the bracelet until I can see clearly.

There, in the center of the bracelet, I find a crudely

engraved double helix, the same shape as the glimmering tether. This, together with the anchoring items, must be what keeps the spirits trapped. The reason for trapping them still evades me, and I feel the beginnings of a headache wrapping itself around me.

"Jace?" Aureus calls. His tone is gentle, the type of tone used to deliver bad news to a child. I turn away from the bracelet, slowly and begrudgingly walking over to Aureus. He doesn't say anything, instead holding up a silver crescent moon with a quartz in the center.

It is the one Aleca was wearing at the feast. I sway, pressing a hand to my stomach as anxiety, sharp and cold, starts in my torso and twists around my lungs. Who has accessed this room without my knowing? How has it gotten here?

"No," I breathe, taking the crescent in my hand. I stare with fear at the cottage, but Aleca does not appear. I meet Aureus' worried eyes. He can tell that I am frayed near to snapping and he reaches out for me. I throw myself into his arms and he holds me tightly, one hand pressed to the back of my head and the other wrapped around my torso.

"I can't do this," I say, my words muffled against his chest. My voice breaks, and with it, my last tenuous hold on my sanity. "I can't…I can't…"

My breath comes in sharp gasps, my shoulders heaving with effort. I feel the way I did in the amphitheater in the moment's following Raznik's death, where everything was too much and I felt like I was drowning. I am drowning again, mystery after tragic mystery converging in on me until I am buried alive. There are never any answers, only more questions.

I want to scream, to cry, to hide away all at the same time. I am only one person, one terribly ill-equipped and entirely mundane person. I did not ask for the burden of leading a Court, and I wish desperately that I could turn it over to someone else. I yearn for the days of innocence, when my parents were alive and my greatest responsibilities were filling pails of water and keeping dinner from burning in the hearth.

Aureus' hold on me tightens and I realize that I am trembling.

"You can do this, Jace," he murmurs into my hair. "You are not alone anymore."

"I am," I say, and I cannot believe that this gasping voice is my own.

"You're not," he asserts. The timbre of his voice against me is soothing. "You have me, and Nesryn, and Lady Cornsilk—"

"Is that me?" Harlow cuts in.

"Yes," I say, and I find my breathing has begun to settle. "That's…what Aureus…calls you."

Aureus chuckles, and the rumbling grounds me. He presses me as tightly as he can and I try to settle into his grasp. His breathing is even, and I find that if I focus on it, I am able to mirror it. He feels me shifting, and murmurs,

"That's it, Jace. Breathe in, breathe out. In, out. Tell me why you are not alone."

"I have you…and Nesryn…and Harlow," I say. "I am not alone. I'm not."

As I repeat his words, I realize the truth in them. Swallowing hard, I reach up and force my hand between us to wipe at my eyes. His hold loosens on me and he steps back, dipping down to meet my eyes. His eyes are burning sapphires in the low light of the room. There is an unspoken question which he must find the answer to in my face. He presses a kiss to my forehead and fully releases me.

"There may be a way to test our tether theory," Nesryn says.

She is all business, as if I have not just had a mental breakdown in front of her, and I have to admit that the consistency of her all-business attitude is what brings me back into my body. She is still staring at the table, picking random items up and setting them down after a momentary assessment.

"My sister, ever the empathetic one," Aureus murmurs to me drily. I laugh, wiping the final, lingering moisture from my eyes.

"I think I can cast a speaking spell on these items. Jace, you can go to the real cottage and investigate it, talk to the spirits. If we're right, and they're being controlled through this diorama, we may be able to break the tethering curse. You need to find a way to get inside that cottage."

Her voice is thoughtful and she's staring at the diorama, not seeing anything around her. She picks up my mother's locket again and turns to look at me.

"Will the speaking spell damage the item?" I ask, looking nervously between Nesryn and the necklace. She shakes her head and I chew my lip for a second before relenting. "If you're sure it won't, then I suppose it would make the most sense to try on an item close to me."

"Are you ready now?" she asks, holding the necklace high in front of her and analyzing it. She unclips it, opening it to the small painted portrait of me and Aleca. "Yes, I think this shall work nicely."

"Now's as good a time as any," I sigh. Nesryn nods, cupping the locket in her hands and bringing it to her mouth. She whispers something and then hands it to me. I take it and stare at Nesryn, waiting for instructions. When she does not offer any, I say, "Now what?"

"You speak," she says, as if I should already know this. "Lift it to your mouth and talk into it."

I do so, feeling foolish, and say a few nonsense words into it. The words echo from a small pendant around Nesryn's throat, and my mouth drops open.

"Good, it works just fine. I'd go now, if you want there to be any daylight," she advises.

I am less than twenty steps into the hallway when I hear approaching footsteps from behind me. When I turn, I see Harlow stepping out from the thick gloom of the entryway. I raise my eyebrows and she mirrors the look.

"Did you think you were going alone?" she asks, incredulous. When I grimace, she rolls her eyes and shakes her head. "Unbelievable. Let's go."

She does not wait for me before she starts down the hall, striding past me and down the stairs. I trot after her, realizing that what Aureus said is true: I am not alone.

FOURTEEN

Wind whips at our faces as we stand in the clearing. Neither of us takes the first step toward the cottage. It stands as ruins today, and I wonder if the discovery of the glamour has ruined it for me completely. The moving air whistles through the trees, and the sky above us is dark with the promise of a storm. Early spring in this Court is always tumultuous, and the storms are unparalleled. They come from nowhere and disappear nearly as quickly, always leaving damage in their wake.

We stand motionless for so long that Nesryn's annoyed voice chimes from the locket and urges us to get moving. With trepidation, I take the first step forward. The ground is spongy beneath my feet, oversaturated by our last rainstorm. I squelch forward, pausing ten feet before the cottage.

The windows are black, as usual, and I cannot see inside of them. The door, though ajar, also provides no visual within the rotting home. If I want to see inside of it, I will have to do it manually.

"Mom?" I call. My voice is hushed, and the wind nearly carries it away. I wait for a beat. There is no response, and I'm not sure whether I'm relieved or more worried. The cottage has never been this still before.

"I'm going to free you all, I promise," I say loudly, hoping that someone, anyone, hears me. "Nesryn?" I ask, holding the cold metal locket near my mouth.

"Present," her voice says. To our left, a tree sways and tips over with a deafening crack, roots pulling up from the ground. Birds take flight, tittering angrily. Harlow and I let out a shout, leaping to the right. "Oops, sorry. I knocked one of the fake ones down."

"Well, I guess that answers whether the diorama is actively attached to the clearing," Harlow mutters. I nod, staring at the felled tree before looking back over at the cottage. We cannot afford any mistakes to happen, not when they could cause irrevocable damage in the real world.

Another gust of wind rushes through the clearing, and my hair whips around my face like snakes. We need to access the cottage before the sky opens above us.

"Can you try to open the door for me?"

The locket is silent, and so are we as we wait. Several long moments pass before the door creaks open slowly. The inside is still dark, no doubt some sort of shrouding spell. It looks similar to the gloom that hides Raznik's office, and I suppress a groan. The idea of walking blindly into a ruined and molding cottage filled with spirits is harrowing.

"Any chance you can get a light in there?" I ask, uneasy. Nesryn does not answer, but then a flickering light illuminates the entryway. It is unsettling to see light with no source. "Stay just like that," I instruct.

Harlow and I creep forward and I throw out an arm when we are a stone's throw from the door. The clearing is eerily quiet; even the birds have gone silent. It is the kind of quiet that precedes calamity of some sort, a silence you never want to hear.

"You can't stay out here forever," Tally says in my ear. I go stumbling forward, landing on my hands and knees in the damp earth. Scrambling back to my feet, I turn quickly to find her. She is leaning against the side of the cottage, arms crossed over her chest. "You know that what you need to find is in there."

She looks as fresh as she did in life, and I am careful to keep space between us as I approach her. There are no tears in her dress, no exposed bone.

"I don't want to go in there," I say quietly, shaking my head.

"You must, Jace," Tally says. Quickly, so quickly that I cannot see her movement, she is in front of me. "Don't you understand? They're getting stronger. The magic is changing, taking hold of us and this land." Her eyes are glassy, and a pit forms in my stomach. There should be no pain in death, no need for tears and terror.

"Who is?" I ask, reaching forward to grab hold of Tally. I remember not to at the last moment, and drop my hands.

"We're not allowed to say," she responds, fear dropping her voice to a whisper. Her eyes dart around the clearing, too chaotic for me to follow her gaze.

"Are you allowed to tell me anything?" I ask.

"At great cost," she responds. Sadness pinches the corners of her lips and eyes.

"What does that mean?" Harlow asks, and I know she is thinking about her brother finding her to warn her about my sister. Tally tears her gaze away from me to eye Harlow, and then, turning her attention back to me, says,

"Take my hand, Jace."

"No," I say, backing away as Tally holds her hand out. The bracelet glints in the dim daylight. I shake my head, repeating myself. She does not care, though, and her hand wraps gently around my wrist.

The glamour falls away and I gasp sharply. My mouth falls open as my eyes rove over Tally. It's as if something has been sucking away whatever has kept her spirit alive. She is little more than a waif, now. Her body, slender in life, is desperately thin and frail. Her face is ripped with age lines, and she looks more like an elderly woman than the seventeen-year-old I once knew. My mouth tries to form a hundred different questions, but my voice will not come to me. The sadness on her face is unbearable, and I clench a fist to my stomach.

"This is the punishment for warning you. This is what happened to me for leaving this cottage, for giving you any warning." she tells me. Her words fry at the ends, as if her vocal cords have atrophied. "Please don't look at me like that, I can't bear it."

"Tally, I…" I cannot think of what to say. An apology doesn't feel significant enough, nor do thanks. I blink rapidly, forcing away the moisture collecting in my eyes. She presses a skeletal finger to my lips, silencing me, and jerks her head at the cottage. The light still shines in the doorway.

"You have to go in," she says, and I realize that she is beginning to fade before my eyes. "Even as we speak…they are working against us…"

Her eyes are frightened, and then she vanishes completely. I look over at Harlow and she nods at me. I return the nod, place a hand on the hilt of my sword, and clear the final feet between me and the open door.

I reach back for Harlow's hand, and she slips hers into mine. Carefully, I press forward, allowing the blackness to envelop me. It squeezes tightly around me, and the pressure of it makes my ears ring. I feel Harlow readjust her grip on my hand, and then we both break through. I massage my chest to allow for airflow, blinking against the sudden dim daylight.

The interior is gloomy, and Nesryn's light no longer breaches the ruins. I lift the locket, asking if she can adjust where the light is. A floating, flickering flame appears through the doorway, illuminating the inside of the house. She must have shoved a candle through the doorway. I pray fervently that she does not set something alight. Harlow squeezes my hand in warning before letting go, wandering to the left side of the cottage to inspect there. I break right.

The air is filled with floating dust motes. A layer of dust, dirt, and cobwebs an inch thick coats everything around us. Dilapidated furniture is stacked against the wall beside a crumbling hearth that has not seen use in many years. Oxidized copper dishes and cookware are piled on a counter in the far corner.

In the center of the room, a broken table commands most of the space. An old candle sits in a grimy glass holder. The cottage is entirely insignificant, and I cannot understand why it was imperative that I enter. I sigh, grabbing hold of the candle from the center of the table. Rolling up to the tips of my toes, I hold the candle wick to Nesryn's flame, hopeful that it will light. The dirt on the wick crackles as fire takes hold.

Tally is nowhere to be seen. I wipe at surfaces, looking for anything that could explain what has been happening. There is not so much as a single rune scratched into anything, and I kick at the wall in frustration. A collection of pebbles comes away from the wall, skittering to a stop in front of my toes.

"There's nothing over here," Harlow says, coming back to my side. "I don't get it. We know there are spirits here. Where are they?"

I shake my head. I am used to finding more questions than answers, but I am growing frustrated despite it. I move on, pausing before the hearth. On the broken shelf built into the stone chimney, a frame has fallen onto its face. I lift it, wiping away the thick layer of dust and dirt. A hand-drawn picture begins to appear and I apply more force, rubbing in circles until I can see clearly. There is a large crack running from the top right corner to the bottom left, refracting part of the image, but I can see well enough.

It is of the Raznik family, of Eambroch and a child Cygnus. They stand before this very fireplace, smiling as they hold up a bucket filled with vegetables together. A sick realization fills me. I am standing inside of their old home, the one they lived in before Eambroch overthrew Lysaar. I understand now why Raznik has chosen this space. There is a sick sort of poetry in Raznik tying himself to the place where his roots began.

I set the frame back down, turning my attention toward the unlit space below. It's a likely hiding place, and I blow a big gust of air out, contemplating reaching inside of it. If we are to find my sister and free these spirits, there can be no corners cut.

Gritting my teeth, I crouch down, sticking my candle as far inside it as possible. There could be anything in the chimney, and I reach up with dread. My hand closes around something hard, but frail, and I bring it down to examine it. A mouse's skeleton sits in the center of my palm and I jerk my hand away with a cry of disgust. The tiny bones tumble from my hand and turn to dust upon impact with the floor. Readjusting my crouch, I stick the candle inside the chimney, twisting my neck to the side so I can look up.

I am nearly nose-to-nose with an upside-down face, so grotesque that it looks more like a death mask than a human. Its mouth is twisted in a snarling smile, baring sharp and rotting teeth. Wild eyes with large, rounded pupils stare at me and stringy black hair falls to frame the face. Unkempt facial hair encircles that horrible mouth, and if I didn't know any better, I would say that the creature looked like Raznik.

A piercing scream fills the air, and it takes a moment for me to realize it's me. I scramble backward, too unstable to get to my feet. I fall flat on my back and Harlow yanks me up. The candle

I held falls to its side, the flame doused by melted wax. Before she can speak, plumes of dust come pouring from the hearth. The cottage begins to shake, and I pull the locket to my mouth.

"Nesryn, get here now and bring Syiera. Bronwyn, too, if she's there. Aureus, stay with the diorama. Bring any magic you have!" My final words end as a shout as the dust settles and something falls to the ground with a heavy thud, landing in a dark heap. I have an idea of what that heap is, and it fills me with leaden dread. I grip the locket in my hand so tightly that the hinge cuts into my palm.

Slowly, stiffly, the heap begins to shudder and rise. The movements are entirely otherworldly, and it only adds to the heart-stopping fear that has seized me.

"What is that?" Harlow whispers in my ear, frantic. We are pressed together, backing away slowly toward the door. My eyes never leave it as I whisper,

"I think it's Raznik."

All of the air in my body feels trapped in my chest, and I cannot get my breathing regulated. My heart is thrumming violently in my ears, warping my hearing until it feels as if I am underwater. I have never felt true fear as I do now. The creature is standing now, wobbling as if it has never done so before. It is entirely shrouded in a tattered black cloak, a hood pulled up and over its head.

"What do we do?" she asks, and I hear the way fright strains her voice and takes it up an octave.

"My…murderess…"

The hiss falls from the creature's mouth, confirming my

fear: this creature is, in some form, Sepyphyr Raznik. My mouth runs dry and I break into a cold sweat along my spine.

He has gained his footing now, and he begins to approach. His steps are small, unstable, and his toes drag along the floor as he moves. The sound is chilling.

"At last," he says. He lifts skeletal hands covered by mottled, waxy skin and pulls his hood from his head. Fright tightens like a vise around my throat. "I've waited for you…for so long."

Right-side-up, his face is no less terrifying. The limp hair hangs like curtains around sunken-in cheeks. His pupils, blown wide and pitch black, make him look like a wild animal. His mouth is still twisted in a smile, and when he opens his mouth to speak, it reveals a second row of sharp teeth behind his first row.

"My murderess," he repeats, scraping forward. He presses a hand to his chest, the same place my sword drove through him only half a year ago. He makes a tsking sound, wagging an unnaturally long finger in the air, and my blood turns to ice in my veins. Harlow is gripping my forearm so tightly that I am confident it will bruise. "You've been most naughty, Jace."

"You're supposed to be dead," I say, hating the way my voice shakes. "I killed you. I watched them burn your body."

"Yes," Raznik says, "but death need not be permanent. If you were braver…you would know…what I know." He speaks slowly, softly, as if each word is a struggle to utter. The underlying hiss is still there, like a snake awaiting its moment to strike.

"I do not care for your riddles, Raznik," I say as coldly as I can. He laughs, and the effect is numbing. Goosebumps erupt along my arms and legs.

"I care little for your wants," he rasps. "I wouldn't, if I were you," he adds suddenly, and for the first time, his gaze slides past me to Harlow. She has unhitched her blade, holding it tightly in her left hand. "Mortal weapons mean nothing to me anymore. You don't want to anger me, do you? You've both lost so much, already."

His mouth curves upward in an insincere smile, and drool drips from his pointed teeth. His is the picture of true insanity.

I feel sick with dread, and for the first time, I feel certain that we are going to die here.

"How are you alive?" I demand. "What have you done?"

The floating flame above us begins to flicker and dim before sputtering out completely. It takes only seconds before another flame flares to light, though it feels like years.

When the room comes back into view, Raznik has disappeared.

FIFTEEN

We burst out of the cottage into the clearing. Daylight is waning, and the first droplets of rain finally begin to fall. I run my hands through my hair, pacing back and forth quickly as I try to think. This is entirely worse than I thought it would be, and I find that I'm yearning for the days of rune circles that made my body go numb. Numbness, I can deal with. Demon creatures with a dubious tie to magic? Not so much.

"What are we supposed to do, Jace?" Harlow asks. Her voice is smaller than I've ever heard it, and it rattles me. Harlow is someone I know to be steadfast and headstrong; her fear fills me with guilt and doubt.

"We wait," I say. "For Nesryn, Syiera, Bronwyn…this is bigger than any of us alone, and he cannot be felled by mortal means. I'm afraid that until they arrive, we are sitting ducks." I pray they arrive soon.

The rain falls in great, fat drops now, soaking our hair and shirts gradually. The clearing is still silent, the songs of birds notably missing. My mother always warned me to listen to the wildlife: if they are silent, something bad is around the corner.

An indeterminate amount of time passes before we hear the snapping of branches and rustling of leaves. We both draw our swords, staring in the direction of the noise. Anticipation sets me on edge, only dropping into relief when Syiera emerges, flanked on either side by Nesryn and Bronwyn. I'm so happy to see them that I nearly fling my arms around them.

Instead, I relay our experience as quickly as I can. Syiera's eyes narrow as she listens, and her gaze slides over my shoulder to stare at the cottage. There is a steeliness in her turquoise eyes; they seem to nearly glow in the ever-darkening evening.

"Corruption breeds corruption," she murmurs. She strides past me, walking around the perimeter of the cottage with deliberate steps. Though she has donned breeches and a tunic for this moment, a silken aubergine cape flows behind her in the wind, making her look every bit as powerful as I know her to be.

"I've left my pendant with Aureus," Nesryn tells me. "The speaking spell is still attached; he will help us where he can."

I nod absently, watching Syiera. The adrenaline has begun to wane, and I stifle a yawn with the back of my hand. Bronwyn whistles and then tosses a small bottle to me and to Harlow. I lift it, eyeing the shimmering green liquid within. I have not entirely shaken myself of my wariness around Bronwyn.

"Revitalizing serum," she explains. "There was no time to get rations, but you need to keep your strength up. This should help."

I uncork it, sniffing carefully. It smells of ginger and lemon. Sensing my hesitation, she pulls two more from her pockets, handing one to Nesryn and keeping one for herself. They both uncork them and tip them into their mouths. They both glow a dim gold for only a moment before it fades again. Satisfied, Harlow and I follow suit.

The effect is instant, rushing through me in a way that leaves my skin tingling. My eyes, dry and scratchy, feel refreshed and the exhaustion I've barely held at bay leaves my body entirely. I desperately hope that Aureus has included Bronwyn's goods in our new trading edict.

Syiera rejoins our party, and her face is grim. I frown.

"I do not like that face," I inform her. She grimaces in apology, but the grimness does not leave her.

"I do not like what I have found," she replies. "It's a wonder your castle has not been swallowed whole by corrupted magic."

She bends to scoop some of the sodden earth in her hands and holds it out before us. The dirt and moss are unremarkable to me, and I'm not sure what I'm supposed to be looking at. Quietly, she murmurs something in a different language.

The dirt and moss lift, hovering over her hands before slowly spreading side-to-side in a triangle of sorts. The space between the dirt and moss sparks, flickering green, copper, and black. The black nearly entirely chokes out the green and copper light.

"This is your land," she tells me. "The green and copper, earth's magic, are being smothered by corrupted battle magic."

"A bid for immortality," I say, suddenly recalling my father's words. "Has he achieved it?"

"How do you beat someone who is immortal?" Harlow asks. Doubt paints her tone.

I shake my head, staring up at the floating triangle of earth. As we watch, another spark of green winks out, overtaken by black. Corruption working in real time. Thunder rumbles distantly and it shakes the ground. Syiera waves her hand, sending the moss and dirt back down to the rest of the earth. The ground shakes again, and I pause. The faraway thunder isn't nearly powerful enough to impact the clearing this way.

I am not the only one who has noticed, this time. Bronwyn's gaze snaps to the earth beneath her feet and then she looks up and locks eyes with me.

"He's coming," a voice whispers in my ear. It belongs to Tally, though I cannot see her. "They both are."

"They're coming," I say loudly, though I do not know who else to expect alongside Raznik. I spin around blindly, scanning the entirety of the clearing with my sword drawn. Harlow has drawn her weapon as well, though Nesryn, Bronwyn, and Syiera all remain empty-handed. They intend to rely on their magic alone.

The trees begin to quiver preternaturally, almost as if they themselves are frightened of what is to come. A metallic screech rips through the air, and I finally recognize the source. I have no time to warn the others before Elouned appears high above the trees, her dark wings spread wide and sharp. With another shriek, she dives to the clearing, hurtling so fast that she is little more than a blur.

She lands before the cottage and rises slowly. Her dress clinks as she saunters toward us, and I realize that she wears a cloak made entirely of razor-sharp feathers. It is a weapon in its own right and promises a thousand painful deaths. Her hair is pulled into a high tail made of a dozen smaller braids with two crisscrossing spikes driven into the base of the tail. I cannot be certain, but I think they are daggers made of petrified bone. Gold-and-crimson eyes rove over the clearing before snapping onto me. I swallow hard and readjust the grip on my blade.

"I thought you ran when I killed Raznik," I call. I sound much more confident than I feel. She bares her teeth at me, and ruby embedded into her canine winks in the final bit of daylight.

"I have always remained loyal to the Commander," she says. Her voice is high and cold as she casts an imperious look at me.

"I had no idea you were so eager to serve beneath me. I'm honored," I respond, droll.

"You!" she spits. She laughs one hard, humorless laugh. "You are nothing and deserve nothing. I remain loyal to the true commander of this Court."

"Why?" I ask, and there is no sarcasm in my voice now. "You're not even from this land. I know what you've done. I know you've abandoned your sisterhood in Dezaiyr, but for what reason…Ifoké?"

Elouned falters; she has not expected that I know her history. That I know her old name.

"My sisters," she says quietly, as if lost in thought. She regains her composure quickly, narrowing her eyes at me. "My sisters," she repeats, and now the word is like a curse from her lips. "Too cowardly to seek real power, too content to allow others to rule over them. Sepyphyr showed me real power."

She shakes out her wings before they settle at her back again, agitated.

"He manipulated you with platitudes," I say. "All he's ever known is manipulation."

"You wound me, Jace."

The hiss comes from nowhere and everywhere at once. Elouned looks up toward the sky, nostrils flaring with excitement. I crane my neck left and right, but I cannot find Raznik. My heart pounds in my chest, and my teeth begin to chatter anxiously. It is one of my least favorite expressions of nerves, nearly driving me to distraction. I flatten my tongue between my teeth, pressing hard to the roof of my mouth to stop the way they clatter together.

As he finally steps into the clearing, a ring of fire erupts around the perimeter, effectively trapping us all within it. They rise high, licking at the air for continual fuel. Wind gusts from the flames, and my clothing and hair ripple in it. The heat, comfortable at first, quickly becomes overwhelming. It dries my mouth and eyes, and I swallow with difficulty.

"This ends here, Jace Grimme," Raznik says. Though his speech and movement have steadied, his appearance remains feral. His pupils are still blown wide, his skin shining and pulled tight against sharp cheekbones. The firelight catches on the saliva-coated teeth behind pale, chapped lips. "This plan has been in motion for years. You and your band of misfits won't be enough to defeat me, now."

"I hardly think you can call the Empress of an empire a misfit," Syiera says, stepping forward. Raznik's eyes widen and then narrow in a cruel sort of glee.

"Indeed, you have a grand power," he says. "Your spirit will provide much life essence for me."

All at once, it falls into place. I look between Elouned and Raznik with horror, and then to the cottage behind them.

"Those spirits aren't trapped because they haven't completed a soul task," I say. "They're trapped so that you can steal their essence. Elouned murders them and shepherds their souls here for you. You've been siphoning from them to keep yourself alive."

If that is what he can call it. He is more of a wraith, than anything. I cannot imagine a single thing worth being whittled down into an existence like this.

My heart breaks for all of the spirits who have been trapped into this cottage, slowly stripped of everything they have after having their lives cut short from them. There is no release in the afterlife without aid, and they have been at the mercy of Raznik and Elouned for so long. Longer than any of us ever could have known.

"They were most interfering in life, but in death, they serve me well," he says. "Those who refused to follow me then have no choice but to follow me now. Rely on me. Give me as much as I want to take. It took us years of experimenting before we finally got it right. I suppose I should thank you for killing me, Jace."

"What do you mean?" I ask, and my blood runs cold.

"We've wrought this magic for years," Raznik tells me.

"Bottled their essence, pushed our magic to new boundaries with no real way to test it. We had to hope that someday, our efforts would pay off. And," he says, a wide, wicked smile forming, "it did. It took time, and effort, but it brought me back. We've bided our time, knowing that someday, you would be foolish enough to find me. You never could keep your nose out of trouble.

"We were patient. Elouned was most attentive, dutifully nursing me back to life, hidden away within the mountains. She brought me the essence I needed, cared for me day in and day out. She kept an eye on my spirits. They've been most disobedient, it would seem. It pains me to punish them the way I've had to. I waited for you, Jace, hid away in that cottage knowing that you'd come looking for your fool of a sister—and I was right. And now that you're here, we can begin. I can take back what was never yours. I will rule again."

"You're a monster," Harlow says through grit teeth. Her voice is hoarse, angry at Raznik's glibness in the face of the fate her brother has been sealed to for nearly a decade.

The realization of just how many of our loved ones have been trapped here for years crashes down on me, and I find myself moving forward without thought. I think of Tally, whose essence has nearly been depleted by her efforts to keep us safe. My parents, who have been stuck without aid. Harlow's brother, his essence so far depleted that he has nearly turned to dust. Parents, spouses, children, all dead and gone and trapped with no way to be saved for so long. The helplessness of them all nearly drags me down.

I stalk across the clearing to stand before Raznik, anger blurring my vision and making my skin buzz. My grip is so tight on my sword that the weapon quivers in my hand. I lift it, jabbing the tip into his chest. He staggers back but is otherwise unaffected.

"You want a fight?" I hiss. "Fine. Let's fight, Raznik. It will be an honor to murder you again."

As if my words are a call to arms, the clearing erupts. Black sparks climb their way up the fire encircling us, as if the land is rising up to defend Raznik. Elouned lunges forward, grabbing me by my hair and yanking me back.

I let out a shout, whirling with my sword extended. She uses the opportunity to wrap an arm around my midsection and takes to the sky. My feet leave the ground and I kick back and forth wildly. We climb higher and higher, until we are well above the clearing. If I should be dropped from this height, it would mean instant death.

"I look forward to watching you die," Elouned says, lips to my ear. I shiver at the heat of her breath against my skin. Without warning, she releases me, taking care to slide my body along the feathers of her cloak. Their edges are thin and precise, slicing clear through my clothing and into my skin. I careen toward the ground, screaming. I am gaining speed, and I realize that she has positioned me directly over a piece of sharp metal sticking upright out of the cottage's roof. I will be impaled by it, and there is nothing that can be done.

Then, my movement is arrested. As if I have hit an invisible barrier, I slam into nothingness. The force of it whips my head back, popping something in my neck. Slowly, I am dragged diagonally away from the cottage and down to the ground. I am dropped unceremoniously on my frontside, and I get a mouthful of peat. My neck is stiff, and the left side of my body burns from the lacerations, but I am alive.

I breathe heavily, pressing my hands into the ground and pushing up with great effort. I see remnants of lavender fire disappearing within Syiera and realize that she is the one who has rescued me from being skewered like a pig atop the cottage.

"Are you okay?" Harlow asks, dropping down beside me. My arms give, and I drop down again. "Here, Bronwyn gave me this. She says you need to drink it."

She uncorks a bottle, and I turn my head to the side to face her. She tips it into my mouth for me, and something bright and citrusy blooms across my tongue. I feel the lacerations begin to stitch themselves in my skin and the stiffness recedes from my muscles. I will never doubt her again.

Harlow offers me a hand and then gives me my sword as I right myself. There is a shout to our left, and I turn to watch Syiera gather lavender fire between her hands. It spins there, growing as she spreads her hands further and further apart. With another shout, she throws it forward. It wraps itself around Raznik, picking him up and throwing him across the clearing.

He rises slowly, and there is a vicious anger in his face. It mars his already-terrifying features so violently that it makes me tremble. Syiera is already gathering up another ball of fire, and Raznik stalks toward her.

Elouned takes advantage of our distraction, pulling Harlow against her with an arm around her neck. Her eyes widen, and her hands automatically lift to try to pry Elouned's arm away. I shake my head minutely, and at the last moment, Harlow shifts her body to bring her hips forward before slamming them back into Elouned. The Valkyrie goes flying over Harlow's body and lands on her back with such force that she is momentarily paralyzed.

I cannot help but let out a cheer for Harlow before I refocus my energy on the fight. Harlow stabs her sword through one of Elouned's wings, and she bellows in pain. Harlow crouches down, one hand still on the hilt of her sword and she yanks several feathers off Elouned's cloak. She sticks them in a leather pouch at her side and rises again. When she pulls her sword out of Elouned's wing, the tip is painted with black blood.

Elouned rises, murder in her eyes as she stalks toward Harlow with a limp. Harlow has rendered her incapable of flight, and it has severely reduced the difference of power between us.

A ball of crimson fire explodes at Harlow's feet, the impact sending bits of earth spraying upward into her face. She reels backward, and another ball of fire goes hurtling toward her. Elouned is angry, now, and she will not rest until she has killed.

I lift the locket to my mouth, whispering into it and praying that Aureus can hear me. A moment later, a large fir tree comes crashing down from our right, forcing space between us and Elouned. The massive boughs wipe her out, trapping her beneath their heft. We stumble away, turning and running from the fallen tree toward the cottage ruins.

I don't know why the spirits have all disappeared at such a critical moment, and I need to find out why. I know they are still tethered to the house, to the clearing. Until we find a way to sever it, they will continue to be trapped. I call for Nesryn and she is by my side in moments. Bronwyn and Syiera take turns against Raznik, but I can see that they are becoming fatigued. He is stronger than he looks.

"I need to get back inside the cottage," I say quickly as we run. "The spirits are hiding somewhere, and I think Aleca is with them. Nesryn, I need your help connecting to them. They've gone completely into hiding."

"I'll stay guard outside," Harlow offers. "I don't know how much good it will do, but—"

"If you become unsafe, get inside," I command her. She nods, and then Nesryn and I rush into the ruins. The blackness squeezes us both before spitting us out. I stumble forward and catch myself on the edge of the table.

Nesryn looks around the cottage curiously, and I watch closely. She pulls a small black pouch from beneath her bodice, dipping her thumb, index, and middle fingers into it. They come away coated in a glittering sapphire powder, and she snaps her fingers to send it swirling off her skin and into the air.

From a hidden pocket in her skirt, she withdraws a long, thin piece of bone wrapped with dried floral garland and a circle with three bells on it. Something lands near the ruins outside and the window furthest from us shatters. The glass lands on the dusty floor with a muffled tinkling, and motes rise from the ground.

Nesryn methodically draws symbols into the air, eyes closed as she murmurs something. She lets out a shout, shaking the bells violently, so violently that my ears burn from the high, bright sound. When she ceases the ringing, the echo of the sound remains. She brings the wand of bone down in a sharp, diagonal line, and then the room glows a bright pale gold. My eyes water from it but I do not allow them to close against the light.

When it recedes, my mouth falls open. The room is filled to the brim with spirits, so many that they begin to blend together. It is impossible to keep from touching them when we are cramped so tightly together, and I watch as the glamours of those nearest us fall away. They all try to speak at once and their voices rise together in one loud din, unintelligible. I throw my hands up and the voices cease.

"They were sealed behind a suppression spell," Nesryn tells me, and I realize that she is panting from the effort of her magic. "You'd best be quick about your task; Raznik will surely learn soon what we've done."

"I mean to free you all," I say, "but I need your help. I know that asking you to work against Raznik and Elouned means that you will be drained of the essence you still have, and I will not force any of you to do anything if you do not wish to. We need help, though. He has my sister trapped somewhere, and he is wearing away the resources we currently possess. If we fall, the entire Nautilus will fall with us."

The room is silent as hundreds of pairs of ghostly eyes regard me. At last, my mother and father step forward.

"Whether we live or die, you are our daughters. We will

fight," my mother says. Tears prick in the corners of my eyes, and I blink them away fiercely. My mother presses her fingers to her lips and then brings them down, toward me. It is the closest thing to affection we can share anymore.

"I'll go," a ragged voice says, and a man steps forward. It is Fallon, Harlow's brother.

"And me," Tally says.

One by one, spirits offer to fight beside us, and then there is but a handful of spirits remaining, unwilling to go. I nod at them, and they quaver before disappearing into a diaphanous light. I hesitate, unsure how to direct spirits into battle. I look to my mother for guidance, and she steps beside me, stepping back into her warrior days with ease.

"We know what this sacrifice means," she says, and the spirits before us nod. "We fight until we can no more. We fight for our own justice, for the justice of those who are yet to come. Those who have had the least of their essence stolen from them, you take the front lines. The weakest will remain at the back. No human will die while we are here."

To see my mother lead as a warrior is something I never thought I'd experience, and I am filled with a reverent sort of gratitude that sends tears streaking down my cheeks. I wipe at them quickly. She has always and will always be the woman I strive to be.

"We will fight together," I say. "Every single one of you will be remembered for what you have done. You will become the stuff of legends passed down through the ages."

The room is solemn, silent, and then my mother takes hold

of my hand. I am unfazed by her glamour falling away. We lift our hands together, and with a shout, we break apart. The rest of the spirits join us with a battle cry of their own, and then the room goes dark as they vanish to the other side of the door.

SIXTEEN

When we emerge from the ruins, the clearing is in chaos. Spirits are everywhere, taking my mother's words to heart. Though they are without weapons, they are powerful together. Their onslaught allows Syiera and Bronwyn to fall back and recuperate their energy. Raznik fights off the converging spirits with inky black magic. Several catch the magic straight on and turn to vapor that rises upward. I hope it means freedom for them.

I grab Harlow by the hand and call for her brother. As one of the weaker spirits, he falls back quickly. Harlow gasps, bringing a hand to her mouth.

"Fallon, what are you doing?" she asks. Her hands reach out for him and then flutter away as she remembers the glamour. His true appearance is a harrowing one.

"I'm fighting, Har," he says. His voice sounds exhausted already. "Jace says this ends today, and I have to believe it. I'm tired. I'm so tired."

"Why are you so much weaker than the others?" she asks. Her voice is raspy, but her eyes are dry.

"It's the cost of leaving the tether," he says. "After I died, I found myself here, without you. I couldn't stand not knowing what happened to you, and I tried to find you for years. It cost me my essence in a large way, but I was willing to give up all my essence to find you."

She lets out a dry sob and throws her arms around Fallon, not paying attention when he turns to the skeletal, unglamoured version of himself. I stand guard over the two of them as they cling to the final moments they have between them. At last, Fallon reaches for me with a bony hand.

"Take care of her," he says.

"I will," I promise. He lets go, planting a kiss on Harlow's cheek before heading toward the fray. She watches him go and then turns to face me with a watery smile. "Are you okay?"

"He never stopped looking for me," she says in a marveled tone. "I…didn't realize how much I needed to know that." She inhales shakily and tugs on her leather brigandine, straightening it. "Think they'll be okay?"

"Better to die by their own choice than stay trapped by Raznik," I say. I stare out over the sea of spirits, wincing when Raznik whips a black tendril of magic out and around the spirit of a woman. Streaks of champagne light twists around the black tendril and into him. The spirit disappears, her essence entirely sucked out of her. I cannot let them fight this battle on their own.

I charge through the crowd of spirits, joining the front lines. A number of spirits have fallen already, not up for the fight against an immortal and corrupted being. I send up a prayer of thanks to them, wherever they now may be.

Raznik's face twists when he sees me. His expression is unreadable. Despite the essence he has consumed, he is weakening against the numbers we have sicced on him. Elouned is nowhere to be seen; I hope she is still entangled in the fallen fir tree.

"Where is Aleca?" I shout. He bares his teeth at me.

"Safe and sound," he taunts. I tighten my grip on my weapon. He may be immortal, but it would still be satisfying to run him through anyway. I refrain, but barely. This is one of those times when I wish that what little magic I have produced would present itself. I know nothing about it, and have only managed it in moments of high emotion. A well-placed shot of magic would take his arrogance down a peg.

"Find the tether, Jace!" Tally cries, wading through the crowd of spirits. "This will not end until you do—oh!"

A black orb hits her square in the chest and she drops. Unlike the other spirits, this spell clings to her, spreading up her neck and down her arms and torso like ivy. It is consuming her; her face contorts in pain.

"Tally!" I scream, and the loss of her comes rushing back to me all over again. I drop to my knees, taking her in my arms. "Tally, no!"

"It's okay, Jace," she says. Her voice is faint, and under my touch, she becomes the frail, feeble shell of herself. My vision blurs. It was cruel enough losing her once to Raznik. To lose her again is unfathomable. He has done this on purpose.

"I'm sorry, I'm so sorry," I sob. I try to rip the magic from her, but it is unmovable. It continues to claim her, the tendrils wrapping up and across her cheeks. Her eyes flutter shut for a moment, and she reaches a hand up to press it against my cheek.

"I'd choose you every time," she says. It is no more than a whisper. Another sob falls from me and I pull her close, pressing a kiss to her cold forehead. Her eyes slip shut. They do not open again.

I hold her a moment longer before I scream for Harlow. Tally's body is still in my arms, the magic preventing her from the same freedom the other spirits have found in true death.

Harlow comes sprinting over, fear splayed across her face. It shifts when she realizes that I am not in danger. She falls to the ground beside me, and I place Tally in her arms, trying to stem my sobs. I cannot find words, but she knows anyway, and she lifts Tally tenderly, carrying her away from me and Raznik, away from the battle.

I breathe in sharp, quick pants, unable to regulate the anger and ache that has taken over me. I rise unsteadily, turning to face Raznik slowly. My shoulders rise and fall with my uneven breathing and my entire body quivers with rage. I am sick to death of Raznik taking the ones who matter most to me.

The ground begins to vibrate beneath my feet, and he has the grace to stare at me in shock. Syiera and Bronwyn appear on either side of me. Syiera takes hold of my left hand; Bronwyn circles my right wrist, my hand occupied by my sword. There is a sudden surge of energy in me. Through my periphery, I realize that they are sharing magic with me. Lavender spirals around the hand held by Syiera, topaz on my right.

"We are with you, Jace," Syiera murmurs. "Focus on what you want the most."

I squeeze my eyes shut, picturing the double helix tethering the diorama to the floor. I want my sister, alive. I want the real tether. I want to destroy every ounce of magic that keeps Raznik alive. I want to destroy him.

The ground lurches beneath my feet, and their grips on me tighten. When I open my eyes, I let out a shout. The cottage, and the earth around it, has lifted from the clearing, leaving a massive chasm beneath us. Raznik stands before us, and for the first time, I see true fear in his eyes. I relish it.

"Jace!" Nesryn calls. "The tether!"

She points to the space beneath our floating island. I pull myself from Syiera's and Bronwyn's hold, rushing to the edge and dropping onto my stomach. They rejoin hands, a renewed surge of magic between them. I grip the jagged earth, peering down below me. Beneath the center of the ruins, a glowing double helix disappears deep within the crater, so deep that I cannot find the end. And there, wrapped in the center of it, is Aleca, still in her gown from the feast. Her eyes are closed, her arms crossed up and over her chest. Her hair undulates around her, as if she is floating in water. She looks unharmed, but my heart stops in my chest. It is a small mercy that there is no bracelet around her wrist.

"Al," I whisper. "Syiera!"

My shout is carried on the wind, and Syiera turns her attention from Raznik to look at me. The magic does not wane; beads of sweat have begun to develop on Raznik's forehead as he presses his black magic forward. A shield of topaz magic absorbs his assault, reflecting it back at him. I hesitate, worried that if I distract them, this island will go crashing back into the ground and kill my sister.

"I cannot do both, Jace!" she calls. It's an answer I expected, but hope sinks in me anyway. I leap to my feet, cupping my hands around my mouth.

"Nesryn!" I shout, desperation making my voice crack. She is the only other one with magic, and I need her. I call her name again before she finally hears me. "My sister! We need to get her out!"

She understands immediately and wades into the sea of spirits who have gathered beneath us to watch. She speaks to them, gesturing up at the floating earth and then to the crater below. I try to follow her hand motions, but she moves too quickly and I lose track of whatever she is trying to tell them.

I scan for Harlow, and find her near the fallen fir tree. Elouned has managed to pull herself out from the tangle of boughs, and she looks haggard. Harlow has her sword trained on Elouned's uninjured wing, a threat that keeps her in control.

"Jace!" Nesryn calls. "They will do it!"

I look back over and find my parents standing at the edge of the crater. They hold hands, staring up at me with sad smiles. My stomach knots. Up here, I will have no proper goodbye.

"I'm so proud of you, my girl," my mother calls. "You can end this, my love."

"I love you both," I shout, and I wonder how many more times I will have to mourn the same losses I have mourned before. Wind wicks tears from my eyes before they can fall. They both press their fingers to their mouths and send their kisses toward me, and I do the same. They turn away from me, talking to Nesryn again.

I pull the locket to my lips, calling for Aureus. He responds immediately, and I try to fill him in on what is happening. I do a poor job, jumping from place to place with very little cohesion. He manages to follow anyway, and I warn him that we plan to break the tether.

"Get yourself out of that room, now. I don't know what will happen," I warn.

"Where you lead, I will follow," he says solemnly, and then the locket is silent.

The fire encircling the clearing has begun to wane as Syiera and Bronwyn continue their efforts. I can see the way fatigue drags their shoulders down, the way it lines their faces, but it does not diminish despite their exhaustion. I stand at the edge, watching as my parents nod to something Nesryn has said.

Carefully, she constructs a bridge out of nothing more than light. It allows them passage to the center of the helixes where Aleca floats entangled. I lay on my stomach again to watch, gripping the edge of the island so tightly that it crumbles beneath my fingers. My parents slowly make their way across the bridge; the force of the magic around the tether pushes back on them.

They work quickly to unravel something, and I realize that

she has been bound with a rope. It falls away, disappearing into the deep, dark cavern below them. I swallow hard; if Aleca cannot be freed safely, she will meet a similar fate. If I have to watch my sister die, it will be my undoing. I squeeze my eyes shut. I cannot let my thinking get away from me, not now.

When I open them, I find Aleca's limbs floating freely. She has been released from the binding rope, though she is still suspended inside the helixes. Each time my parents touch the helixes, they flare but do not release her. Desperation grows in me as magic begins to weaken. No one can keep this up for much longer.

I yank my sword from beneath me. The blade—sharp, diamond, and not of mortal make—gleams in the firelight. I cast it below me, and the trajectory of it lands in my mother's hands. She holds it up to me and then turns on the tether. In life, she was deadly with a sword; I trust she is the same now.

She brings it high behind her shoulder with both hands, swinging hard and meeting the helixes with a loud, bell-like toll. They flicker, and she does it again. Over and over, my mother drives the sword against the tethers until cracks begin to split in them. Aleca drops down the chain and my father grabs for her.

Despite my mother's continuous battering against the tether, it does not give. I roll onto my back and rise, rejoining Syiera and Bronwyn. Bronwyn is pale from over-exertion. I jerk my head at her and she drops her shield with a gasp. The sudden shift sends Raznik's magic careening over our shoulders in a violent streak. It hits the fire and flares before disappearing. He stumbles backward from the sudden lack of resistance.

"Enough!" I shout, stepping in front of him. He looks weakened, and I can see the effort he has to make to draw from his reserve of magic. Another toll of the helixes sounds, and he clutches at his chest. The tether is tied to him as much as it is to this land.

Syiera pauses, a web of lavender spinning between her hands. I shake my head and it dissipates. He sucks in gasps of breath, his entire body heaving from the effort. There is no sound except for the whistling air and the crackling of the fire trapping us within the clearing.

"You can't keep this up, Sepyphyr," I say. "Look at you. You're already dying again. Your magic was never going to save you. If it was, it would have well before now. You've been losing your hold over the spirits for months."

He snarls, blasting a jet of magic at me. I drop to the ground; the magic skims my shoulder on my way down and I hiss against the searing burn. He aims another at me, misjudging and instead pockmarking the earth beside my head. I throw my arms over my head to protect it from the descending spray of earth. He never was one to go down without a fight, regardless of whether it was an evenly matched one.

Another bell toll rings out, this one louder than before. It leaves my ears ringing in the wake of it.

"We're nearly there!" Nesryn shouts. The island begins to shudder and then we are descending back toward the ground. If we don't get Aleca out now, we never will.

The sky has begun to lighten with impending dawn, and it casts a blue-pink light over the land. There is one final, keening bell toll. Light bursts from beneath us, casting out across the entire clearing. It is blinding, and I slam my eyes shut against it. When the light recedes, the once green and lush clearing is a perfect scorched and smoking circle, the grass dead and brittle. The ring of fire has disappeared completely, leaving a ring of smoldering embers in its wake. Raznik falls to his hands and knees and I race over, grabbing him. We are hurtling back toward the ground; the speed makes it difficult to remain upright. As the floating mass we are on rejoins the earth, we are thrown to the side.

I leap up, looking around wildly. My body aches from the sudden impact of earth against earth.

"Aleca, where's Aleca?" I demand. I race around the perimeter, trying to find my sister. In the wake of the tether being destroyed, every single spirit has disappeared. Aleca is nowhere to be found.

"No, no, no!" I say, whirling around where I stand. "No, she's still here, she has to be somewhere! Aleca!" My voice is shrill with desperation. "Al! Aleca!"

Wheezing laughter pulls my attention back toward the ground where Raznik struggles to pull himself up. With the tether gone, he has little tying him to this life.

"You…and your family…all you've ever done is meddle," he says. His words are slow and slurred. "What a delight…it has been…to be the reason…you all die."

"She's not dead," I say, though I do not know who I am trying to convince more: him, or me. "She's not."

He is standing now, clinging to the side of the cottage for

support. Black magic flickers in his right hand, but before he can cast it at me, it flares and fades. My heart thrums against my chest, so forcefully that my clothing quivers.

We are at a standstill—he has no magic, and I have no weapon. I turn on my heel, searching again for any sight of my sister, my sword, or my parents. I know I will find none of them. My gaze lands on Harlow, who still has her weapon trained on Elouned. She jerks her head at the woman, and I frown as I try to understand the message she is trying to convey. Then, as subtly as she can, she pulls the tip of a metal feather from the bag at her hip. Realization dawns on me and I sprint over to them.

As I reach for the clasp to detach the cloak of feathers, Elouned grabs my wrist in a crushing hold, ripping a feather from her shoulder with her other hand. I crumple beneath her grip, twisting and dropping onto my knees. She holds the feather millimeters from my neck; she could kill me in this position without a second glance.

Harlow stares at me with frightened eyes and I manage to point at the hollow of my throat. She nods, and I close my eyes as she maneuvers the tip of her weapon between me and Elouned. The blade drops for a moment before swiping up, and the cloak falls away from around her throat. Without the weight, Elouned's hold on me falters. The hand holding the feather shoots out as she tries to regain her balance, but it is enough for me, and I break from her hold.

Harlow gingerly hands me the cloak, careful to keep their razor edges from nicking me. I rush toward Raznik, opening the cloak wide in my hands. I twist my body sideways, heaving the cloak behind me before bringing it down in a sideways swipe. He lifts an arm to protect himself, but it is of no use. He is too weak to defend himself.

The feathers slice into him, one after another, until he is little more than a pile of smoking ribbons on the ground. There is nothing to suggest that these tatters were ever once a sentient creature. The final pieces float to the ground, landing atop the pile where they lay motionless. With the tether destroyed, there is no essence left to keep him alive. The feathers come away slick with black blood. Corrupt blood.

Elouned lets out the bellow of a wounded animal, and she tears herself from Harlow's grip to race forward. She drops to her knees, lifting the scraps of Raznik's remains in her hands.

"No, my love!" she screams. "What have you done, what have you done?" Her grief sends chills down my body. "You," she howls, looking over her shoulder at me. Her eyes are ice-cold despite the pools of tears. This is the second time I have taken him from her, and she intends to repay the favor. She places his remains on the ground again, rising and stalking toward me.

She does not need a weapon to take my life. There is never a more dangerous person than one who has nothing to lose, and this is exactly the position I've put her in. I am still holding her cloak, my only line of defense. I cast it aside, as far from us as I am able; it is as much a weapon for her as it could be for me.

Her wings erupt behind her and though she cannot take air, she lurches forward at me. Her hands lock around my arms, and her wings curve down to trap us both within them. She slams me to the ground, bringing her hand up behind her. The back of my head bounces off the ground from the impact and black spots burst in front of my vision. It returns just as the sharp finger armor on her middle and pointer fingers makes a straight line for my face. I turn my head just before they can plunge into my eye. She drags them down my cheekbones, slicing through the skin there.

Blood drips down my face, into my mouth. I spit the taste of iron out. She brings her hand up again, this time piercing just below my collarbone. I manage to press my hips up, forcing Elouned onto her back. I straddle her with a leg on either side, pinning her arms to the ground when she tries to reach for me. Now, with a safe vantage point, the others are able to help me.

Syiera and Bronwyn rally for one last show of magic, and they work quickly to weave a net of glowing cables around Elouned. She is trapped there, and though she fights against the confines, she finds no freedom. I slide off her, and struggle to my feet, wiping my face with my arm. My dirty sleeve comes away streaked with crimson.

"Bronwyn, can you and Harlow please escort Elouned to the dungeons?" I ask tiredly. "I have promised a reunion to someone, and I intend to make good on that promise. Oh, and try to get her in through the lower entrance; I'd prefer the least number of eyes on this as possible."

Harlow yanks Elouned upright, and together, she and Bronwyn disappear into the trees. Now it is only me, Syiera, and Nesryn. Nesryn steps forward, a rare show of sympathy on her face. I turn away, unable to bear it. I know she believes Aleca is dead.

"Jace," Syiera says softly. I stare resolutely toward the trees, as if I have not heard her. She sighs, and then I hear the two of them retreat. I am alone again in the clearing.

Slowly, unsurely, the birds begin to chirp and sing again. I stand motionless in the center of it all, my only company the ruins of the cottage. Now that Raznik is dead, they are truly just ruins. There is no spell that blacks the windows out, no spirits peering from within. The cottage, once home to Elouned and a hidden affair with Raznik, is little more than kindling for our next bonfire.

I drop into a squat, picking up a large stone that has fallen from the foundation. With a scream, I hurl it into the window. The glass shatters into the cottage. I pick more stones up, throwing them into window after window until they are all blown out. The last of my stamina leaves me, and I fall to the ground, sobbing. I pick up jagged pieces of glass, clenching my fists around them until they cut into my skin. I barely notice the pain. To die now would not be enough to relieve me of my sorrow.

"Did I miss something?"

My head shoots up, and the glass falls from my hands. The sound of blood rushes to my ears and my heart throbs uncomfortably in my chest. I rise slowly, shakily, and turn to find my sister standing behind me. I let out a shout, sprinting toward her.

I slam into her so hard that we both go staggering backward. My arms wrap around her tightly, and she wraps hers around me, wheezing from the impact of my body against hers.

I pull back, gripping Aleca tightly by the arms as I survey her.
My vision is blurred with tears, and I pull her into me again,
pressing a hand against the back of her head.

"I thought you died," I say weakly, my voice breaking. "I
thought…oh, Gods, but you're alive, and you're here! How?
How are you here?"

"I just…I just came from over there," Aleca says, jerking a
thumb at the woods in confusion. She stares at me as if I have
just grown a second head, and I laugh giddily. "Why are you
dressed like that? What happened to your face?"

"Later," I say, taking her hand in mine. "For now, let's get
out of here."

We do not look back.

……†……

They are all gathered in my office when we return at long
last. Bronwyn jumps up with a cry, rushing over to hug Aleca.
Syiera is not far behind, and she swoops Aleca into an embrace
of her own, much the way a mother would her child.

Harlow is by my side in an instant, drawing me into a kiss so
relieved, so insistent, that it leaves my lips bruised. I cup her
face, planting a softer kiss against her mouth before she loosens
her hold on me.

"I'm okay," I say hoarsely. She runs a thumb along my
cheek, her gaze tender.

"Jace," Aureus says. Harlow steps aside to allow him space
and he pulls me into a tight embrace, planting a kiss on my
forehead. "Gods, I thought we lost you both," he murmurs

against my hair. The anguish there is palpable, and I tighten my hold around him. "I'm so relieved to see you."

"Oh, Jace, I have something for you," Aleca says. Aureus releases me and I step past him. From within her gown, Aleca retrieves an item and holds it out for me. There, in her hand, is my sword, the diamond blade still as sharp and bright as the day I received it. I take it with a gasp.

"Where did you find this?" I ask, running my hand over the surface. I bring it to my lips, pressing a delighted kiss to the cold blade. I thought I would never see it again.

"I dunno," Aleca says. "I was at the maypole, and then suddenly I was in the woods with your sword in my hand. Everything between that is a bit of a blur."

"Do you remember anything at all?" Syiera asks.

"All I remember is that there was this insanely bright light, and my parents were there. Then I heard a woman's voice tell me that I had the choice between staying in the light or returning to the life I knew. Obviously, I wasn't going to stay in some mysterious light alone, so…"

She shrugs. I narrow my eyes, staring off in thought. My head throbs and I rub a hand along my forehead as I try to follow her story. There is something I am missing about it, but I am too tired to figure it out.

"A woman?" Aureus asks. He cuts eyes over at me and raises his eyebrows as if this is significant information. I stare at him blankly and then it dawns on me.

"Karishua!" I exclaim. "It has to be, why else would Aleca have my sword? It was swallowed up when the tether broke."

"Your goddess?" Aleca questions. I nod and her eyes go wide. "Remind me to leave her an offering."

I don't know if I'll ever figure out why or how she chooses to appear in my life, but I'll never doubt her again, not now that she's brought my sister back from veritable death.

"Ask me to remind you tomorrow," I say, stifling a yawn behind my hand. "For now, all I want is a hot bath and some rest. The Courts leave in the morning, and I can't see them looking like this. All of you deserve the same. I cannot tell you how grateful I am for each and every one of you." I pause, meeting each person's eyes. "You have saved me, my sister, and most importantly, you have saved my Court, all at great risk to your own safety. I will never be able to repay you."

"We'd do it all over," Bronwyn says. She smiles at me, open and genuine. I extend my hand to her, and she takes it, shaking firmly.

"With any luck, we'll never have to again," I say. "Please, go get rest. I'll have staff bring you food and hot water."

They need no further encouragement, and file out of my office one after another, their shoulders heavy with the efforts of a battle hard won.

EPILOGUE

"Tell me why I am back here, young lady."

Healer Rex's voice is stern, and I flush at the admonishment.

"Job security?" I offer. He tsks at me and I sigh. "I hope sincerely that this is the last time for a long while. There was…an incident last night. It has been resolved."

"I'm glad to hear it," he says, slathering burn paste on my shoulder. He has already put a generous layer of my lavender lemon juice salve on my face; the citrus burned viciously at first before turning into a buzz soothed by the lavender and oil. Carefully, he wraps my palms tightly with gauze and a sticky strip of fabric and then pats my knee. "You're good as new," he tells me. "Or at least, you will be in a few days."

"Thank you, Healer Rex," I say earnestly.

We exit together, parting ways when I reach the dining room where all the Court delegates have gathered for a final breakfast together.

When I enter, the room is filled with conversation, with laughter and the promise of a future. Instead of chatter ceasing upon seeing me, it swells to welcome me, pulling me in with ease. I settle beside Syiera, and we share a private sort of smile.

By the time our meal has ended, she has extended an offer to host the Courts at the citadel in Apaiji in the coming summer season. I am filled with a renewed dedication to my Court as I watch the Courts take their leave, disappearing into the forest and mountains as the sun rises high in the sky. It is a beautiful day, and it carries the promise of newness.

Before the Dezaiyr delegation leaves, I pull Omarose aside.

"I believe I made you a promise upon your arrival," I say, leading her down to the dungeons.

"I try not to make a habit of being in the dungeons of a foreign Court," she drawls.

"I know this does not look promising, but I hope it will be worth your time."

We come to a stop before a cell and the guard offers me the key. I fit it into the lock, turning it with a rusty sort of click. The door swings open, and we step inside. Omarose inhales sharply.

"Ifoké," she says. It is simultaneously a curse and a prayer. She reaches a hand forward, hesitating.

"It seems for a time she found residence deep within our forest. Our land is not hers. She belongs in Dezaiyr," I say. "Bring her home."

"Thank you," she tells me. For the first time, there is no undercurrent of a challenge, no unspoken threat. I nod, and she holds a hand out to me. "I look forward to the years to come, Jace."

I take it, the victory curving my mouth in a relieved sort of smile.

"I do, as well."

......†......

The Apaiji delegation are the last to leave. Harlow and I bid them our goodbyes with tight hugs and promises to remain in contact. I squeeze Aleca tightly, pressing a long kiss to her cheek.

"Do me a favor, Al," I say. "Let me come to you, from now on?"

"Deal," she says, laughing. "I love you, Jace. And you, Harlow. Please take care of my sister for me."

"I will," she promises. Aleca throws her arms around Harlow, disappearing within her enveloping hold. When they part, Aleca wipes her eyes.

"You'll both visit, soon," Aleca stresses. She hugs us each again quickly and then is out the door and down the stairs.

......†......

In the weeks following the departure of the Courts, normalcy begins to creep back in.

When Nesryn left for Alymere with her parents, Aureus chose to stay back, offering to stay on as my official advisor. I accepted without hesitation and he promptly brought me through every single room in the castle to find the biggest and best one.

Raznik's quarters were destroyed when my mother broke the tether. The outside walls of the castle remain untouched, but inside is another story. The moment the tether exploded in the clearing, it exploded from beneath the diorama as well, charring and decimating everything inside the room. It is only due to my warning that Aureus was able to get out of the room in time. The unfortunate truth is that whatever answers we could have found there are lost to us forever. We will never know the full truth, and we must be okay with that.

I meet with my mind healer, Lilith, relenting at last and telling her everything. I spare no detail, speaking until my voice gives out. The freedom I feel from relieving myself of these secrets leaves me feeling lighter than I have in years.

I make good on the promise I made to the hundreds of spirits who sacrificed themselves to bring Raznik's reign of terror to an end. Near the funeral Pyre, I erect a tall obelisk etched with a traditional memorial poem. I leave flowers for them daily. A separate stone has been laid for Tally, whose body remained even after the spirits disappeared. Harlow dug a grave, staying by my side as I said my final goodbyes to the girl who sacrificed everything for me, in the end.

Garyn and I break ground together, building a sturdy bridge that officially connects our lands for the first time in a century. A large basket appears atop my desk one day, and when I pull back the cloth cover, a note flutters to the ground. I pick it up, recognizing the writing instantly.

"The first of many trades to come. W."

I rifle through the collection of goods there, healing pastes, oils, and, in the center of it all, a single bright green pear. Warmth fills me.

Though Harlow maintains her home in the village for some time, she spends more and more time at the castle. The day she arrives at my door with Beans in her arms, a sheepish sort of smile on her face, is the day I finally confess to her that I've fallen in love with her.

She stays in the castle after that.

There is still much healing to be brought to my Court. There is much growth, learning, and peace to be found. Progress will not come quickly, nor will it come easily, but I have faith that it will with time. I will continue to undo the corruption and isolation brought to this land. I will continue to fight for my people, not against them. We will enter into a new era as one.

We will rise, together.

Acknowledgments

Another chapter of Jace's story comes to an end, and with it comes my continual gratitude for the people in my life who have helped make it happen.

Nicola, who continues to be a cheerleader for me and Jace, and who first made Jace's story a possibility back in 2020 when she took a chance and gave me the honor of being the first-ever fiction book published through Unbound Press. Thank you for your unending enthusiasm for the stories I bring you;

Jesse Lynn Smart, my editor who gave me amazing feedback and pushed me to expand and bring more life into the novel deposited in her incredibly capable hands;

Leah Kent, who once again created the very image I had in mind for the cover of this novel;

My parents, for never once doubting that I'd become a published author, for never trying to quell my whims, art, and many phases of life, and for loving me endlessly;

My sister, Colleen, who continuously supports me, showing up for various events and pushing for my books to added to bookstores and libraries all over, and for encouraging me all along;

Kathryn, my once-and-always Vlor partner and cheerleader, and who also collaborates with me always (I once again thank you for Bronwyn);

Ashtin, who lovingly peer-pressured me into finishing this

novel and who loves these characters almost as much as I love them;

Lindsey, my very own Aureus, and someone without whom I would be lost;

And, finally, my wife Sarah, who has a Saint-like amount of patience for me, who taught me how to throw her over my shoulder in the middle of a coffee shop for accuracy, who always answered my, "Can I read you this?" with an enthusiastic, "Yes!," who provided me with support, encouragement, love, and empowerment, and who reminds me every day that I will never, ever be without love.

(Also, my cat Milo, who cannot read, whose entire personality I ripped off for Harlow's cat, Beans, and who, as I type this, is crawling up my leg for ear scritches. May you always be a Muppet, Milo.)

About the Author

Having been writing since the first grade (SO many stories about dolphins), it was only a matter of time before a story found its way into the world! You can be sure there are always a few more irons in the fire.

My main gig is as a social worker. I try to imbue my work into my writing-my greatest hope is that I can remove stigmas around mental health and inspire people to be their most authentic selves. There is no growth in comfort, but there's also no growth if we aren't providing that safe space to grow.

I live in Vermont with my wife, Sarah, and my spoiled rotten furry babes. I can be found on Facebook under Amy Babiarz (there aren't very many of us), or at my website, acbabiarz.wordpress.com. If you're interested in seeing a lot of pictures of dogs in sweaters and cats being menaces, you can follow me on Instagram at @ababiarzwrites. I wish I understood Twitter (or X, I suppose) but I don't, and honestly, I'm too scared to ask at this point.

About the Cat:

Milo (Beans) is a giant grey tabby cat intent on escaping his cushy life at all times. When he's not trying to escape his home, he can be found squishing himself into various boxes and baskets, watching the birds on our back porch, and obtaining his snuggles when his humans are at their most vulnerable in the bathroom. Being a muse isn't easy work, but he's rewarded handsomely for it.